KAY BOYLE

Plagued by the Nightingale

With a new Preface by the author

PENGUIN BOOKS — VIRAGO PRESS

PENGUIN BOOKS
Published by the Penguin Group
Viking Penguin, a division of Penguin Books USA Inc.,
375 Hudson Street, New York, New York 10014, U.S.A.
Penguin Books Ltd, 27 Wrights Lane,
London W8 5TZ, England
Penguin Books Australia Ltd, Ringwood,
Victoria, Australia
Penguin Books Canada Ltd, 2801 John Street,
Markham, Ontario, Canada L3R 1B4
Penguin Books (N.Z.) Ltd, 182–190 Wairau Road,
Auckland 10, New Zealand

Penguin Books Ltd, Registered Offices:
Harmondsworth, Middlesex, England

First published in Great Britain by
Jonathan Cape Limited 1931
First published in the United States of America
by W. H. Smith 1931
This edition published in Great Britain by
Virago Press Limited 1981
Published in Penguin Books 1990

1 3 5 7 9 10 8 6 4 2

LIBRARY OF CONGRESS CATALOGING IN PUBLICATION DATA
Boyle, Kay, 1902–
Plagued by the nightingale/Kay Boyle; with a new preface by the author.
p. cm. — (Virago modern classics)
ISBN 0 14 016.212 7
I. Title. II. Series.
PS3503.O9357P5 1990
813′.52—dc20 90-7041

Printed in the United States of America

KAY BOYLE

was born in St Paul, Minnesota, in 1902. She was educated at the Cincinnati Conservatory of Music and the Ohio Mechanics Institute where she studied architecture. Her first marriage to a Frenchman took her to Europe where she remained for thirty years. Much of that time was spent in Paris where, as part of the legendary group of American expatriates who lived and wrote there in the twenties, she knew Robert McAlmon, Bryher, Nancy Cunard, Gertrude Stein, Ernest Walsh, Sylvia Beach, Ezra Pound, William Carlos Williams, James Joyce, and Caresse and Harry Crosby. She returned to America in 1941 and embarked on a distinguished academic career. She was a lecturer at the New School for Social Research, New York in 1962, Fellow at Wesleyan University, Connecticut in 1963 and Professor of English at San Francisco State College between 1963 and 1977. She was also a Fellow at Radcliffe Institute for Independent Study in 1965 and Writer-in-Residence at Hollins College, Virginia from 1970-71.

She has written, edited and translated more than thirty books in all, including novels, short stories, poetry, children's books, essays, a memoir and an anthology. Her first collection of short stories was published in 1929 and her first novel, *Plagued by the Nightingale*, was published in 1930. She won two Guggenheim Fellowships, in 1934 and 1961, and she won O. Henry Awards for the best story of 1934, *The White Horses of Vienna* and of 1941, *Defeat*. She received an Honorary D. Litt. from Columbia College, Chicago in 1971 and from Skidmore College in 1977. She is a member of the American Academy of Arts and Letters.

Kay Boyle has been married three times and she has five daughters and one son. She is a Professor in the English Department of California State University, San Francisco.

Plagued by the nightingale
in the new leaves,
with its silence . . .
not its silence, but its
silences.

MARIANNE MOORE

PREFACE

Once any work of mine is in print, I find re-reading it a painful operation – an operation performed without anaesthetic, and very difficult to bear. As long as a poem, a story, a novel, has not been committed to publication, revisions and revivifications can be made. But to examine a piece of my writing with the knowledge that it is too late to save it from its failings, its inaccuracies, is close to tragedy. Perhaps the one way to deal with this unhappy situation is to look upon one's published work as though it were the writings of another author; and indeed it was another, much younger writer, who wrote *Plagued by the Nightingale* over fifty years ago.

In re-reading here and there through this book, I have learned a number of things. I have learned, for instance, that one tends to see the landscapes of the world in much more vibrant colours when one is young. The mountains and valleys and seas and skies that I write of now are bleached of pigment compared to the sea-scapes and skies and mountains of this book before me, and I find myself dazzled by the blazing of colour in contrast to the dullness of bourgeois life described in the pages of *Plagued by the Nightingale*. Or is it quite simply that while opticians supply the ageing with glasses so that they may see more clearly, they fail to explain that the sunset actually becomes less brilliant as one grows older, and that the green of the sea is less green, and the gold of the sand is tarnished by time? Not knowing which truth is truer than the other, I have turned for help to the words of others who have analyzed and evaluated better than I am able what the young author of *Plagued by the Nightingale* was seeking to say.

One critic of half a century ago wrote of it in *The New York Times Literary Supplement* that "the whole book is invested with that elusive quality of charm, a book that for all its dreadful pages may be read with pleasure." Although this might seem to imply a degree of schizophrenia in the novel, it is undoubtedly a recommendation. Another critic pointed out that the author of *Plagued by the Night-*

ingale speaks of the horse's ankles, whereas horses don't have ankles. They have fetlocks. (And were this book a student's endeavour that I was grading, I would have pointed out that the adjective "sweet" is used far too often throughout). A fine critic and author, Hugh Ford, wrote recently of this book that it is "the story of colliding cultures, of the divisions separating generations . . ." Perhaps it is; but I think there is one quite isolated thing that the young American woman discovers when she enters the daily life of the French family. It is not a specific of the colliding cultures Hugh Ford speaks of, but quite the reverse, and it is clearly stated at the beginning of Chapter XII, as Bridget reflects on one startling difference between her husband's French family and her family at home. ". . . her own family had scattered their children out like dice," she now saw. Her family "had not held them close together this way in the hollow of the hand". Everyone in her family had been dealt with as an individual, "with his own individual way to go," she was suddenly aware; and while it was easy to know when family members approved of something, or disapproved, it was never with a finality "it would break your heart to defy." She knew now what had never occurred to her before, that she had wanted her family to be "a loving Jewish tribe, to be all the more fierce for each other because there is the same flesh on our bones". In her fear of being "one person alone, unrelated . . . afraid to have no family at all", the American girl puts her hand gently through her French mother-in-law's arm, and "the responding pressure gave her a curious assurance". Here, she was not asked to make choices in life, to be on one side or the other; no demands were made "except that she be gentle, and that she be good and kind".

But there was no way that this could be sustained, and the meaning of the book may perhaps be that there is always in life the necessity to choose. This would seem to be borne out by a confession the author herself made thirty-odd years ago. "I probably write out of a feeling of guilt," she said. "I feel guilty for every act of oppression that is committed in our time. I write about the commonplace things, the day by day acts we accept as part of our routine, to indicate how these seemingly harmless acts can lead to official oppression. I believe I began this in *Plagued by the Nightingale*, and am still writing the same story today." But another critic reviewing the novel fifty years ago in *The Bookman* echoes the earlier quote which implies a split between matter and manner. The author has written on "two levels", this critic points out, "the explicit and the implicit; the flowers she gathers on the upper level distill, drop by drop, a bitter brew on the unseen level, and it is that potion that in the end accomplishes her tragic effect . . ."

Bitter brew though it be, I shall now take on momentary responsibility for this book, and – despite my impatience with the past – compare Bridget with the other young American women who hold the centre of the stage in my early novels. It is all too evident that I present these quiet-spoken, romantic, and self-sacrificing young women as victims of circumstances or of less sensitive individuals than they, and I deplore the over-weening justification of self this signifies. Yes, my novels are in large part autobiographical, and yes, I consistently depict in the best possible light these young American women who win the hearts of one and all (well, almost all) by their gentle ways. But is it not possible – no, more than that – is it not probable that Bridget is the victimizer? Did she not, a voluntary and biased intruder in their midst, make victims of the French family on whom she passed her ruthless judgments? They did not cast her out either by word or deed. It was she who sentenced them to eternal exile from the company of intelligent women and men (with the exception of Charlotte, Annick, and Luc) by caricaturing them in fiction. She outraged every tenent of the French family's life, religious, social, and political, and had nothing to offer in recompense except her own confusion.

(Before I again renounce any responsibility for the authorship of *Plagued by the Nightingale*, I feel obligated to point out that in my second published novel, *Year Before Last*, the same victimizing American girl betrays her devoted husband, destroys her marriage, and shatters the life of an eccentric, middle-aged Scotch woman, all in the name of high virtue and glorified romance. In a later novel, *Primer for Combat*, the presumably maturing American woman sacrifices (or attempts to) her husband, children, and home for the sake of a wildly glamorized ski-instructor. Yet she, at the expense of the other characters involved, emerges as a woman of high integrity.)

As if all this were not enough to place in question the probity of the young author of *Plagued by the Nightingale*, there is a final, damning fact which I feel should be brought to light: Luc, the handsome, young, French doctor from Rennes never existed in reality. He is a total invention. This is the way his presence came about: on leaving Paris some time in the late 'twenties, a kind American friend of the author's took the manuscript of *Plagued by the Nightingale* to New York, and in due course showed it to a publisher he knew. The publisher reportedly read it with a certain interest, but pointed out that it was all very well for the French sisters-in-law to long for a husband, but why not give some evidence that there was an eligible suitor on the scene? This would provide a romantic sequence and develop a story line which the book now lacked; and he added that he would like to see the manuscript again if this suggestion were worked on.

Did the young author recoil from such a desecration of the novel she had slaved over for years? Did she proudly disdain this outrageous compromise? Not for a moment. Gone were the days of unviolable integrity when Harriet Monroe of *Poetry Magazine* agreed to publish a poem the author had written at the age of thirteen, and which her mother had submitted to the magazine. But Miss Monroe wanted the last line changed, or, better still, quite simply deleted. "You must decide what you want to do," the poet's mother had said to her. "If you don't want to change it, then you should write Miss Monroe and tell her what your decision is." So the author-to-be of *Plagued by the Nightingale* wrote humbly to Miss Monroe that she did not wish to make any changes in her poem. But fifteen years later, the self-same author leapt into action at the New York publisher's suggestion, and eagerly created a wholly fictitious character. When the book was published in 1931, a reviewer wrote in *The New Republic* that in it there were passages of prose "which crackle and snap with electric energy . . ." This would seem to be an accurate enough description of Luc, "this gleaming, god-like man" who comes striding up the driveway "bearing the sun in the roots of his hair . . ." And to think he didn't even exist.

But in all fairness, I can say of the book that it is one of the many records of a young woman's troubled search for the old landmarks by which we choose the way that we must go.

Kay Boyle, San Francisco, 1980

I

THE GRASS blind quivered in the window, fluttering against the window frame green sweet wings veined delicately with light. Downstairs there were voices, and the copper odour of tea drifting up the stairs.

She came gradually to be awake, lying soft and rested in the plumed bed, deep in the protective palm of his family. The summer afternoon had come in through the window and swooned upon the floor. A feminine world echoed in the stairway, a new world polished hard and capable even in Nicolas' room, tied in dim bunches of lavender among the linen, undisturbed by the rose petals which had fallen and which moved sedately in the breeze across the floor. She could hear Nicolas breathing as he slept, and below them the assertion of life: Maman's voice tiptoeing across the sound of china. A strange feminine world mounting with the girls' feet on the stairs.

The girls had opened the door and peered tentatively in, and Bridget turned her head to them, looking at them over the lengths of counterpane that rippled from her chin. They saw that she was awake so they scurried softly in. First Annick scurried through the door, and then Marthe, and then Julie, coming to the bed and leaning to touch her cheeks with dry quick mouths.

They whispered questions to her, but she smiled and shook her head to them that she had not understood. The girls moved softly away around the bed to the couch.

"Five o'clock tea!" cried Annick to her brother, speaking her slow strange English. They had brought warm water to wash and Nicolas' polished shoes. They moved quickly, softly in the room, adjusting the fresh warm towels and the fluttering blind. Bridget could hear him rousing and responding to the girls. Presently they went off, out the glazed door into the hall and down to their own known world.

"They speak too fast, Nicol," she said. She was washing at the little white stand in the clear still oval of water below the primroses of the basin's edge. Nicolas lay watching her from the couch, the yellow dart of the brush over her hair. He sat up, blank and indolent, sitting as if stunned with sleep, leaning absently over his shoes, and she came to him with the basin of swinging water to wipe his face and palms.

"But you mustn't wait on me," he said gently.

She washed his face under the smooth black temples and hair. His skin was dark and fine, with his face turned away from her, averted like a child's from the water, and the hair growing up in his soft neck, dark and perfect like a child's hair. She washed him, aware of his face soft and defenceless in her hands, his fine nostril threaded with hair and turned in aversion from the little blue rag and the water.

"You make it so difficult," she said. She hung above him, above the perfect piercing sweetness of his flesh, and her hands and voice were turned almost roughly upon him in harsh conscious pride.

"It won't be long before you understand everything they say," he remarked vaguely when she had done with him. As they went down he leaned upon her arm, and the stairs shone so that each step reflected their descent.

The family was waiting in the salon. Papa's face clung to the triangle of three black moles and his brow was gathered up under the smooth white elegant cap of his hair. Maman's sharp quick hands drew chairs for them, setting their cups at the table. She was the hard centre of movement around which fluttered Annick and Marthe and Julie, the three girls. Bridget sat down among the family in the salon selecting from their speech with Nicolas words that had meaning for her—"*Californie,*" and words of the sea. A full afternoon of impatience had preceded this, she knew. An impatience smooth with silence, revealing nothing beyond their solicitude for the two travellers.

Maman's protruding eyes examined them as she talked. Her nose was long and high, and her eyes moved quickly back and forth across the bridge of it, her hands rising and falling with her words, pouncing upon the handle of her cup or down to clasp her black heavy knees. The girls listened and laughed and stole shy looks at Bridget's hair and her thin hands. The sisters were dark like Nicolas, but with a blown, ruffled darkness. Annick's cheeks were raw with colour, her gaze sweeter, her glances at Bridget more direct and more sustained. Julie was small and apricot-fleshed, with a boy-voice. Marthe's neck thickened down like a tree-trunk into her body. But nowhere was there the blood of Nicolas. He sat fragile and worn, his eyes bare and vaguely hostile before the full, cream lids that arched below Papa's brows.

Nicolas was telling them of the ranch and Bridget smiled tentatively at Annick across the tea.

"*Les montagnes*," she cried softly. Her hands shaped shadow and ice between the tea urn and Papa's vest. Annick nodded eagerly. The clay mountains—Bridget was thinking of them solid and blind as chalk with paths lacing them like veins in the flesh. She smiled at Annick. Nicolas, she concluded, was telling them of when he had first begun to know. His long hand moved down his leg from the thigh to the knee, gentle, caressing. His hand lingered on the narrow cap of his knee. His eyes were quietly on them, remote from pain or fear. And Maman leaned sharply forward and touched him with her insentient fingertips, speaking to him almost in impatience with the shrewd untranslatable wisdom of one who has never yielded to pain. She spoke rapidly, including Bridget. Nicolas smiled.

"She says that the summer's rest will set me up," he said to Bridget. "She says that Jean's is incurable because it began in the trenches and went too far without the proper care."

Papa stirred forward and spoke to Nicolas. His voice was short and final as if he had put a judgment on his son. He sat back, tossing one heavy leg across the other, clasping his fingers across his vest. And Maman cried out against him, appealing to them all with her open palms. Nicolas laughed aloud, as if he were not concerned in it at all.

Papa sat tossing in his chair. The smooth cap of his hair slipped back and forth as his brows lifted and fell, and he lifted his hand and counted off the victims slowly on his long fingers.

"Ton grandpère, ton oncle—le père de Jean—ton cousin. Maintenant, ton cousin Jean . . . et toi . . ."

The colour swelled in Maman's face. The girls murmured together in protest. Nicolas laughed.

"I have only come into my heritage," he said to Bridget.

Maman diverted them, speaking rapidly of her eldest daughter, of Charlotte and of Jean who were at the seashore with their children. Her voice rounded and smiled about the babies. One had been ill, teething, she rapped her front teeth with her nail. Her hands shaped their limbs, their perfect heads, the hair cut across their brows. Her lips receded in fatuous lines of pride. She sat in repose, transfixed by her emotion, with her eyes looking blindly down her nose. And then she leaned suddenly forward, the glow of pride diffusing her in motion, her cheeks hanging forward as she spoke. Softly and personally she pressed Bridget's knee with her hand, speaking so personally, so meaningly to her, and the girls nodded and smiled in a soft murmur of assent.

"*Et vous* . . ." said Maman so meaningly, so softly to her. Bridget looked away in confusion to the bright points of antagonism which glowed in Nicolas' eyes. And suddenly he threw back his head, his lips pulled up under his moustaches, and he laughed: "Ha, ha, ha! Ha, ha, ha!"

"Well, never five I hope!" he had cried to them. "Never that! Charlotte, whose wisdom I respect, exaggerates on that score, on that score, my dear parents!"

Maman observed the gathering anger on Papa's brow and dropped five lumps of sugar in his tea.

"I fear," Nicolas had said, "that you shall never have the pleasure of distributing boxes of sugared almonds in honour of the baptism of my child."

And he had left the room.

II

THE BRIGHT shawl was striped in purple and blue and speckled with corn-yellow sand. The stripes curled and curved under the sun and under the bare legs of Bridget and under Nicolas' long dark legs. Bridget's fingers pecked at the soft woven fringe.

"Will you swim, Nicol?" she said. But no, he would not swim. He smoothed her arm with the tip of one finger. Papa had brought them fresh fruit in a little grass basket and Nicolas would rest his legs with him awhile as he sat sucking absently at pomegranate skins. The water was before them, half sea, half river washed full by the tide, and beyond was the firm edge of rye and pasture, with the river embracing the fields and their charmed crescent of sand. Behind them their beach coiled away to the poplars and the wood.

Bridget went down to the sea and put a toe in the sharp tide. The cold rose in her stifling as she plunged. Her toes were spread wide as if pierced with needles of ice and meshed in soft drifting fingers of weed. Presently she was submerged in a rich ringing warmth, turning slowly upon her back in the warmth and filling her eyes with the clouds, and the shadows of them that floated across the sea.

She had come out of the water and Papa's voice and eyes turned suddenly to Nicolas made her aware of her long angular body coming to them up the sand. Nicolas watched her strangely and sharply as she came, masking his eyes as if to enable himself to observe her in some new way, to see her in complete detachment from himself. His face was waiting before her, without emotion, like the carved echo of the reproof in Papa's glance.

And so he lay there, looking down his long legs to his wife, and wanting suddenly to see her as if he had never seen her before. But as he watched her coming up to them his eyes grew intimately and tenderly upon her, and his small warm smile spread out below his eyes. Bridget sat down and pulled the shawl to her across the brittle sand. Papa rubbed his coated arms and trembled with mock-cold.

"*Froid?*" He cocked his eyebrows at her.

"Oh, no. *Chaud,*" she said.

She flushed, and his lids hung heavily upon her. She wondered if his voice had remarked upon the swim, disapproving because her legs were bare. He watched her as she sat wrapped in the bright shawl.

Nicolas had leaned his cheek against her arm and Papa watched them, fumbling the little pale seeds of an orange out over his lips and down into the sand. Every move flung a shadow across the stained globes of his eyes. Any speech between them was snapped closed behind the click of his false teeth slipping in and out of place. Down at the bend of the sea-river were sail boats swinging their bleached wings against the sun.

The roan filly was *pleine,* Papa remarked. Bridget had seen her with her belly hard and glossy as a full chestnut and her hoofs shattering across the yard. Charlotte would be desolate when she knew. She had kept the little horse in the triangle of clover with her nostrils cool as wax. Jean had even talked of a belt of chastity. They laughed. A fine silver one, buckled and carved with the crest and the *omnia vincit amor*. Papa shook with his words, stroking his full sallow hands. He looked laughing up the beach, brushed the tears from his eyes and made a gesture of silence to Nicolas. Maman and the three girls, with a nun amongst them, were proceeding towards them down the beach.

The girls swung their bags in greeting, Maman nodded forward, and the nun lifted her arms and waved small red hands to them from her penguin body. Bridget walked to meet them over the sand, and when she had come up to the women her face was pressed between the white cloth of the nun's cap and the flesh of her cheek. First one side and then the other.

"*Ma petite* Breedget."

Tante Dominique held Bridget in her stubby arms. A bit of lip rouge had scarred the pure wing of her cap, and Bridget looked at it with shame. At lunch Maman had told them that when her sister was young they had searched in the nine leading boot shops of Paris for green kid slippers sufficiently small to fit the foot of Tante Dominique. Her hands were red and misshapen with gout, lying inanimate as gnarled roots on Bridget's shoulders.

But Papa's story was one that made them laugh all the harder. The two Pibrac sisters, he had told them over coffee, had grown up in St. Servan where he had been in barracks, and there, in the company of the other young officers, he had set eye upon one of them as she emerged from her home. Her face had been masked with a violet veil, for it was but two years after the death of both her parents, and her figure concealed by a bustle, but her shapely foot had won him. The following week his father had called and proposed his son to the aunt who had acted as guardian to Mesdemoiselles Pibrac. He requested that Mlle. Pibrac be permitted to meet the promising young lieutenant, and it was not until the very day of the wedding, Papa recounted, that he had discovered his mistake. He had seen his bride but twice and on the third occasion she was for the first time accompanied by her sister in bridesmaid attire. As she lifted the hem of her skirt to step into the carriage, the toe of her boot was revealed and Papa had clapped one hand to his head and the other to his heart and exclaimed that this was the Mlle. Pibrac he had wished to marry.

Maman's laughter had rung out the heartiest of all at the close of the story, and she had set off on foot to the station with the girls telling Bridget that she was off to meet her rival. Her only rival. There had not been another in thirty-two years. And now the beach flung a yellow arm about them all. Maman and Annick went off to sit with the men and the others went up over the knoll to change into their bathing things, and Bridget to dress. Annick smiled up as the others walked away, taking out her work and following them with long clear glances. She did not bathe, not even on their own isolate beach. She could not have gone up with them and laid off her clothes, and she could not have finally subjected herself to the water. Once out of her clothing it would have been as if she had put her identity aside, betrayed and abandoned herself. And as Annick turned to smile up after them, Bridget was aware of the suppressed other look of half-revulsion for her exposed legs and arms.

Tante Dominique disrobed behind a rise of ground over which her shoulders and back swelled, pulling fiercely her rough grey shirt over her bent neck and head. The black nun's dress lay folded square on the grass below the crisp angles of the cap. The small white moon of her tonsure gleamed among the frail old hairs of her head. Tante Dominique in the faded blue suit ran off down towards the beach with the grey trousers of the suit slipping down over her tennis shoes and the delicate blue veins in her calves.

Marthe and Julie undressed rapidly, putting carefully aside their long white garments. Marthe was tall in her long embroidered shirt, crouching down on her fine white legs. Julie's back curved softly, the colour of apricots deepening in her armpits and fading up over her small breasts. Their bathing dresses had sleeves to the wrists and sagging skirts, and in these they leapt away, like ugly ducklings, over the grass to the beach.

Bridget dressed and walked away up the sand. There were no shells, only the flat wet ochre sand and the tide now drifting down. The beach was widening, but so slowly, without perceptible secession, widening the distance between her and the detached cries of the bathers. She walked in the light lax sand, watching the continuous flutter of water at the edge. The advance was so apparent, and yet the water was really withdrawing from the land. There was the soft break of the low wave, as though the water were advancing, and then the long sucking silence, and then again the little hurried rush of water and the arch and shatter of the wave. Out beyond, the river centre was dark and profound, an intense blue, flowing swiftly down. And again and again the little gasping wave came out of this deep silence, a white stroke splashing and scattering along the edge of the sea.

When Bridget turned she saw Annick and Nicolas walking up the beach to her. The bright shawl hung from Nicolas' shoulders and trailed a flaming fringe on the sand. He strode steadily forward, dark and gleaming with sea, and so far now from disease or despair. The colours of the shawl were swinging behind him as he came, and Bridget thought that maybe it was true, maybe that here he would be made strong and that really there was no fear. Tears fled into her eyes as she went to him, and behind him his sister walked short quick steps, up and down.

Now that Bridget was dressed, Annick could bear to see her. She took Bridget's hands, feeling them in her own and fearing that Bridget had taken cold. There was a guilt, an atonement about her now, because she had hated Bridget's body.

"I love you, my sister," she said softly in English, and her voice went blind and meaningless in the strange tongue.

Bridget clasped her hand.

"I love you, too," she said.

Nicolas was singing as he walked behind.

III

THE WORLD, edged with a little lip of pure mud, floated round and round them. Afternoon warm and blue and humid shimmered about the fat heavy heads of the elm-trees over the wall, and the straw roof of the pig-house was flung down like an old hat under the chins of the elms. The terrace proceeded sedately from the wall, drawing up with a gesture of disdain the fresh new yews from the edge of the pond. And Charlotte's house strode up upon the terrace, its erect line assailed by white wings and the roof scarlet as the crest of a cock.

The world floated round and round them, the low hills with the poplar row and the river, the soft afternoon coiled about the elm heads, and the terrace withdrawing the glossy yew from the touch of the pond.

"Oh, tomorrow!"

Maman threw her hands up to the house, her face blazing with joy.

"Oh, tomorrow!"

The girls burst into talk. From the bank Papa waved an

exultant cane, his face a vivid triangle about the pale loose folds of his chin.

"Nicolas, Nicolas!" he called.

Nicolas turned the boat and rowed obliquely through their circular world to Papa standing impatiently in the mud, prodding the shimmering air. His eyes danced beneath his lids.

"Nicolas, Nicolas!" he called. When they had drifted close in the row boat, he pointed it out to them. Maman and the girls leaned perilously to see. And there it was, untouched by rain or tide: a footprint of the youngest grandchild still patterned in the mud. A week's absence had it survived, a week trembling on the brink of Charlotte's and Jean's return from the sea. Oh, why had they ever had to go? Oh, why were families torn apart; oh, why hearts rended? It was as if that portion of the family had departed in miraculous death, leaving the individual and unblemished glory of their being.

"A week. They have been gone a week now," said Maman, rapidly crocheting in the boat. A week, a week, they have been gone a week. A week of horror without the children, without Charlotte, without the bridge games with Jean. Rarely did son-in-law so adequately fill the gaps: his fortune, and his presence as a fourth at bridge, his property adjoining theirs which really made one great expansive park over which in-laws, colonels and aides-de-camp could roam at ease. There was a satisfaction too in having him a first cousin, as long as the Church had blessed the union, for he was so used to their ways. Even his partial paralysis was no detriment, for were there not five children to inherit it and carry it on in their blood? And just because he walked with two canes they were assured that he could not wander far afield. He was still an active participant in billiards and croquet.

In two days Bridget knew their photographs by heart. Through Maman's gestures and indications she knew which one was Riquet, which was Mimi, which Monique, which Jeannot. Riquet had planted all his vegetables upside-down, Jeannot was beginning to show some weakness in his limbs, for, oddly enough, it was only the male members of the family who were liable to this corruption of the bone.

In Charlotte's house the bedrooms of the children opened out from the parental bedroom like the four fingers from the palm. In each could be seen a half a wall of river between grey satin window curtains, and grey four-posted bedsteads mirrored in the floor. The Christs were in silver at each head, with unpodded mistletoe laid across the pierced fine feet. In Charlotte's room the console and the prayer-chair stood in pools of sun, the yellow plush blooming like rich flowers with elaborated stems.

Maman threw open the rooms to Bridget, walking heavily on her heels and leaning her head and her round shoulders forward. Her fingers smoothed the embroidered bed-spread, flecked the lace skirts of the candlesticks. "Tomorrow."

Below them on the terrace, Papa and Nicolas walked up and down. Up and down they walked, bruising a path through the short sweet grass. Maman touched the fresh linen in the *armoire*, straightened a ribbon's crease with her moistened thumb. At the end of the road where the fishermen's houses were gathered close to the river, a *fête* had been in progress all day. Now the singing and the notes of trumpets overflowing on the wind came through the windows in remnants of sound.

Nicolas was squatting down in the shell pathway to examine the poppy heads that were folded away from the prick of the first young stars, and the wind struck major notes across the wall. The family were shutting the long windows and drifting off to bed. They were unreal, suspended in a mechanical dream that would be realized on the morrow. They talked dimly together through the halls, of the children, and of Charlotte's written orders to the houseman and the cook.

"Tra-la-la-la," said the trumpets, and Nicolas danced over the garden to Bridget. They took hands and went down the path and through the door in the wall to the road. A little green bell hung above the door, announcing that someone had come in or gone out, and this bell Nicolas muffled with his fingers as he pulled the door closed behind them, so that the family should not know. Bridget waited in the road, elated with this, for it made more perfect the illusion of their escape. Between Charlotte's wall and the family's wall they walked down the road together, arms pressed together, elated under the dark still trees.

"Did you used to go off this way?" said Bridget.

"When? Five years ago?" he said.

"No. When you were really young. When you were really young here did you used to go off this way?"

"Yes," he said. "Sometimes." He left it there, as if there was nothing more to say.

"I pasted a photograph of the Duc d'Orléans on the door so that every time anybody went through they beheaded him in—in, what?"

"In effigy?"

"Yes," said Nicolas, "in effigy."

They walked on into the sounds of the *fête*. Rockets were curving and spinning over the little houses. The fishermen's houses were squatting in the webs of green nets that hung drying from door to door. Lanterns of bright metallic paper glittered like humming-birds above the people, strung by festoons of daisies away from the the terror of the stamping feet. The feet were in boots of yellow wood and stiff lacquered leather that never betrayed the bend of the foot.

Across the wharf stamped the feet, and the bugles stated and restated the unembellished theme. Even Nicolas could not make out the human meaning of the dancers' cries, but he and Bridget came in among them and were taken into the fierce broken rhythm of their dance as though they were never strangers, accepted and almost unobserved by the fierce indifferent dancers. They joined hands with the others and stamped across the blond wharf.

It was almost as if they were taking part in an articulation of the sea, with casual sea-creatures who had no human bond. Off they went, swinging and stamping in the dance, with the fresh flesh of the hard indifferent dancers striking and ringing in their palms. Presently Nicolas was drawn out into the centre of movement by a girl with hair white and dry as ashes under her velvet cap. Her hands, swift and muscular and steel-hard, guided and swung him in the dance. She spun him like a dark meteor, her hands like cold running steel upon him, dark star-flesh and luminous flesh whirling to the sea-rhythm of the music.

The lowered instruments dropped them into silence, and Nicolas walked steadily away on Bridget's arm. In the road, beyond the touch of the cones of light, Nicolas fell down upon the grass.

He lay in the grass with his face pressed close on Bridget's palm.

"Help me," he said. "Help me. I am afraid."

She felt him touching and trying his legs in the darkness.

"Lie still, Nicol," she said.

She lay beside him in the grass, pressing his hand. Above them there were the stars, calm and incurious in the rich chains of darkness.

"You danced like a dark star, Nicol," she said.

His palm was suddenly withdrawn from her, leaving her without identity in the immensity of darkness. She groped for him across the grass and came upon his fingers riveted hard as steel to his face. She wrenched at them, seeking to pry them open; she kissed his fingers to soften the relentless mask under which his face and his tears were bared.

"I danced like a bag of bones," he said. "My legs spraying like powder from the knee caps. That, you see, is the rotting of the bone."

Back was going his mind, thought Bridget, back and back. Back to all the ancestors in the salon, the one who bathed in milk, and the one who sang, the one who channelled his inspiration in parallel lines, renaissance façades, and the delicate grillwork of Bastilled France, and the one whose disdainful fingers lingered on a satin knee in Charlotte's salon, his face recoiling from each impinging stroke of the brush. . . .

"Philippe was destroyed at twenty-five," said Nicolas. "He continued his life painting flowers on silk. Isn't it funny?" he said. "Isn't it funny? There's nothing better than that for me."

They lay for hours, extinguished in the darkness, with the slow setting planets descending before them, and clouds moving across the stars. Beyond in the grass was the soft nuzzle and crop of gypsies' beasts set wild for the night. It was a long time before Nicolas could get up on his knees, and upon his feet, and stood with his arm across Bridget's shoulders. They went forward a few steps together and she could feel his body leaning down upon her and then he drew up and away in his own strength as if the blood as he walked were flowing down in him like new bright wine.

She walked close to him, moving with him so that she swung with the motion of his body. It was all she wanted, to be close and quiet with him, contained in his rhythm. She had no wish to speak, for maybe if they did not talk of this thing it would have no real importance and it would go away. Perhaps if they ran very hard down the road, it would be left behind. Just to leave it there in the grass, heaped with scorn, with the leaves that had fallen low over it, heaped with the pitch of night, tarred and feathered with cat-tails, let it be.

Down the road they went, down, down, down. Her heart was singing like a harp.

"Listen," she said. "Nicolas. Nicolas, I am so strong I could carry you in my hand. I could toss you over my shoulder and let you flutter in the wind. Mountain. Nicolas. Mountain. MOUNTAIN."

"Grain of sand," he said.

They had come to the door in the wall and they leaned against it and laughed. Suddenly the bugles sprang out, mocking them because they must tiptoe up the family's stairs.

IV

THE THREE girls came to breakfast in spotless white. Annick and Marthe and Julie came in from the garden with plates of strawberries, stooping in their white linen to salute Bridget's cheeks. If the name of Charlotte, their own Charlotte, were mentioned, they began to chatter like wrens. They drank their bowls of milk and coffee thinking of Charlotte who was on her way home to them, and of her husband, and of her beautiful home. Annick was more gracious, for her spirit hovered about God as well. More and more often in these latter years had her spirit turned to God; and she would have turned completely to Him and entered Tante Dominique's Order had it not been for Papa. But she could stuff and bake a cod as could no other member of the household, and her pure, pure voice, so clear like the ringing of a festoon of silver bells, could read from the *Revue des Deux Mondes* to him as could no other. Edith Wharton was beautiful read aloud in Annick's clear ringing French across the card table while Maman snapped her cards and hummed upon her game of solitaire. If Annick's soul recoiled from certain incidents however delicately described, Papa consoled himself that the greater number of hours a day were her very own to turn completely to God's glory. He did not like the group of shabby wretches under ten who recited their catechism to her in the garden every afternoon. Nor had Maman any patience for them. They considered themselves a human, fallible Colonel and his wife, and this daughter too perfect to be considered a rebuke. Perhaps a saint, but certainly not an example for ordinary human conduct. What in the world would become of the nation if every good Catholic looked upon things as Annick did? Her bedroom was cold as the tomb, hung with paintings of the Blessed, with a stern crucifix across the wash-stand, and no *bidet* thrust out of sight.

And now that the day of Charlotte's return had come, Maman had begun to reflect upon the wash. So that the regal pines of the *parc* need not be hung every week with ballooning sheets and the rest of it, the linen would be hustled off to the attic and there hung away and once a year there would be such a washing as would call the sun out from behind any clouds. Clothes like duck wings, and the bodies of four or five washerwomen bending over at the stream that ran down through the grounds and with wooden spankers beating the life out of dish cloths that had been waiting a year for it. At breakfast she had a haggard look under the eyes, and Papa explained to Nicolas that she had kept him awake half the night wondering if she had ordered enough of the bars of Marseilles soap, and enough of the crystals to boil the linen to get them spotless as feathers.

Charlotte and Jean and the children would return by motor so that it was impossible to know at what hour it might be. Maman spent the entire morning showing Bridget how to make a darn and raking the gravel driveway into the finest of designs. When she was done, the approach to the family's house looked as though it had been combed and waved.

It was almost noon when Nicolas came out of Papa's *bureau.* His mouth was turning its ends up in his face, so that Bridget knew he was in a rage. Down to the summer-house he came to her, throwing a regard of disdain upon the shrine Annick had erected for him when he had departed for California to make his living, into the summer-house and flung himself into a chair.

"Papa says we should have a child," he said. "A dear little child to run around and call us mama and papa. I can give it paralysis, what can you give it, my dear?"

"Let's pretend we're very rich and give it a fortune," said Bridget. Suddenly she put down the sock she had been learning to darn and began to cry. She sat very still and tight in her chair and the tears rushed down her face.

"How do you like my family, grain of sand?" said Nicolas.

She sat pressing herself tight and stiff in her chair. Through the great torrents of her tears she could see the garden, orderly and prim.

"What are we going to do?" she said. Her voice was unrecognizable, squeezed thin and sharp. "What are we going to do?"

At that instant the gravel sparkled and spattered apart and into the driveway sailed a handsome motor car with sides as sleek and luminous as tar. The whole summer world became suddenly alive. Marthe and Julie appeared at the windows, waving and shouting aloud. Maman and Papa hastened through the door, Annick's bicycle fled through the gate and she leapt lightly down.

But the word "Charlotte" perished on their lips. From the car alighted two gentlemen. The first was Nicolas in miniature with a bang cut straight across his brows. The second was ruddy and blond with a gleaming small moustache.

The voices turned, with scarcely a shade of disappointment, to "Luc" and "Pierrot," "Pierre" and "Luc."

Bridget was suddenly amongst them all. Here was Pierre, the doctor brother, said Nicolas, and here was Luc. Pierre's face was like a bit of parchment against his father's ruby lips. The tip of his pale nose inadvertently touched and recoiled from the tuft of black hair in Papa's ear. He saluted Bridget's hand.

"How are you accustoming yourself to our France?" he said in his fine polished English. He looked pleasantly and brightly about for a chair. Down in the green tin chairs they all sat, and Pierre sat talking, first to one and then the other of them, with his small fine hand pressed down on his immaculate knee. What a fine little man he was, telling them that he had been called to an *accouchement* at Saint-Malo, that everything had passed very well, that Luc had distinguished himself again as his assistant, and that here they were! Marthe and Julie were in quite a flutter, and Annick's colour was even deeper in her cheeks. But their glances were not for their elder brother, but for the young doctor who was talking respectfully to Maman about her strawberry beds. It was he who had presented her a year ago with the speckled setter dog who had streaked his smart coat with its dusty paws. But he brushed it off laughingly and rubbed Picot's silky ears back and forth across his smooth head.

"*Vacances, vacances,*" Maman kept cawing out of her vulturous old mouth. "*Vacances, vacances.*"

And the girls tittered together and leapt like butterflies when he finally said:

"Next month I shall take my *vacances.*"

There were many things to show him that had been altered since last he was there. The cement steps to the summer-house he had not seen before, nor the collection of post-cards of lower New York which Nicolas had brought to Annick. In the course of their excursion around the grounds he tripped over a croquet wicket and fell upon the grass. The indignity of this made the colour fly up in his face, and great was the consternation of

Maman and the girls. But he jumped to his feet, laughing, brushed himself smartly off, and said it was nothing.

"*Rien, rien,*" he said, but the girls were far from reassured. They could not spare him. For the life of them, they could not silence their dismay. Nor could the sight of a stout woman who came pedalling with great dignity down the drive. She delivered a telegram to Maman, and as Maman read it aloud every face fell: Charlotte would not be home until the following day.

V

EVERY summer the same thing faced them, but this year was a special year.

It was June, and the country as northern as ever, but never had the roses bloomed more beautifully, and never before had Nicolas returned with an American wife. Had she possessed a fortune, and had she been able to speak their tongue, life in the country that year might have been an even more buoyant and promising thing. But nothing could dim the wonder of Luc being thirty that year and now in a position to choose a wife; now with a neat little *pied-à-terre* at Rennes, his work in the clinic, and his vacation to be spent as usual with the family of Pierre, everything pointed to the fact that the time had come.

Every summer for ever the same thing had faced them like a new and blazing spring: Pierre's return from medical school with his fellow student, Luc, and then the return of the two young doctors from their work in hospitals and in the war. This year it was the return of the young men who had built up and owned their own bright *Clinique*.

Annick had had more years of correspondence with him, and all winter for many winters letters had gone back and forth between the country and Rennes. Annick was Luc's own age, and now at thirty they had the healing of the ill in body and soul like a common weal between them. However the three girls looked at it, it must have seemed to them that Annick and Luc were the ones to share a common life.

But in Marthe were moments of rebellion. If she were not handsome, her hair had a deep and natural curl and, God forgive the thought, her leg was prettily turned. Up she came with a petrol lamp and a photograph of Luc to Bridget's room.

"Luc," she said, almost screaming the word at Bridget so that she would understand. "Luc. Luc."

She indicated her upper lip in description of his moustache. How smartly it rode his lip like a neat little jockey perched in his seat! Luc, Luc, Luc, said Marthe. She thrust her head forward on her long neck and screamed with stifled laughter. Marthe had smuggled two cigarettes away in the pocket of her gown, and they sat on the edge of the bed smoking them together. Luc, Luc, Luc, she said. There was eight years' difference between them. Was it a great deal to have eight years' difference between the man and the woman?

"*Huit ans*, Breedget," she whispered but it shrilled across the room.

But surely she felt there were many things she could give him that Annick could not give. She was filled with high spirits, almost an hysteria of spirits. All of the time she wrote letters everywhere, to everyone. In detail she described her small room to everyone, everywhere, and Bridget had known before she had come to France where each book, each foot stool, each photograph was placed. A full-length reproduction of the Comtesse de Noailles hung above her bookcase. Oh, the mystery of that seductive face! And Madame Roland's round common likeness was pressed away in secret with a few pansy flowers. Oh, the courage of those hips, those haunches!

And if Marthe were asked to make mayonnaise or slice tomatoes she cried for hours like a child. Her mind must have been in a confusion of ceremonies, and now she tried to dance a little before Bridget in the room. Powder she wanted, and rouge, and to be whirled away, away, away in a delirious dance. Luc, Luc, Luc, she said, dances this way, and this way, and this. Away she went in a confusion of medical balls and ceremonies.

"Dansons," she whispered, *"dansons, dansons."*

They would be friends, they would, they must be friends. They were exactly the same age. It was a lovely age for girls to be. *Dansons, dansons.* They danced across the room, very badly, stepping on each other's toes. They would be friends, they must be friends.

That very night Annick wrote to him that she had finally persuaded Papa to allow her a fortnight to teach the little waifs in the charity camp at Cancale. "I shall probably not be here when you first arrive for your vacation," she wrote, "and must thus forgo a few days of hearing from you by word of mouth of the clinical work. But there will be much to talk about, especially after a return from Father Bimont, who is now organizing a pilgrimage to Lourdes in the early autumn. I am hoping with all my heart to be one of their number."

What they were to Luc, the three girls, nobody knew. No one had any idea what was going on in his mind, but one thing he must have felt of them all and that was that no matter what was going on in the world, they remained as they had always been. Whatever happened in the world, it never shadowed or altered them in any way, and whatever year he came back, they were there with their legs grown a bit longer and their hair, but in them there was really no change. In his letters to them, there was no difference. If he sent Annick a mother-of-pearl rosary from Lourdes, he was sure to send Marthe a statuette of Jeanne d'Arc from Reims, and Julie protested that it was because Luc considered her a child that he had sent her the replica of Mont St. Michel in a glass ball that flowered with snow once it was shaken. But the small points of delight in her eyes when she spoke of it were snuffed out when the conversation turned to something else.

As a boy, Julie would have possessed smooth black hair and a ringing voice. As a girl she was apologetic for her rough ways. For years the relatives that had gathered at family festivals had told her, had remarked upon her fingernails, regretted that her hair was straight and oily and that her eyebrows met upon her nose. Mirrors she would pass with her head averted so as not to see, and she was the one of them who did not fear the rain but who would walk out in it, hunching her shoulders up around her neck so that the less that would be seen of her the better. This was exactly what she felt. Out in the rain with the wind masking her and the rain falling down her face, she would for the first time lift her eyes, and here her voice was in its right place, shouting against the elements.

What a torture it was for her to seek out Bridget and show her the glass ball in which the snow fluttered down all over Mont St. Michel. On the bottom side of it Luc had written "*Bien à vous.*" She stood shaking the ball in front of Bridget, shaking it with her face set and almost angry. But she took care to point out to Bridget that Luc had written on it "*Bien à vous.*" And Annick came in with her sweet soft step, with her letter to Luc unsealed, coming to read it aloud to Bridget before sending it away. It was part of a lesson for Bridget, part of her French instruction to hear the letter read in Annick's sweet clear voice. Each phrase she lingered on and explained again and again in a thousand ways so that Bridget would understand.

Luc. Luc. It was like a spring bubbling unceasingly, escaping drop by drop from the heart of each one of them. Luc and Luc and Luc.

VI

THE MORNING clouds tossed back the tennis ball and the cedars murmured together at the gate. Marthe and Julie ran around the pink tennis court unbalancing their racquets at the ball, and Annick on the little canvas stool painted carefully on her knee a likeness of the gravel drive, the rose garden, and the Chinese *tilleul* whose boughs in the warm summer air dripped down like yellow wax. Nicolas was stretched on the *chaise longue*, irritably swinging his restless legs.

"My God," he said to Annick at intervals. "My God."

"There is no sin but the betrayal of the aesthetic," he finally said.

Far down the road a klaxon sounded and the family shattered into agitated bits. The girls threw down their racquets and raced to the open grill. Papa folded the *Ouest-Éclair* with trembling fingers, and Maman hurried up to them from Charlotte's house. The maids were clustered down the door, blue and white strokes beneath the glass shell of the portico.

"I will not move," said Nicolas. "My life has been twenty-five years of *répétition générale* of my emotions. From the first cook's flowered corsets to the present moment, nothing has changed the *religio loci*, nor the distribution of moles upon my father's face. . . ."

The klaxon at the gate screamed him into silence, and immediately the limousine proceeded slowly through the open grill. The girls ran forward, clinging to the doors and to the steps, kissing through the clear panes the four fresh faces of the children, and Charlotte's smiling face. When the car stopped Charlotte leapt out to them, holding the baby in her arms, her eyes flowing with tears. Ten days it had been, ten endless days! She kissed them quiveringly, laying the baby in Maman's eager arms, and stooping to kiss their faces with one soft tanned hand drooped upon their shoulders.

Then she ran past them to Nicolas and Bridget who stood apart. She was as tall as Nicolas, but strong, with a deep bosom and a flat broad back. When she turned her face away, her body seemed to belong to someone else. It was so strange a thing below those sweet brown eyes, the small snub nose, and the warm childish mouth. She pressed her brother against her, and her wet cheeks against his face. Five years it had been.

"*Mon petit frère*," she cried as if her heart would break.

Her eyes were black under her full heavy lids, her face white and polished as porcelaine. She turned to Bridget and kissed her cheeks, putting her cool quivering hand in Bridget's fingers.

"*Ma petite sœur*," she said. She looked deeply into the strange new sister's eyes.

She called to the children, holding out her hands to them, gathering her black satin coat around her, the embroidered sash; the sprays of monkey fur that shredded at her wrists tickled their four noses. As she turned, the toe of her slipper caught in the hem and tore the lining from the satin, and her tanned fingers fled over the tear, her diamonds flashed brilliantly across the cream satin and gleaming black, and her long nails ripped the torn satin out and flung it carelessly away.

"Oh, Charlotte!"

Maman's grieved voice reproved her, and holding her grandchild close she stooped and gathered up the piece of brilliant satin, smoothing it carefully into repair.

"Oh, it doesn't matter!" cried Charlotte. "The children now!"

She drew them forward, proudly to Nicolas and Bridget: the three with their bare thin legs in sandals and their hair cut straight on their foreheads, Jeannot and Mimi and Monique; and Riquet hanging back in the arms of his aunts, averting a flushed shy face and black bits of eyes under his corn-white hair.

Behind them all was Jean descending heavily from the car, leaning on Papa's arm and on the chauffeur's shoulder. Forward he came, like a risen Buddha, swaying forward on his useless legs, his cheeks like apples, his eyes heavily lashed and intensely blue.

"*Ben, mon vieux,*" he said. He collapsed in tears on Nicolas' lean dark breast.

"What a change you must see in me!" he was sobbing, "what a change! I've had a terrible time; what a time I've had!"

Nicolas stood motionless under the weight of his brother-in-law and cousin who was crying his eyes out on his shoulder. It was evident that he knew not what to do. If he attempted to lift his hand to soothe Jean's shoulder, the poor man sank into the crook of his arm and made him totter. If he made an effort to recapture the canes Jean had let fall, the stricken man sagged at the knees. It was Maman who saved the situation and removed the great sobbing man to her own bosom. There the world diminished to the string of jet that clutched her throat and in her arms Jean gradually recovered.

"Now, Jean," she murmured, "just think how fine it is to be home again. We can have a game of bridge right after lunch, you know." She was chuckling in his ear, but two wrinkles of distress scarred her forehead. "They've made you chocolate cream for dessert, Jean," she was saying, "and a *brioche* for tea! Now there!" He had lifted his head and was beginning to smile. "Now give your nose a good blow," she was saying, "and have a look at Nicolas' Bridget!" Jean was now smiling adorably from face to face with a perfect tear-drop gleaming on each black lash. Enormous dimples appeared in each cheek and he wiped his vast face and his long moustaches clean of all his recent emotion. "You see, we're going to make Bridget nice and fat," said Maman. "And then she can go off to Paris and buy herself a little Nicolas at the *Galeries Lafayette*!"

Jean smiled and smiled. After he had kissed Bridget he smacked his lips as if he had tasted something good.

"Yum yum," he said. There was a perfect white part down the middle of his hair. "Yum yum, yum yum."

The three eldest children had begun to hop up and down, clapping their hands together.

"Oh, we'll have a little cousin," they cried. "A little cousin, a little cousin!"

But suddenly they turned shy and fled down the drive. Maman and Charlotte were leading the way, and once in Charlotte's great salon, the family relaxed. Charlotte and the children were home, moving about in their rooms, and the baby pleasantly and distantly crying. They were all back now, even Nicolas back from the States with his young wife. Here was the family wholly restored, relaxed in Charlotte's salon and awaiting the call to lunch. Beyond on the drive the gardeners in white smocks were sweeping away the fallen acacia blossoms and poplar leaves.

VII

THE CHURCH was new, with a broad white nave. The wooden saints that flanked it had faces as red as fire. More shame to Annick, said Papa. For it was she who had been obliging enough to retouch their faded countenances. A wave of shame rose in her whenever she passed the gaudy *Christophe* in the vestry door. In time they would fade, but to her it was a source of great anguish that while Charlotte's children were small, at least, this would be one of the family jokes and jibes. All through their childhood they would hear Papa talking about it, and somehow this might alter their opinion of her. It might even give them a frivolous conception of religion. It might in some way lessen the dignity of God.

With bowed head and clasped hands she was advancing to take the sacrament at the altar, when she heard a titter rippling under the bowed round hats of Charlotte's children in their pew. Her heart was suddenly stricken cold and for the sake of her own pride she ventured one furtive look in their direction. Their heads were shamelessly lifted from their hands, and they were stifling their laughter at the sight of the *enfant de choeur* who had tripped upon his gown and fallen flat on the steps of the altar. With measured step she advanced, her thoughts in relief turning again to God, her steps bringing her to the priest's encrusted robe and to the delicate flesh of Christ which he stroked down the lifted waiting tongues.

In ecstasy Marthe follow her sister down the aisle. Annick's head had been bowed, but Marthe's hung low like the humblest servant of God. Annick's step had been slow, but Marthe's feet moved as if she trod a shining path. Her elbows were held far from her trim grey suit, her fingers were clasped as if in an agony of delight, and under her lids her eyes threshed back and forth. Once at the altar she fell with the greatest abandon upon her knees and the stormiest emotions caused her bosom to rise and fall. When the priest stood before her at last among all the others she flung back her head, revealing her long full throat, her jaw fell open and the flesh of the Saviour slipped easily down into her very soul. For a full minute after he had passed her by she held the lace curtain of the altar under her chin, her fingers trembling with ecstasy. With what emotion she swayed back and blindly stumbled into the family's pew. She fell quivering against Bridget, seeking out her hand.

Sedately, with dignified tread, Annick resumed her seat. Once a month she took the sacrament, but every Sunday Marthe reeled to the altar with an emotion that never lessened, flinging herself in the most terrible abasement at the feet of the priest. With a breath of relief the children's heads suddenly lifted from their hands, and they all filed demurely out into the court-yard of the church: Maman and Papa and the three girls; Bridget and Nicolas, Charlotte and Jean, with the four children making their four abrupt bows as they passed the holy place.

In the sunlight, Charlotte turned to them all, disclosing her smile. She broke into talk. Her breasts rose, swelling the gold tulips of her blouse, her fingers flew over the buttons of the children's jackets, shaking light through their hair as she pulled off their tight hats and tossed them away into the waiting surrey.

"Yes, Maman, you must drive with us. Yes, yes, Papa, you must drive back with us. Jean will be so glad."

Monique had pressed softly in among them with her face below them and her small head turned away.

"And thou," said Charlotte, shredding her fingers in Monique's hair. "Thou wilt walk with Tonton Nicolas, my child."

Monique swung her head up a little between them and gave Bridget a queer long look through her lids. Her mouth was dark as a plum and her face was thin and golden with wine-silk eyes. Bridget took the small cold fingers in her hand and they walked after Nicolas and Jeannot. Monique put her feet delicately forward on the cobbles as she walked, glancing softly and shyly up into Bridget's face. She was like a bright sleek little animal, a fallow deer turned sensitive and keen to human approbation.

Nicolas walked ahead with Mimi and Jeannot, the boy. They had come to the confectioner's shop and had stopped to exclaim against the pane.

"Oh, *babas au rhum*!" they said. "Oh, *marrons glacés*!"

Tinkle of lemon sticks on the plates, spun baskets pink as doves' feet, flamboyant sun. They went through the shop door and Monique's plum mouth melted in baba juice.

"Nicolas," said Monique. She murmured his name softly and solemnly in her tart.

"*Tonton* Nicolas," chided Jeannot sharply. "*Quel enfant!*"

Bridget and Nicolas sat quiet, watching them. They thought of the children as their own, maybe, with their own blood mingling in the children's bodies. And they sat exchanging small smiling glances over the children's heads, pleased with the rôle of *père* and *mère de famille*. But something like a fury had begun to possess Nicolas, and he started to blaspheme at the sun that was shining too brilliantly on his face, and at the sweetness of the cakes that were sticking to the children's fingers.

"My God, how my shoes are pinching me!" he said. He had suddenly turned yellow and wan, and he sat raging with the ends of his mouth turned up in his face. Bridget felt he was ready to kill them all.

"It would have been better if they had died in my sister's womb!" he said. Just so many more they were, so many more to be sick and disappointed with life.

"To be born with a fortune," he said. "Look at Jean, that miserable creature, born to a fortune and not an idea how to enjoy it! Look at my father, with money put away in the bank to buy nice husbands for Marthe and Julie! Wouldn't it have been nice if I had been born a German and could have marched right through Brittany and murdered the entire family! Not one of them would I have spared. Imagine knifing Jean to the heart!" He sat grinning and swearing at the sun. "Maybe Charlotte would have been saved, perhaps I would have let Charlotte survive. But imagine the joy of slowly killing Maman, extracting her front teeth slowly, and ripping Papa up the middle!"

He sat in the confectioner's shop with his thin legs stretched out in the sun, thinking up the ways in which he would murder them all. Jean, the head gardener, would be bled like a pig.

"The only nice thing about the war," said Nicolas, "was the five French officers I saw hooked up by their jaws in a deserted butcher shop. We came through the town in moonlight, and here were the five gentlemen who had perished some days back, hanging all by themselves by the jaws where the Germans had put them. Sense of the ridiculous, what?"

Suddenly his eyes filled with tears.

"I want some money," he said. "I'm tired of being poor."

All the way home his legs were as strong as legs could be. He took them the longest way so that he could point out to Bridget the place where he had played under the pine-trees in the deep moss as a boy. He had remembered these trees as the highest, the thickest, the most magnificent in the world, but somehow they had diminished now in grandeur.

"It's because you've turned sour, grain of sand," said Bridget.

"Oh, really," he said.

"Sour, sour," said Bridget. But she felt that something was taking place in him that she knew nothing about. She felt he was turning remote, and he was rankling in her like a dim wound in her spirit. He was going cold in protest against the family, and a bitter shadow had fallen across his will. Something shiftless was becoming of him, as if he had forgotten why they had come to France.

"All summer you are going to be at peace, and rest yourself," she said. "And then when you are strong, we shall find work to do again and go away. There are countries everywhere, and when you are strong we can go anywhere at all that we want to go."

"It would be easier to kill Jean," he said.

Before them in the woods the leaves were running like honey along the boughs. How had such thick streams of sunlight ever run into this black northern world? The children were in it, up to their naked knees, prancing and shouting through the woods. Soon they were at the river, and although Charlotte's house and the family's house were there visible through the trees with the road running between the two, Nicolas sat down on the bank and told Bridget the story of the famous sail from Saint-Malo to the country place which he had made with the entire family when he was eight years old.

VIII

BRIDGET lay in the grass watching the sky and the deep green bosom of the elm that stood unruffled against it. A mild bright wind was bellying in the clouds and swinging them steadily across the pure lakes of the sky. The afternoon was tapering down to dinner.

"You'll catch cold," said Papa's voice beside her. His voice bowled down his white vest to her.

"What are you doing there?" he said. He was thrust up between her and the clouds, containing his agitation. His fingers twitched at his sides. "You must sit up in a chair," he said.

She went back with him to the family where they were gathered upon Charlotte's terrace, and there Papa drew up the long low chair for her and patted the cushions under her.

"There," he said. "You must sit up in a chair."

Nicolas looked up over his book, observed Papa's round back leaning to settle the cushions, and turned back to his page again. Maman looked up quickly, alertly, like a bird, and smiled quickly under her nose, and then her fingers returned to their work upon the web. Annick smiled softly and discerningly at Bridget.

"The clouds are so beautiful today, Bridget," said Annick, as if they alone knew. She sat looking at Bridget as if they alone were aesthetically allied. In her fingers was a narrow coarse bit of crochet work that she was working into austere edgings for her under garments.

Jean's yawn fell together and he folded his paper, smiling. Charlotte was coming vigorously across the terrace, carrying the baby against her shoulder while the other children ran about the blue skirts of her dress. She smiled deeply at them all as she came. Her black hair was like a close cap and curled down over her ears and neck. She smiled with the pale triangle of her mouth. Maman watched them over her glasses as they came, her face soft and contented over her nimble fingers.

Charlotte brought the baby directly to Bridget and put it down carefully across her knees.

"Oh, Nicolas," Maman cried out, "oh, Nicolas, isn't your wife lovely so!"

Nicolas looked slowly away from his book. He stared darkly and blindly a moment at Bridget and then he smiled, plucking his fragile amiability from a remote and sardonic source. His eyes dropped from them and returned to the page. Back and forth went his eyes across it as he read. Bridget saw the leaf turn and felt the baby move slightly in her arms. Its black clear eyes were mildly discovering her face, making a slow adventurous voyage across her nose, down her cheek and over the movement of her breast.

Here was the family united again, united with such intensity as if it had survived its first separation. Maman had begun to talk to them all as she worked, and Charlotte was sitting idle, smiling at them and looking out over the sea. Not too far out, but close at the little waves that were murmuring against the terrace wall. Suddenly the church bells pealed and pealed out over the summer fields. They came rocking and ringing out on the warm air: a soft hesitant note and then a warm full peal and volley of sound. The family stared into each other's faces. Maman lifted her head, cocking it and listening sharply.

"Not a baptism," she said.

"It is war," said Papa grimly.

Nicolas lowered his book for a moment. "If it is war," he said, "I'm not going to fight for your damned country," he said. "I'm not going to fight for your damned country."

"Oh, shame, shame," said Maman.

Charlotte walked quietly around to the drive, and Bridget gave the baby to Annick who had clasped her hands and begun to pray. Up the drive she walked with Charlotte, quietly to the gate. The peal of the bells was turning frail as the wind shifted, and the fragile petals of sound drifted along the air. Then the wind turned towards them again with the full clanging stroke of the bells.

Peasants on bicycles were flashing past on the road, and they did not turn their heads to Charlotte's questioning voice crying after them. People on foot were running in their loose heavy boots, running heavy as horses down the road. An old woman fled past with two blue pails swinging in her hands.

"Fire!" cried Charlotte.

She took Bridget's hand and they started off in short breathless runs down the road. Below, the road escaped from the trees and curved out across the green rye and the wheat. They ran a little apart, and children with pails clattered between them, while the full clang and clatter of the bells rang out ahead on the road. Around the turn the wheat rolled away and low knolls of mustard weed glittered against the dark coils of smoke. Smoke in a full throbbing river, flowing upward, dark and magnificent.

Bridget's hands were cold as she ran, and running she saw from the corner of her eye the golden body of a ripe pear hanging under the sharp black pear leaves, near the road and ready to fall. She looked at Charlotte, and Charlotte smiled quickly at her, running at her side and smiling quickly and secretly as though they alone were aware in this fleeing dark and brilliant world.

The red tongue of the road licked slyly along the gorse, and now the smoke was above them, and only the trees before them were withholding the opaque wall of heat. Beyond the trees were the walls of a stone house like discoloured teeth erect in flame, and above them a sky sucked white by fire.

It was the last of the row of thatched houses which began the town. Charlotte said, without passion, that if the row went the town would burn. People were running the length of the street to the pump with their buckets, and when they returned the fire-fighters hoisted the full buckets up the ladders and emptied them down over the flame. Charlotte and Bridget stood in the field before the house listening to the soft rush of the torrent of flame and the gentle smack of the water striking the fire. And then began the soft, soft boom of the collapsing stone. The bells were ringing as if their sides would split, but on another plane of sound.

Presently Maman and Papa emerged from the trees and came into the solid volume of heat. Maman walked quickly, with her shoulders humped forward, her hat on and a coat for Bridget across her arm. She came to them with Papa and then she hurried away into the confusion of people in the lane. She spoke to the agitated people, moving her hands and directing with her sharp old finger. There was a cessation of movement, a visible break, and the men on the ladders were left calling out for more water, shouting aloud although their voices were burned dry in their throats.

Then the people in the street began moving again under Maman's words and the directions of her hands. They were busy forming two lines in the lane from the burning house to the pump. The empty pails fled up one chain of hands to the pump, and then down they swung full again in the other hands to the men on the ladders. There was a magnetic current of energy in the two strong chains of hands, and the great full pails came swinging steadily down until the slaps of water on the flame were thinning out the smoke against the discoloured sky.

Like charred bits of sapling, a few swallows began to curve down in the fading smoke across the wheat and there was a faint stir and sigh among the people like a recognition that it was almost at an end. The water flowed steadily down from hand to hand, and the bells struck slowly now, and without panic, rocking off into silence. The people had begun to chatter over their swinging hands. And presently, perceptibly, the pails began to come slower and slower, to come at intervals, and the men on the ladders stood empty-handed. Faces peered curiously up the line.

"*Envoyez l'eau!*" they shouted.

A murmur gathered down the line, swelling into one great cry.

"*Envoyez l'eau!*" cried the fire-fighters on the ladders. Maman walked down between the waiting people.

"The pump is dry," she said.

Slowly the flame grew up again and the men leaned out from the heat, crying wearily and angrily at the people.

"Your mother is a fool," said Papa. He followed after her with his cane. And suddenly the bells started out again over their heads.

The people were grouping together again in lines, but this time with greater spaces between them so that there would be enough hands to reach out of sight to the pump that was farther in the town. Charlotte and Bridget went into the lines, filling two empty spaces and waiting for the full buckets to swing down the lane. Charlotte's tanned hands gripped the wet handle each time it came, her diamonds shone, she smiled easily each time she swung the full bucket on. This activity became a new and absorbing thing to them, quite apart from the fact of the fire. When Bridget lifted her head she was amazed to see the flames still glaring through the empty window sockets of the second house, and to see the geraniums writhing back on the sill. The men were even mounting the roof of the third house to wet the straw.

The buckets slopped steadily down the line and the empty pails fled back to the pump. There was the soft rush of the flame and the brittle split as the timber fell. The second story had collapsed and the next house was burning. A young man was crawling up over the thatch and hacking the burning roof away. His hands were red on the axe he held, and his sleeves were rolled back on arms as white as milk. In golden flakes the burning roof fell away in the evening.

There was a sudden blind quiet, a relaxation of hands, and the people stood idle, watching up the lane from which no miracle of water descended. Presently the lines fell apart and Charlotte and Bridget walked into the town among the scattering people. The women were frightened now and they had begun to carry out their linen and their vessels from their houses, and to set them away in safety in the wheat. Charlotte and Bridget stopped to help bring out a great carved cradle and a chest of drawers. The village people had scattered, following Maman out of sight in search of another pump.

And now the lines were forming again from a fresh pump under the church, in the very bowels of sound. The distance between hands was wide and arms stretched out to reach the outstretched arms. The men were beginning to sing to the rhythm of their hands, singing slowly beneath the sound of the bells.

"J'ai un chien qui gueule tout le temps . . ."

Bridget swung the buckets.

"Et une femme qui en fait autant . . ."

Bridget closed her eyes and felt the bitter flame hollowing her nostrils, the taste of flame in her mouth. A half hour . . .

"Je m'en fous, je suis élégant . . ."

In an hour the third pump had gone dry. The people broke apart, some starting off with Maman down another street. It was night and the moon had begun to hollow white valleys in the streets. Bridget followed the others down the cobbles, wandering along in mild panic. Charlotte had disappeared. They had come to an arch in the houses with a moonlit courtyard beyond. And in the centre of the court a fountain stood up in the light with a strong dark chain of water stringing from the stone lion's mouth.

They rushed to the arch, the dark figures, crying aloud and swinging the empty pails. But the gate was closed before them, and they all stood transfixed at the bars of it, defeated and silent in the pure hollow warble of the water.

And then two lithe ones ran up and swung themselves over the gate and the pails were tossed after them. The two lithe men ran back and forth, filling the buckets at the fountain and hoisting them high over the grill-work to the ones who were waiting there in the street. And now they were too few to form into lines and they spread themselves out in the little street, far from the cries and the sounds of the fire. Bridget was left at the gate with a man who swung the bucket over and down and she took it in her hands and ran with it down the street to the next woman who ran on with it to the next. Bridget was in a panic of weakness, running with the sharp slap of the water on her feet and hands. Her mind was working calmly and rationally with these people, blank and thoughtless with them, and consumed in action. But her body she felt was almost in death, straining fiercely up from the buckets.

Suddenly motion and sound ceased as if they had all been suddenly snuffed from life. And then faint triumphant cries rang out of the silence.

"*Vivent les pompiers, vivent, vivent, vivent les pompiers!*" the people were crying.

Bridget dropped her empty pail and ran on with the people. The woman who had swung water from her was weeping and she caught Bridget to her and kissed her cheeks.

"*Vivent, vivent les pompiers!*"

Bridget came down among the people, past the piles of fine linen and polished heirlooms in the wheat. The two walls of the house stood charred against the lingering plumes of smoke. The men were taking long gulps of cider and resting their weary bodies before a final soaking of the smouldering wood. Their faces were wet and raw, and their raw hands smoothed their forearms as they talked. Charlotte was among the little groups who were talking with the men who had fought the fire, and when she perceived Bridget she came down to her out of the circle of heat and light.

She came along, putting her wet weary hand in Bridget's hand, and they walked away together through the trees. Maman and Papa had gone on before them, she said. It was almost midnight in the icy-jewelled watch on Charlotte's arm.

"What will Nicol say of us?" laughed Charlotte.

And Bridget suddenly thought of him. Nicolas, Nicolas. As if she could ever escape the rift and pain in her heart.

IX

IT WAS a good day for Nicolas and he was with the men down with the big net opening the dam. They could see them from Charlotte's terrace, working in the water, and Nicolas was striding with his bare legs through the shallow pond helping to adjust the net so that the fish would be stranded in it when the water fled through.

Charlotte had fetched her hat, and with Bridget she turned away from the family and walked up the beach with the children. Riquet plodded beside them with his short legs spread apart and his fat knees knocking, and Jeannot fluttered from rock to rock with his green net. The little girls walked together, winding their arms with sea-weed.

"When we can talk more easily together, you shall teach me many things," said Charlotte. It was always in the future for them, what they should be to each other, promised and secret and unseen.

Charlotte rested her soft hands on her hips.

"To walk from here," she said. "I do not walk gracefully. Will you teach me to swim?" She lifted her fingers over her breasts. "I want to be slender. We shall walk a great deal together, Bridget." She took Bridget's hand and she stood touching the smooth flat flowers on Bridget's wide hat. So much they would be to each other, so much, so much. She stood murmuring to Bridget, and touching her wax flowers, touching the bright beads in Bridget's neck.

It was Monique who came between them, carrying them little seas in her palms.

"I am afraid of Monique," said Charlotte with her shy brilliant smile. She pressed Monique's plum mouth with her finger. "Monique is my confession. I must keep my finger over her lips, this way, saying hush, thou must not betray me!"

She laughed softly in her throat.

"And thy lids down, Monique, over the betrayal of thy eyes!"

She closed Monique's lids with quick touches of her mouth, and Monique danced away, smiling under her closed eyes. Jeannot watched in derision.

"Open your eyes, Mon," he cried.

The sharp cold sparks of the sea fled before them, and Monique stood still in the sand. Jeannot, with his net, turned impatiently away after a brown sloping wing.

The shadow of the poplars quivered across the sand and the cries of the men as they worked back at the dam drifted across the beach in the sea-wind. Bridget walked on with Charlotte, and Charlotte talked to her of pictures, of photography, and of painting. With her hands and her eyes and with simple words she talked so that Bridget comprehended it all. And with such bright shy awe, with such reverence that hands and fingers could interpret the sensations in one's body. All pictures, even bad pictures, were really beautiful and a wonder to her because with hands and fingers one could imitate life. Even Bridget's pictures. They looked like nothing she had ever seen on earth, but to Charlotte they were beautiful, they were to be cherished in wonder.

Bridget listened, and she responded with her few hesitant words, but she kept hearing the remote cries of the men drifting down the wind. She listened, and she was in a tremor of apprehension. Charlotte talked blindly and brightly on, but Bridget kept turning and turning to the sounds of the pond and the stroke of the red crest of the house. But it was all beyond the curve, and hidden, with only the absolute knowledge in her heart that Nicolas was in pain. She went on with Charlotte, but it was unreal to her, the sea and the sand, the full swell and slope of the sea, and the fine dry slipping sand. She went on in terror, quieting her cold fingers in her palms. Whatever in act had come to him was of no importance: the manner of death was indifferent. But she knew that he was done, and in her heart she saw him so clearly, done, and lost to her, with his will sapped out in a new tide of pain.

She thought of him, and she was numb with terror. She listened to the men's fragmentary cries on the wind, and she thought of Nicolas dead and submissive under the solid weight of the pond, with his face like a sharp white shell beneath the glittering chains of water.

"I should like to be the epitome of grace," said Charlotte. "Do you think my arms are too large?"

It was a long time before she was ready to turn back to the terrace for tea. The pond, as they came to it, was still, unbroken and alone, and beyond on the terrace the table waited quietly under the tea cups. Jean was sitting with his stick dangling between his loose knees, and Maman and Papa were playing bridge with the two girls. Beyond them on the lawn, Annick was teaching the catechism to her urchin boys. There sat the family, so unconcerned, playing and talking under the deeper boughs and the thin light.

In the brass sides of the kettle, the wall of the house and the geraniums at the windows were reflected blind white and scarlet and green. Maman had finished the blue sweater for Charlotte and she tossed it over to her between plays. Charlotte stood up above the tea table and slipped the sweater down over her breasts, turning this way and that before them all so that they might see the fit of the belt and the turn of the sleeve.

"*Chic,*" she cried. "Do you like it, Bridget?"

So quiet was the air, so tranquil. Bridget felt they were secured on a safe sweet island, nodding, browsing softly upon a quiet sea. So safe they were, so safe. What a world of women who lived without avarice or despise, what a woman's world built strongly about the men's fortune and the men's fortitude, what a staunch, sweet world that could never fail. No fire or flood to blacken or to rot them, no death final enough to destroy them all. Wipe them out and they would go on living securely in the palm of God. Their fingers busy with a thousand kindnesses, their hearts touched by poverty or solitude. And this strange, hard, bitter thing in Bridget that could have cried aloud. This perverted thing in Bridget that closed like a fist in their faces and that said: "Where is Nicolas? Where is Nicolas? Where is Nicolas?"

"Where is Nicolas?" she said.

But here was Madame of the Dépêches again, pedalling with grim dignity down the drive. A ripple passed through each heart, and the blue envelope was put in Maman's hands. She cawed sternly with apprehension, she ripped it open with one nail. And as she opened her mouth to read it to them, the whole world blossomed, burgeoned, burst into hosannahs of song.

Even Annick came to hear, abandoning the souls of her young pupils to kneel before her mother for the tidings. Luc, Luc swelled in the throat of every singing bird. The afternoon that had come so near to swooning in the heart suddenly sprang lightly from eye to eye. In two days Luc would be in their midst for his month's vacation. Luc, who was to these three virgin women a French career that they had studied for in cathedral naves, had languished for in convents, in their communion veils had learned to bow before, burn candles to, this man who each of the three knew must mean a lifetime crowned or doomed for ever—he who had made no sign of life to them except to brush his hair back, trim his nails clean, shave and scent his face! These girls have gone into confessionals to you, have pulled out their words as smarter girls pull out their eyebrows, crying for patience and a generous heart that would relinquish you to one another! This was the year that Luc would speak his heart out, if heretofore he had performed no miracles but forgot to answer letters, rode trimly on the backside of an ambulance, contended that Anatole France had espoused his secretary and not his cook—but women in menial ways were all one to the family—cooks, secretaries, pastry-doughers, clerks, or even that ignoble Madame de What whom they had cut in the street from the day she had fallen so low as to invent a soap that smelled and sold. Luc was to come, and each one knew that this year his decision would be made—Luc was to come, Luc about whom all romances were written, all plays staged, all histories inspired.

Once the excitement had lulled into a drenching calm of delight, Charlotte suddenly put down her cup and her eyes turned round and vague.

"Where's Nicolas?" she said, looking about at them all.

But Maman had just trumped Julie's ace and the game was too diverting for interruption.

X

ONLY AFTER dinner did the family begin to concern themselves with it. Nicolas, it appeared, had never returned to tea. A fury and anger was growing in Bridget's heart, and a terrible fear, as if the family had done away with him. She knew so well all that he was holding against them in his soul, right or wrong he was holding it against them. If the good devoted family that he had would insist upon his birth, would insist upon bringing him into it, he was thinking, then they must take the responsibility of the disease they had in them and give him the means to fight it as well. So much had he talked to her of it that she thought of the illness as a thing that was the family's possession and that had nothing to do with themselves. The disease was the family's as much as the *pelouse* or the gate or the wall. They were allowed to share it because the family was made up of good people who opened wide their hearts; this was the way Nicolas talked to Bridget and whichever way the truth was she knew in her anger that it was the family and the best that was in them that had turned his heart so cold.

Down, down, down to the bottom of the pond, to the valley of the river, had they pressed his heart with their thumbs; down, under the torrents of bridge games, under the grim Sundays of thunderous mass. Nicolas, Nicolas, she whispered in every room of the house, Nicolas, where are you, what have I done too to drive you away? Annick had taken her wheel out and ridden off to the village to seek him, and Marthe had wandered down the road. Whether it was an occasion for panic or for reason, no one could decide. Papa was following Maman step by step as she squatted among her strawberry plants, a plate balanced in one hand and with the other picking off the ripest fruit. He had several conflicting theories which he was describing to her in every corner of the garden.

These were the things they were all doing to keep it from their minds that something had taken place. No word, no gesture betrayed them nor caused them to look into each other's eyes.

"But he has walked too far," said Charlotte in the midst of Jean, Julie, and her children. "And finding himself too weak he has merely sat down somewhere to rest."

But suddenly the tears rushed from her eyes and she flung herself into Bridget's arms.

"My darling, my darling!" she cried with her eyes still so beautiful and unscarred by her weeping.

But this in itself was a signal of defeat and Maman and Papa who had come leisurely down the drive now hastened forward with consternation in their faces.

"Poor child, poor child!" said Papa. Suddenly his face diffused with anger.

"Has it occurred to you, Jean," said he, "the truth of what has happened?" In his desperation he appealed to the one other man of the family who happened to be present. "What has certainly happened," he went on, quivering with anger, "is that my son has gone off with another woman."

"Ah, Papa," exclaimed Maman in anguish.

"Your unfortunate brother," continued Papa, turning upon his wife, "did precisely the same thing at Nicolas' age. There was a striking resemblance between the two, they both played the violin, and Nicolas' radical opinions since his return to France can be explained in no other way. He has turned against the gentle influence of his wife. It should be evident to you all that he has gone off with another woman."

He placed his trembling hand upon Bridget's shoulder and his moist eyes looked into hers.

"Or there is one alternative," he said. "There is one alternative, poor child, and we can all of us but pray to God that it be so. Your unfortunate young husband has met with foul play. Given the choice, I, as his father, have no hesitation and I feel sure that you all of you share my feeling. If he is lying in the bottom of some ditch, we can but rejoice the day we find his dear body and put it to rest among those of his own flesh and blood."

"You are insane," said Maman. For a moment her eyes flashed wildly at him. "What of your own brother, Auguste, and the madhouse of his home?"

"Is this quite the time, quite the time to bring up stories of my relatives?" cried Papa.

"Yes, oh, yes, it is the time," said Maman, lifting her voice like a weapon so as to pierce their ears. With Charlotte she walked rapidly down towards the pond, hurrying Bridget off between them. "Yes," said Maman, "why he should tell all the stories on my side of the family is extraordinary, *extra*-ordinaire, *extra*-ordinaire." Her voice was challenging, sparring with, piercing the descending evening to its very heart. "His brother Robert who lives in Saint-Malo today," she sang in Bridget's ear, "has had the most extraordinary life. He married a Creole with a great fortune in her own right and six months after their marriage they had a son." Her voice was more muted than the soft waters of the pond which ran in the wind across the ringlets of stones. "Not a word would he hear about it, but surely he made up his mind never to be her husband again, and being a lawyer in great demand, he would leave her for days at a time to plead a case in Paris or other cities."

Here they were close to the edge of the waters and Maman flung up her chin as if there were nothing weighing upon her mind.

"One night he encountered your Papa and asked him to come home with him to dine. There was his wife hiding behind the door and before she saw that your Papa was with him she had leapt on his back, ripped the coat from his shoulders and flung him to the ground."

"La, la!" said Charlotte as if the story were a new one to her.

"She had the kind of warm blood that could not do without him," said Maman, shivering a little as if a chill had run down her spine. "And if he would not come into the same bed with her at night, she would go after him and tear the night shirt off him and claw his back. I saw the scars of it myself."

Down they walked, the three women, arm in arm, listening to the silence of the pond. Bridget saw the sharp ears of the first stars over the trees and she tightened her arms around her mother-in-law and Charlotte.

"She finally had a very handsome young man every night in the house, and then your uncle could come home in peace from the courts and get a good night's rest," Maman went on. "Robert was a good Catholic and as there could be no question of divorce for him he closed his two eyes to what was going on under his own roof. But she brought things to a crisis and she sued him for divorce to have her own way."

Bridget was listening and miraculously making out the sense of the story, but a strange thing had begun to happen in her thoughts. Before she had gone two steps further she knew that Nicolas was somebody else. Until this moment she had thought of other people, outside, strangers, and as herself and Nicolas one sign and signal of purpose and youth, one figure-head carved against the surf of the world, one spirited high will. Now she knew that they were not. Nicolas was this woman's younger son. This was Nicolas' sister who held her in her strong brown arm.

"When the case came to court," went on Maman's voice, "your uncle asked to plead for himself. It came up in the Paris Tribunal and all of us were there to hear your uncle plead the case of the church against the demands of passion. Passion it was she had for him," hissed Nicolas' mother. "Passion, passion."

The sky was as black as pools of ink between the shining stars. Why did you turn from me too, whispered Bridget. She took out her pride and stood it up and shot it through and through a hundred times with her despise. Nicolas, Nicolas, she whispered, and the word led her to no glamour. There it ended, there.

"Never had he been so brilliant," she said, "and he asked as if he were asking for his life that this woman be restored to him. The professional men and all of us cried without shame," she said.

"Poor Maman," said Charlotte, ready to weep at the thought of it.

"And the poor wretch lost his wife in spite of it," said Maman, "while the son was awarded to him. Here was he with his wife gone and another man's son left with him over night."

But now the mother exclaimed aloud and started back.

"Why, what have we been doing?" she cried out.

Bridget and Charlotte looked down as well and saw that they had indeed in their preoccupation been walking through the shallow waters of the pond. Already their feet and ankles were submerged and on and on they had been walking without a thought for where they were going.

There they stood ankle-deep in the water, Nicolas' mother, his sister, and his wife. Never before had the three women been so close. They leapt apart in fright at the sound of their own laughter, and then flurried together again and clasped their agitated hands.

"I saw Nicolas," whispered Charlotte.

"It was Nicolas I saw," said Maman in a strange grieved voice.

And indeed Nicolas was standing beside them, beyond on the path.

"*Qu'est ce que vous faites là?*" he said. It snapped across the little space of water to them. He looked a hideous, thin figure standing there, snapping his sharp ugly words at them. Even in the fresh light of the stars his face was as yellow as bile.

Out of the water they splashed to him, and Maman's concern was now for their three pairs of streaming shoes.

"Ah, Charlotte, your grey suède ones too!" she cried.

Suddenly she put her old hands on Nicolas' shoulders and absently kissed his averted cheeks.

"Where have you been?" said she.

How she could bring herself to say these casual words was a miracle to Bridget.

"Nowhere," said Nicolas as he glowered upon them.

"My little Nicolas," said Maman as though she were drawing a painful subject to its close. "Shall we all go home together now?" said she. "We have all been deeply grieved at your absence." She took his arm.

Charlotte could no longer hold back her tears and she pressed against her brother's side. And Bridget watched them in sorrow and concern, thinking that if she were a woman this was the way she must be. She must speak out to him even if it sounded like complaint, but maybe it was this, she thought, that whenever a woman spoke out without reflection it was really some complaint she was making. Everything she could think of to say to Nicolas was no more than a complaint against him because he had done what he wished to do.

"Am I nothing at all to you that you could abandon me here with them all?" she flung with all the whines, the tears, the protests into a dusty corner of her womanly heart. The womanly heart of me, said she in silence, has nothing to do with where you were or what you did with your bunch of miseries.

"Nicolas," she said for the first time. "How's your bunch of miseries?"

"They're doing very well, thank you," said he. Then he turned on his mother. "But I'm not going home," he said. "I've had absolutely enough of it. Every time I sit down or stand up or go to the Vater or come back from the Vater, your husband asks me when we are going to have a child. It's wonderful to have an old Colonel in the family," he said. "All the devotion, the thought, the consideration for the fatherland. Why don't you have a child yourself, Maman?" he said. "You're only sixty-five. I don't know what you've been doing with your life," he said.

"Hush," said Maman.

"Listen," said Nicolas. "We haven't any money, Bridget and me. We have no money at all, you know. And I've got this thing in my legs that you passed on to me and that I would probably pass on to my son. I haven't any money at all, I don't know what I'm going to do, and this morning Papa said he would give me fifty thousand francs if I would have a child."

Suddenly a silence fell upon them all. A terrible silence stopped the beating of their hearts. How would they lift their heads to this, how look into each other's eyes, Bridget did not know. Without daring to see their faces in the uncertain light, Bridget took Nicolas' hand. Suddenly he stooped and kissed her mouth.

"Mountain, shall we go home?" she said.

"Do you know, Nicolas," said Maman as they all walked up the path around the pond. "Every other year the trees here by the water were thick with nightingales. Never a summer has passed but that they came back to us and sang all night here in the trees. Even in Charlotte's garden there was one nightingale that had his nest in the acacia tree before the house."

"Papa said they would be sure to come back this year," said Charlotte turning her head this way and that as if to catch some sound of them. "But they're so late, perhaps Papa is wrong."

"Hush, hush," said Maman in reproof again as they regained the wall.

XI

How Luc managed to turn the rabbit over, to get the rascal who was running like quicksilver through his fingers, over and flat on its side, over and pressed perfectly flat down with its teeth nosing through the neat split in its upper lip, was a thing that rattled the girls together like the sticks of a fan.

With one finger putting the soft fur back, he pointed out to them the white sore in the rippling flesh close in the rabbit's side. The place they saw was alive with maggots but the three girls had nothing but real pity for this sight. Dismay or horror had nothing to do with what they felt, and once the rabbit had been cleanly scraped out with a pruning-hook of an instrument and a sponge of iodine had been sopped into the immaculate hole in his side, the little beast made the sprightliest leaps across the run and started in shredding his lettuce leaves with, not his heart even, but the end of his nose fluttering, which was the usual thing. The cold eye was upon them, however, and upon Luc who was wiping his blades clean on the grasses and fitting the ivory hilts of them back into his case.

This was the first moment that Luc had appeared really as a surgeon to them, really out of college and ready to meet gaping flesh and the pulse of wounds. They had known of the years as an interne in hospitals, but never before had he stood out to them so as a perfect equipment against death.

"Against suffering and death," said Annick's solemn mind.

She could not take her eyes away from the fine young man whose fingers were snapping the case of instruments back into his hip pocket.

"Against suffering," thought Annick with her hand raised suddenly against her bosom as if to protect her own heart. He was patting the smooth haunches of his breeches with his open palms. Julie, who could hardly bear to lift her eyes to him, observed that the cups of his knees were as shapely as porcelaine demitasses and bulged not a whit above his leather puttees.

"Poor beast!" said Luc pleasantly, with just the proper cold impersonal tone required to set their hearts ringing aloud with the flavour of his pride. In deference they turned and followed him out of the vegetable garden.

It was Marthe, or so it seemed to all of them, who had gone a bit too far. She had hemmed six handkerchiefs for him and in the corners had embroidered his initials with hairs from her own head. This was the thing the country girls did, and the poorer class girls in Saint-Malo, for their men who were going to sea. Even to Marthe herself it seemed the most unthinkable thing to have done, but after the operation upon the rabbit had been performed she felt that all sense of reason and proportion were lost. Indeed in *L'Illustration* were paintings of women, high and noble women, who flung themselves at the feet of a great artist, who shouted themselves hoarse before the footlights, and tore their bouquets to shreds to shower him with petals.

Fleeing up the stairs she met Bridget descending and she grabbed her in her arms.

"Luc," she whispered to her, "Luc. The handkerchiefs."

They went into her room together. The Comtesse de Noailles looked at them with profound understanding. Marthe's trembling hands fluttered a bit of powder on her nose, shriekingly she dabbed her cheeks with the faintest blush of rouge from Bridget's bag.

"Just because I was born here, here, in this house," she was saying to her face in the glass and to Bridget, "is it any reason why I should be different from what other women are? In Paris they would do this, Bridget, and anywhere but in this house a woman would be doing this. But just because I am here, with the family as it is . . ."

Down the stairs they went together with the handkerchiefs folded away in Marthe's pocket. The entire family was settled on Charlotte's terrace. Maman was stitching across the white web of embroidery stretched upon its frame, and the Cross was growing slowly under the deliberate stroke of her needle; the stalks and the petals were growing strongly under the elaborate *fleur-de-lis*. Annick and Julie were sitting beside two deep-bellied baskets with broken boughs of acacia and yew piled beside them on the ground. With their bare palms they were stripping off the small bitter leaves from the yew branches into one basket, and into the other they were plucking the fresh pink acacia blossoms from the fallen boughs.

Jean sat with his slack knees fallen together and his wide hairless hands clinging to his cane. Click and patter went the yew leaves into the basket, shiny they were, like slivers of patent leather. The basket of acacia blossoms looked softer than swans-down, and rich and deep with colour and smell. Charlotte was working a little, idly and gently, here and there. She was moving in a kind of maze of love for them all, turning her head now and then to the cries of the children fluttering up from the garden side of the house. Papa was reading the *Ouest-Éclair*. Luc was with Nicolas somewhere, somewhere not very far for they could hear their voices talking together.

Bridget and Marthe as well sat down beside the baskets and set themselves to work. Tomorrow was the village *fête*, and early in the morning the girls would be up in the square sprinkling out a carpet of flowers all around the church. A deep path of yellow saw-dust would leave the church door and wind through the streets wherever the religious procession was to pass. This would be flanked with banks of emerald yew, and decorated with beds of acacia. The Crown of Thorns, they said, would be drawn in with saw-dust and the pierced bleeding heart with acacia heads. Annick had sketched it out with crayons on a bit of paper. The village people would hang the fronts of their houses with enormous sheets so that the procession might pass along unsullied walls.

Beyond in the stable they could hear the slow heavy panic of hoofs as the ailing cow was led in and tied up for an injection. Jean lifted his heavy loose head and sat listening.

"Ah-ha, they're giving her castor-oil!" he said. His head wobbled from side to side with laughter. The girls responded with their high happy laughs and when they had subsided, Riquet watched them all from under his lids and then slowly and gravely repeated his father's words. A wonderful moment it was for them all that a child of three should say the words so well, so amusingly, and with such charm. Monique flung her arms around her little brother and kissed his flaming cheeks.

"Angel," murmured Charlotte. She caught him up across her bosom.

"Riquet. Riquet. *Petit* Riquet," she murmured in his neck. He leaned away from her, patting her smooth face with his hands.

Down the drive were sweeping two dove-grey nuns with their little faces flushed in the heat beneath their stiff white veils. Charlotte set Riquet upon his feet and turned her face against the drive.

"Charity. Do walk with me down to the pond, Bridget," she said. "Maman, tell them I'm too busy to talk, and give them something, Jean. . . ."

She put her round bare arm through Bridget's arm and they walked slowly and easily away over the grass.

"They sell dresses and pillow-slips," said Charlotte. "I've bought enough for three lifetimes. You shall have a lot of them, Bridget, when you have your home, your place, and your babies too——"

Suddenly the colour mounted in her neck and cheeks and she touched Bridget's hand.

"Isn't it silly the way we say these things?" she said. She pulled Bridget's hand against her bosom. "Feel it there, Bridget," she said, "feel my heart there beating with love for you."

Bridget clasped the long lovely fingers that pressed against her own.

"It was so terrible a thing for Papa to say to Nicolas," said Charlotte. "Darling, so terrible a thing to buy a little baby right out of your heart that way! And such a little bit of money, too!" she laughed now and showed her small white teeth a little savagely. "After all a very little bit of money, you know. Well, maybe that's the French Papa part of it. What could you do with fifty thousand francs after all? For a year you could live very nicely in Paris, of course, oh, very nicely, but after that what would you do?"

The pond was perfectly still beyond the bright breasts of the ducks as they streamed through the water. At the edge of it Charlotte stooped and made a soft caressing sound through her teeth. At the sight of her the ducks changed their resolute direction and came towards her over the glossy water. Beyond the outer wall of the pond was the sea advancing up the river-bed, a bright blue widening blade. White crescents of movement were soaring above it and dipping down upon it as it came, their clear cries drifting back from the far bit of sea and rising over the luminous mud and the pond. The pond was like a deep sweet bell hollowing and echoing the clear cries of the dipping gulls.

"You understand," she said, looking up from her hands in the water, "you understand how I feel about children. This life here, it is the life I want. Ever since I was sixteen I have worn Jean's picture in my locket. He went away with his cousins to one of his father's *estancias* in North Africa, to see the work and the life and to work there himself. It is from there the income comes to him and his father thought it wise that Jean see the ranches himself and how the sheep were tended and how the work was done. A wonderful future for a young man, you know, but he couldn't stay away from me and I couldn't go off to live there and leave the family. So in two years he came back and we were married. We are first cousins, you know, so we had a dispensation from the Pope, and this is the life I want, being so close to the family. Maman and I cried for three days before I got married, and when I went away for my fortnight's honeymoon I was so lonely that Jean had to bring me back in two days."

They laughed, and Charlotte turned her head over her shoulder, laughing. There were Maman and the Little Sisters of the Poor pursuing them down the long slope. Charlotte rose with dignity, put one arm about Bridget's waist and drew her slowly on around the edge of the pond.

"But I know there are people who live differently," she said. "Even my own children may choose to live differently. I do not speak of this, but it is the way I feel, it is so," she said.

She walked slowly and steadily, watching the reappearing points of her suede boots as they proceeded.

"I do not know about music," she said. "Some day you and Nicolas will listen to Jeannot and Mimi in duets at the piano." Her small pale mouth gathered earnestly about her words. "I want one to play the violin, one the 'cello, and one to sing. Mimi has the piano for her own, of course. But what instrument shall we give the baby?" She laughed aloud. "You must decide that for me, Bridget. I shall love it. In Paris I took them to a concert and they hated it. Even Monique. So grotesque. They laughed like imbeciles. Was it because they were too young?"

Charlotte's glance darted back over her shoulder. They had lost Maman and the two nuns. So they walked leisurely on up the orchard, talking together and examining the small green apples that were beginning to swell under the leaves. There too, Charlotte said, there had always been a nightingale who had sung at night among the great black leaves. Presently they had come along the little path through the pine-trees and they lingered a moment by the umbrella-bushes at the grill. But this year he had forsaken them, said Charlotte, and she stood putting the leaves aside with her fingers, touching them gently and hushing her voice as if she thought she might come upon him then in the tree.

Nicolas and Luc were in a garden shed as they came down through the *potager* to the house. The two young men were in white gardeners' smocks dyeing sacks of saw-dust red and apple green, and setting them out in wooden frames to dry. The family was in a fever of devotion for their church, but it was evident that Nicolas and Luc were enjoying themselves with this business because they had nothing better to do. There they found them working with their bare forearms stained green.

When Nicolas perceived Charlotte and Bridget approaching he turned back to his work, avoiding Bridget's eyes, turning away and setting new silences between them. Charlotte exchanged a word or two with Luc and then drew Bridget on around the house to the terrace, to the girls stripping the yew leaves and the acacia into the baskets, to Maman's needle in her hand again piercing the great white web. But the air was cool and ruffled as if a storm had scarcely passed. Papa was tapping the ground spasmodically with the tip of his cane.

"But what has happened, what has happened?" asked Charlotte softly looking into the faces of her mother and father. She could not bear things to be hidden away and made gloomy, sinister secrets. They all loved, they were all of the same blood, and they must share one another's pains.

"Your sister Marthe," said Papa rising, "has done an inexcusable thing."

His weary eyes, bleared with remorse, looked upon his children.

"She has made certain advances to a young man who has shown her no marked preference over her sisters. He is a guest amongst us all and I have no doubt you all are aware to whom it is I refer." He looked ominously under their brows and into the very depths of their beings. "Find it in your hearts to forgive this unfortunate young woman if you can," he said. "I cannot bring myself to do so."

His exit was marred by the fact that he had forgotten the *Ouest-Éclair* on the tin table and that he must a moment later return to fetch it. But this did not lessen the intensity of Marthe's grief, and as soon as he had departed for the second time, she flung herself at her mother's knees in a paroxysm of weeping. Her terrifying sobs rang out across the pond and Maman immediately stopped her needle-work and soothed the head that had fallen upon her lap.

"How times have changed, my Marthe," said Maman. "The courtship of Papa was another matter." Her hands were smoothing down the soft hair in Marthe's *nuque*. "Up to the house they brought him one fine day and the first thing he said to me was would I play the piano for him? This is what I did for your dear Papa, I played 'Euranie' and he sang the words to it, and every time I looked up from the keyboard at him I saw him with his head thrown back and his open mouth singing above me. 'Euranie, oh, Euranie,' " warbled Maman now above Marthe's quiet head. All the girls burst into peals of laughter. " 'Euranie, oh, Euranie,' " cawed Maman over the terrace and pond.

"When he was out of the house my aunt said to me, 'Well, how do you feel? What do you think of that young man as a husband for you?' 'What do I think?' said I. 'I think he has the finest set of false teeth I ever saw in my life,' I said. And the next time I met him was at the church door when I married him, for in spite of his false teeth I had been very much taken by the gallant young lieutenant."

Marthe's laughter rang out the loudest and the most hysterical at the end of this story. Surely they had heard it before, but now it was a great relief to them. It was wonderful to laugh and laugh in the warm summer afternoon and to know that Papa himself was perhaps fallible after all.

XII

MAMAN and Bridget were seated deeply in the grey cushions, and Papa and Nicolas faced them from the little drop-seats of the limousine. Papa's hands, in immaculate suede, were gathered one upon the other on the silver beak of his cane, and Nicolas' profile watched away through the window to the white road that ran out before them.

Maman talked on, as if in spite of the two men who sat so stolidly in silence: Nicolas setting himself away from them and turning a dark blind mask to Maman's voice. Bridget listened and responded with her own few words, and Nicolas sat with his face averted from whatever they had to say, protected from them and invulnerable and still in his resentment and pain.

Bridget had begun to think of her own family and how they had scattered their children out like dice and not held them close together this way in the hollow of the hand. There was nothing in the world she expected of her own people, for they had no idea at all of family life or what a family should be. Everyone was an individual to them, with his own individual way to go, and they never interfered. It was easy to know when they approved of something or when they did not, but they never came in between with a severity it would break your heart to defy. But in this way they were separated people at last and it was only another kind of perversity in Bridget—in me, she thought, it is the perversity of weakness that asks my own family to be a loving Jewish tribe, to be all the more fierce for each other because there is the same flesh on our bones. Because I am afraid to be one person alone I am insisting they protect me with their interference. I am afraid to be alone, she thought. There is no necessity to be one person alone, unrelated. I am afraid to have no family at all, she thought; no one, nothing, I am afraid. Gently she put her hand through her mother-in-law's arm as she sat talking beside her. The responding pressure gave her a curious assurance. She was accepted so because she was Nicolas' wife, she thought, but there was a deep satisfaction in possessing a title that made no demands except that she be gentle, and that she be good and kind.

They were riding to Saint-Malo in Charlotte's limousine and the object of their visit was to call upon Oncle Robert. The son his Creole wife had carried but six months was doing his military service in the colonies and Maman remarked that when Robert was not off on a case, he was at home a lonely man. The town appeared bit by bit before them, low and hooded under its high wall, with pieces of the ultramarine harbour glittering among the tree-trunks of the little *boulevard* which ran half-way about the town. At the farthest end was the bright firm sea and the rocks of the harbour, and quiet sturdy boats of merchandise bulging in past the wall.

The family sat heavily and importantly down in Oncle Robert's frivolous salon to wait, with their peculiarities variously repeated in the eight mirrors which had been built in amongst the panels of the wall. The windows, between lengths of white embossed satin, faced Dinard and the sea. Indeed the family was far too solid and human, embraced as they were by the exquisite arms of the gilded chairs, with their stout clean boots bruising the deep creamy carpet and its fine design of gold. Maman and Papa sat heavily but with a great appearance of ease in all this splendour, but their voices had sunk to whispers and they looked with reproof upon Nicolas who sat silent and arrogant, stretching his long careless legs in disdain.

Oncle Robert's entrance was preceded by the austerity of three tortoise-shell cats striped in deep black. Their loose rich fur slipped rhythmically down and up their narrow shoulders as they walked. The low rose-velvet chair had been left unoccupied, and now Oncle Robert hastened into it, plucking a white thread away from his black velvet knee and settling himself far, far back into the chair until the unsoiled soles of his velvet slippers faced them.

"Imagine me," he began at once to them, "caught in Paris at the moment of your arrival, my children. I was in despair. My feet were bewildered in the gardens of Versailles, my heart flirting with the gold-fish in the Tuileries, and my voice, incidentally, hopelessly entangled in the law courts. When I freed one portion of my person, I found I was even more firmly secured at still another point. Imagine it, darlings!" His hands exclaimed. His hair was cut in a straight white bang across his delicate brows. "The Chinese porcelaines in the Louvre were weights upon my metaphysical ankles," said he with a flurry of gaiety, "and the Athenic bodies were cool detaining hands upon my arm. . . ."

Papa's lip receded from his false teeth in laughter.

"My daughter-in-law," he said, "understands but two phrases of the French tongue, my poor Robert: 'I love you' and 'I am not cold.' "

Maman's voice and laughter revolved in protest.

"And what more need a woman know?" asked Oncle Robert looking with his proud little chin lifted from one to the other. "But you are speaking economically, no doubt," said he with a gentle wave of his fine hand. "You were always, my dear Auguste, willing to sacrifice whatever imposed upon the success of your delightful repartee: the truth, or the accomplishments of your new daughter." His eyes moved rapidly over Bridget, proceeded to Maman and Nicolas, and were arrested again upon Papa's exposed teeth. "Permit me to suggest"—the hard contemptuous beads of his eyes examined his brother's face—"that there are capacities of comprehension infinitely more exact than the drum of the ear. There is the spine, Auguste——"

"The spine?" cried Papa with a burst of laughter.

"The spine," repeated Oncle Robert, but two little flags of colour had begun to wave on his cheek bones. "The spine, my dear brother, the contraption, you understand, that runs down the middle of the back. There is also the iris of the eye, and there is finally the London Calendar which has a motto for every day of the year." His delicate hand drifted across the rose-velvet chair to the polished desk in *acajou* and with one finger he lifted the solid pages of the *Calendrier Anglaise*. "Which has broadened my knowledge of foreign tongues to the extent of"—he looked at Bridget with a frail wavering charm suddenly balanced in his eyes—" 'two is company, three is a crowd.' "

Bridget laughed. The tortoise cat relaxed across her knees, fixing her straight in the eye and revealing its deep saffron belly.

"We have made an appointment with the specialists to see Nicolas," said Maman brightly, stirring in her chair as if to hasten the arrival of tea.

Oncle Robert lifted his hands in horror.

"Do not mention the word doctor to me!" he said with real feeling. "I have coughed myself tediously from salon to salon. All during my sojourn in Paris my hands were violet and my chest murmurous. Do you know what it is"—he pointed his voice over his arched fingertips to Bridget—"to be cold to the roots of your being, and fire as futile as jewellery on your hands? Oh, how I have shivered and shuddered—there is no place, incidentally, where one can shudder as hollowly as Paris. Now, London," he said, "after all London has its open fires and its grogs. London," he said. He was suddenly startled by the discovery of Nicolas' profile yawning against the long piano.

"Nicolas, my dear boy," he said. "Have you been ill?"

But the tea table became the centre of agitation, for the soft stroke of a yellow tortoise-shell paw was curving whipped cream from the fluffy meringue.

"He too has been ill," remarked Oncle Robert, lifting the cat gently away between his thumb and forefinger. "Barking like a fox. I've been in despair."

"Really, Robert," murmured Maman in mild reproof through her tea.

Oncle Robert's fatigued body fluttered on the rose-velvet, his eyes returned a hundred times to proudly pierce Bridget's gaze. They were not friends; from the outset they suspected one another.

"How lovely of you to have become one of us!" he said. "I tell you frankly, Auguste, that were I but twenty years younger I would have asked you for your new daughter's hand!"

"They will stay with us," continued Maman down her nose, "until Nicolas is out of the doctor's hand. Then they'll be off to Paris, or to wherever Nicolas has the most advantageous offer. Will you talk to people about him, Robert? Will you ask the old General if he knows of any openings?"

Oncle Robert's nose hung over his long pale hand.

"How extremely interesting!" he murmured. "You know, I'm afraid I've forgotten the details of Nicolas' work. Ah—just what is it you do, Nicolas?"

Maman's voice stepped brightly in between them.

"He managed a ranch in California, you know. He speaks English. He knows about livestock and horses and crops."

Oncle Robert broke a fragile biscuit between his teeth, recoiling slightly as if the crumbling of it grated upon his ears.

"Doubtless there is a great demand for that sort of thing in Paris," he said vaguely.

Nicolas laughed aloud. "Ha, ha, ha," said he under his moustaches. He leaned back on the piano and shouted with laughter. Suddenly he threw out his long legs before them.

"My dear uncle," he said bitterly, "examine me carefully. My lower limbs are not yet entirely useless, and under the circumstances you can understand that I am not eager to propagate the race. Nevertheless," said he, "nevertheless, my dear one, your estimable brother has offered me fifty thousand——"

Papa solemnly rose.

"Let me explain this to you, Robert," said he with his fingers twitching in fury at his sides. "My son and his young wife find themselves in an unfortunate position. I have offered them this sum to start them off in life together and to establish a little family . . ."

"I wonder how you feel about it, Bridget, my dear," said Oncle Robert rather gently as he turned his sharp little head to the windows. "I mean, about the curtains. I'll tell you what happened to them. Would you ever believe it, they were the loveliest cream colour, just about the same shade as the carpet, or perhaps half a breath lighter. And didn't I have them cleaned, indeed I did, and, believe it or not, they came back as perfectly spotlessly bleached as you see them."

He looked proudly about him to see what had been the effect of his astonishing story upon them and his eye fell upon Papa who was still standing up on his two feet.

"My dear Auguste," said he, "do sit down, I beg you. NOW, the question *is*, would you have them dipped or would you leave them just as they are?"

XIII

JUNE was indeed a wonderful month that year, but the fifteenth was the most beautiful day of all in it. If it was not yet rightly summer, still the feel of it was in all of them and the girls' bare arms were already turning tan. True there had been some slight change in the plans on which they had counted so much: in the first place, Pierre had decided that he could not take his vacation at the same time with Luc for if he did so it meant leaving the *clinique* to subordinates. Secondly, Papa had withdrawn his consent to Annick's departure for the charity camp at Cancale. She made no mention of this. She came down to coffee and milk one morning before Luc's arrival with her eyes raw with her grief. And from this they knew that she was not going away.

But on the fifteenth Luc had already been four days in their midst, and his charm and his beauty were warm generous things that he gave out in handfuls to them all. He had taken photographs of the three girls, he had bought them each a small brown leather case containing two silver-topped bottles. But on the morning of the fifteenth he came down to the table with a new wonder and glory about him. His curly hair was combed back with a more drenching comb and his skin was as clear and delicate as a child's. It was the stubborn little moustache on his lip and the well-shaved look of his jaws that brought up the matter of respect and pride. His eyes were so beautiful on this morning that they should have been anywhere but there in his professional, stubborn head.

Almost the first words he uttered after he had swept his clean serviette across his knees were: "Well, Annick, shall we have a set of tennis together right away after breakfast?" he said. And this was really the first definite advance he had made to any one of the three of them.

As soon as they had all risen from the table, Julie lost no time in flying out of the family's garden, through the gate in the wall and down Charlotte's drive to break the news to that branch of the family. Like magic appeared the camp stools and the garden chairs and the striped umbrellas, and when Annick and Luc appeared with racquets and balls in hand Charlotte and Jean, Maman and Papa, Marthe and Julie and Bridget were already seated along the edge of Charlotte's court. Maman and Charlotte were exchanging a few deep looks of understanding and it was generally considered more or less a lapse in delicacy on Nicolas' part that he had chosen to remain at home and read while this important episode in the life of his three sisters was being enacted.

Maybe it was true that Luc himself had never at any time suspected that the family had definite designs upon his future, but surely it must have been evident to him that he was a romantic figure to the three unmarried girls. But in that terrible moment when he put his racquet upon the rosy court, carefully placed the four spotless balls in its exact centre, and stood up to roll back his sleeves, the three pairs of eyes that fled from wrist to elbow as he turned his linen up and over must have seared the golden *duvet* from his flesh.

As sprightly as a top he whirled across the court, skimming the balls with a quick steady stroke across the sagging net. One, two, three, four, they went. He and Annick were getting warmed up, and Annick was hurrying down the lawn after the four balls he had spun away. Her sweet prim legs were hastening in all directions across the green, and suddenly Luc, with two easy nut-cracker movements of his white-clad legs, had vaulted across the net and was beating the bushes with his racquet by her side. The search for the balls seemed a signal to the family to turn their heads away. The women-folk bent over their needle-work and Papa cleared his throat deeply as he opened the *Ouest-Éclair*. Only Maman felt she owed some solace to the terror of Marthe's fixed bright smile. "He is lost," said Marthe's glassy eyes to them all. "I have lost him." Her crochet needle had fallen twice from her trembling hand.

"How peaceful it is!" cawed Maman to her brood. One furtive eye was watching Marthe's fingers. "What a gentle and peaceful life we have here when we consider the size of the world around us. Consider New York, for instance," continued Maman. "Those postcards of Nicolas' give us some idea at least of how many many men that one city alone contains! Bridget, now what would be your idea, approximately, of how many men there are walking at this moment on one side of Broadway, New York? Now, listen, Marthe!" admonished Maman. "For after all a fact like this should be of interest to all of us, and particularly to young women who know very little about life!"

She kept a wary eye on Marthe's agitation but Papa suddenly folded the *Ouest-Éclair*.

"It is the sorrow of my life," he said gravely, "that one of my sons did not enter the army."

"Such a lovely life!" exclaimed Maman charmingly turning her head to Bridget. "A six-hour day for a man, really," she went on, tossing the fat twist of wool back and forth on her needles. "One fences, one rides . . . So nice for the women," said Maman daintily. "One travels, meets congenial people, dances, plays cards . . . the Colonel was always home half the day with me, always for tea."

"I never had one unpleasant experience," said Papa in a grieved tone.

Hardly had he finished speaking than Annick and Luc came running back on to the tennis court, flushed and laughing together and bouncing the four recalcitrant balls.

Annick possessed an unfortunate underhand serve, but Luc met it gallantly and soon accustomed himself to tossing the balls back in easy bounces. Some of them soared almost out of sight among the heads of the towering pines and when these finally descended on Annick's side of the net, they surprised her by bouncing close to her feet and, as they rose to her racquet, by suddenly swerving away. These balls she greeted with a little squeal of amazement and was unable to return. Her face was very flushed and sweet as she played, very earnest with its trim little nose winged with white.

Never for a moment did Luc's charm and patience give way. As he stroked the ball over to her slowly he called out words of advice as to where she should place herself and how receive the ball. All the more admirable was this, thought Bridget, because he was not a good, patient man. In him there was a gleaming devil that glittered and stung under his cool smooth control. Over the net went his quiet counselling voice, saying this and that to Annick as though she were a sister whom he loved and must guide and direct in all her actions. And every note of that quiet brotherly voice was a terrible stab in the hearts of Marthe and Julie.

"It's ever so much better than last year," he was saying as he began his serve. "But, perhaps, Charlotte, you know, maybe a little bit of something more could be done to the court, you know, to get it a bit smoother. Now, there you are, Annick, right where you are. Now, that was a good one. You're ever so much better than last year," he said.

He was like a brother who had grown up with them all and surely, thought Bridget as she watched him playing on the inadequate court, if he came back to Pierre's family every year this way it was because he had no people of his own, because Pierre had been his friend for fifteen years, and because they welcomed him with enormous feasts and simple excursions, and because he was free to wander where he wished. But the one thing he was free to do, he never did, for whatever his plans for the days were they included the entire family. He never went away alone to a dance or for a weekend. He was their guest, and perfect as a host he was, considering their habits, their preferences, and what to them was a special occasion more than he ever gave a thought to himself.

Because he was such a perfect gentleman, and because his perfection in this idle month of the year was always for them alone, what could they do but be in a fury of love before it. He would have shamed any prince had he put a uniform and plumes on him, and on a surf-board he would have been a miracle on any sea. But all this was for them and their two fresh country houses, his fine arms for the old oars of their row-boat on the pond, and his body to plunge and stretch in the privacy of their sea. He belonged to them. When he exhaled a breath, they were entitled to draw in the same air that had just passed through his lungs.

"Now take this with your backhand swing," he was counselling Annick, and Maman was smiling with pleasure under her nose. But as he turned and stooped to gather the balls upon his racquet, something fell from the pocket which was placed over his heart in his white summer shirt. Although he recovered it at once, every eye had recognized it. And his face had undoubtedly turned a shade deeper as he tucked the handkerchief Marthe had embroidered for him back into his pocket. He thrust it, almost absently, into a pocket of his trousers, but the fact that he had asked Annick to play tennis with him suddenly dwindled in importance. The family no longer hung upon every word he said to her, and presently Papa began to yawn and then wandered off towards the hen-house, and Maman decided to write a few letters before lunch.

XIV

THE SPECIALISTS had examined Nicolas and said that there was really little to be done. For the moment the local doctor could shoot him with injections such as they were giving Jean, and maybe in Paris in the laboratories where they were making a study of such things, there might be a cure. But the best they knew was that he must get away from the habit that he could not use his legs, no meats, no wines; and sea-baths and the sun would be a fine thing. What it was, quite, nobody knew.

"The sins of the fathers . . ." said Nicolas to Jean. "Oh, well, dear one, think how our fathers must have sinned and sinned. . . ."

"Oh, dear, oh, dear," said Jean. Tears had begun to gather on his beautiful lashes. He had no inclination to cry for he really enjoyed his illness very much. Because he could scarcely walk, it was natural that he do nothing at all, and no other life could have pleased him so much as this one of sitting perfectly still in the heart of the family. What he did not notice was, although Papa confided it to Maman in piercing whispers several times a day, that his mind was beginning to decay as well as his legs. But he felt that every now and then a little display of grief would do him no harm. And he found it the simplest thing in the world to do just before lunch when he had not had nearly as much breakfast as he had wanted.

"Now, don't cry, my little Jean," said Charlotte kissing his broad bland brow. "Just look how beautiful the acacia is all around us." Its flowering branches were dripping to the ground. "Why shouldn't we take a journey to Paris, just you and I, with perhaps Monique, and see what the specialists can do. If we find one who knows a lot, Nicolas too can go to him. Now, let us make plans for a little trip to Paris!"

"Oh, no," he said wiping his eyes. "I can't leave Maman and Papa. I can't leave my little children," he said.

The most delicious odours of cooking were beginning to

emanate from the house. Jean looked up and his appetite gathered in bubbles on his lip.

"What I should like to do," he said smiling happily, "would be to take a trip to Lourdes!"

"Well, why don't we?" cried Charlotte. "We could take Monique——" wherever she went the little girl must come—"and it would be a wonderful thing."

"That would be a good easy way of getting cured," said Jean mischievously as if he had got on to his own sly ways. "It certainly would be no trouble," said he. He looked around to see if Maman or Annick were in hearing, and then he continued: "To put down my canes and walk. I don't like the idea of having a long cure in a clinique with injections and what-not fifty times a day. But if Our Lady of Lourdes would do it very quickly, that would be all right.

Charlotte suspected some blasphemy in this, and she shook her head.

"Of course, Paris would be lovely," she said. "After all, there's the Opera, and it would be wonderful to have some new clothes, some cloaks and frocks, and some hats that run around the back of the neck!"

She was like a little girl, clapping her lovely hands together and dancing about them with her hair in the heat curling over her ears. She clapped her hands softly on Bridget's cheeks, and in a sudden burst of love she kissed Bridget's eyes and the corner of her mouth. Rich and seductive odours of chicken in the *marmite* with mushrooms and peppers were replenishing their nostrils with delight.

"What wonderful lives we are going to have!" cried Charlotte. "Bridget, Bridget, think of the wonderful trips and lives we are going to have!"

"But let us decide not to take a trip," said Jean. "We are very happy here, if we went at once in to lunch."

But nothing could quench Charlotte's joy in them all and Bridget began reproaching herself that it was her own shabby spirits that had discouraged Nicolas. He was ill, and with his father opened like a book of wrath before him, he was unhappy, but what was this but the start of their life together, for until now they had really done nothing at all. If once they were in Paris there were many things they could do to make a life for themselves, and if once he would not take things to heart the months in the country would be a repose for him. They were not trapped, she thought as she looked at him, in no way were they trapped.

On this day they were having the mid-day meal in Charlotte's house with the creamed chicken and the children and Charlotte and Jean.

"What I would like to do now," said Nicolas going on with the conversation, "would be to take a few little trips about."

Charlotte opened her eyes wide with wonder. To her it would seem the easiest thing in the world to do.

"But you can't without money," said Nicolas. "Or with just a little money. I don't see anything romantic in going third class."

Charlotte seemed to understand this very well.

"But haven't you any money at all?" she said. Jeannot looked up at them in horror as he heard his mother's words. "Maybe a few thousand francs?" she said.

"About two," said Nicolas. "I thought maybe I'd get well right away, at once. But here I am."

He looked very grim and bitter, eating away at his creamed chicken. The thought of his illness had preyed and preyed on him till his cheeks were hollow and his eyes worn deep in his head. But the anger of the whole thing was that he expected something of his family. They had brought him up close in the warm safe bosom, and now he felt that they could not evade it, that here was his plight and it was they who must do something about it. The fifty thousand francs was an insult because of the conditions it imposed; it did not, so far as he was concerned, exist. It was nothing at all.

It was nothing at all, and yet he wanted that money very badly. When he talked about it to her, Bridget thought that he would do almost anything in the world to have enough for them to start life together in Paris. He would do everything to have it, except he would not have a child. For nothing on earth would he have a child with his illness in its bones. The family talked of the future as if Nicolas and Bridget were two normal healthy young people starting out in life, but it was not so simple as this no matter how they looked at it. In every detail of their living now, Bridget had submitted to him. We are not trapped, she thought, we are not trapped. But she had no plan for escape from the family; she vaguely knew that some day when Nicolas was better they would go to Paris and they would survive.

Escape, said she to herself, escape. It is not a matter of Nicolas' escape from the family, but from his own miseries. Somehow they seemed unimportant to her, the illness, the poverty, because they were in love. Even if Nicolas had, in the bosom of the family, divorced and disjoined himself from her in his despair, she never doubted that they were in love, that they were more in love than anyone had ever been.

The truth of this was even more apparent to her than ever before when Luc came skipping down the drive and joined them for coffee. It was not his habit to leave the family at any time, but here he was stepping through the dining-room window of Charlotte's house, and as he sat down among them Nicolas said to her in English:

"Well, what do you think of Luc?"

It was some time before Bridget replied, for the wine was so good, the strawberries had been as big as plums, and she was lost in absorption in a minute examination of the way Nicolas' hair grew on his temples. It was almost impossible to believe that anyone's hair could grow so perilously beautifully near the wing of his eyebrow, or that an eyelid could curve and open in just that way.

"Luc," she said finally. "Luc?" as though it were the first time she had ever heard the name. "Oh, Luc," she said. "I think he is very nice."

Suddenly she looked at him, and over Luc's coffee cup for the first time their eyes met and held each other.

XV

THE THING had now come to be accepted among them all that whichever sister was uppermost in Luc's affections, Julie at least was entirely out of the running. Never had Luc singled her out in any way, so that when there began to be talk of holding a picnic on Castle Island Julie herself said that she had never in the least cared for these immense picnics. "With hordes and hordes of people," she said. Maman did not at all consider the family a horde and was very much affronted by Julie's terms and attitude. On the morning of the planned departure for Castle Island there was a slight scene concerning the matter in Maman's bedroom. Tears were shed. Not by Julie, who had been ordered to come whether she wished to or not, but by Marthe, who felt that her younger sister should be allowed to do as she wished and saw no reason why, if her sister were remaining at home, that she herself should not wear the new white sneakers which the Galerie Lafayette had deposited at the door.

The sneakers were Julie's but they fitted Marthe to a T, and the inference was that if the rivals had been reduced to two, that the third who was now playing no part in the drama should contribute her all to one sister's success. Marthe lay on Maman's bed, biting the pillow a little to stifle her sobbing. Nothing, nothing would appease her except the white sneakers with their shiny black soles.

"But Julie is going with us," said Maman, "so that settles that. She will wear her sneakers and you, Marthe, will wear your buckskins which were quite grand enough for you last year, so why shouldn't they be this?"

But it appeared Luc had seen the buckskins every day all summer last year. There was no stemming the tide of tears.

"Well, so did he see your sweet face every day all summer last year!" cried Julie in a rage now. "And do you think he remembers it any better than anybody else?"

Annick had quietly listened, but it was evident that this scene had made her sick at heart. Every detail of it, and the principle behind it as well, had sickened her to the depths of her soul.

"My sisters," she said, "this is what I have decided." Her calm face and her unperturbed voice alone should have been a rebuke to them without the necessity of the words that followed. "I think it is Marthe who is really suffering the most, and for this reason I too am going to remain home from the picnic. Marthe and Luc are very companionable together, and I am sure that if she goes off happy in the shoes she wants so much that surely everybody will be happier today on Castle Island."

Maman looked at her with pride and admiration. What a sacrifice it was, she felt, how much more than human from the lips of the one among them all who had received a special mark of attention from the young man! It was almost more than God Himself might have done under such circumstances.

"What a pity that all my girls," said Maman sharply, "do not consider others as Annick has just done!"

"What a pity!" said Julie tartly. "For then we'd all stay home from Castle Island and Luc could fish with Nicolas all afternoon. It's exactly what the poor *type* would prefer anyway!"

Nothing can describe the look which smote Marthe's face at her sister's use of the word *type* in reference to Luc. She rose trembling from the bed and stuffed her handkerchief into her quivering mouth. Without a word she went into her own bedroom, and presently they heard her calling the servant to bring up her buckskin shoes. Bridget and Maman insisted that Annick be one of the party, and Maman finally conceded that Julie—"my *garcon manqué*," she called her as she admonished her to get her hair washed while they were absent—might stay at home.

The two row-boats had been lifted out of the pond and carried across the dam wall to the salty river, and there they were bobbing quietly at the little wharf at the end of the road. A flock of servants was packing them tight with hampers, and Nicolas manned the oars of one boat, while Luc settled himself in the other. As if there were no question in the matter, Marthe stepped into Luc's boat, showing the really beautiful calf of her slim leg as she did so. With the greatest care, she tucked her linen skirts under her haunches. Maman and Papa and Annick followed her lead, and at the last moment Charlotte—with her three elder children—fled down the road and with cries of laughter climbed into Nicolas' boat. Bridget and Charlotte sat on the back seat holding the rudder rope and squinting at the sun.

"You look a sight, darling," said Charlotte, "with your hair behind your ears!"

And if this was not the funniest thing in the world that had ever been said, it was pretty nearly so, for they sat shrieking with laughter.

"All set!" cried Nicolas.

"Heigh-ho!" responded Luc. And then he suddenly discovered that Julie had been left behind.

"Why, where on earth is Julie?" said Luc.

Maman, already in a drip of perspiration in her black tailored coat, cried out:

"It's all right, Luc, it's quite all right," she said. "Julie was not feeling quite well and preferred to stay at home."

But even though Luc was a doctor he would not take this as any good excuse.

"Oh, no," protested Luc. "I say, we can't leave Julie all alone like this!"

"Not all alone," cried Marthe. "She's going to have lunch with Jean."

"Oh, no, I say," said Luc. "Julie must come along. It's going to be a lot of fun, and Julie's young, too, she's the youngest of us all. She must come along!"

Ah, the wormwood of these words to Marthe! She sat with her face as bitter as gall. But there was nothing to do but send little Jeannot back with a message for Julie that if she did not come Luc simply refused to go to Castle Island at all.

They sat waiting and bobbing on the water and Bridget could feel the freckles leaping one by one agilely upon her nose. Castle Island seemed scarcely a stone's throw away, with its fluffy little woods growing all over it and its ruin of a castle hanging perilously to the rocks. There was nothing honest about it, except the little growth of oaks, for the island itself joined the mainland miles and miles up the river, and the castle had been built in ruins to make a picturesque spot in the Rance. The River Rance seemed now quite a worthy river, for the sea was in, and flowing up as it did from Saint-Malo, was offering them quite an expanse and swell of water. On the first downward turn of the tide, shrimp fishing would be lively along the rocks at Castle Island, said Papa. In anticipation of this several triangular nets had been placed in the waiting boats.

Down came Julie and Jeannot together, running at top speed hand in hand. From far up the road the sneakers on her feet had fluttered out as white as the wings of a dove. Oh, what rancour was written upon Marthe's young face! But Annick, for the first time that morning, looked extremely peaceful and at rest. Her sweetness was an actual living thing, and whether it was through pride or through humility, the real truth was that if others were not happy, she was unhappy too.

Had they known that the island had already been invaded that day, the plans for their picnic would have undoubtedly been postponed, but once they had moored their boats and dragged the hampers ashore there seemed to be nothing to do but stay. An entire regiment of English people was scattered all over the island. Some were perched on the peaks of the quite sizeable boulders and the ruins of the Castle were peopled with many English faces. Many of the gentlemen in the party wore little white canvas hats far back on their perspiring foreheads and the ladies wore light-coloured washable skirts which were short and wide and gave their limbs free play.

The island consisted of a small smooth beach surrounded by high jagged rocks, of a steep rocky precipice on which hung the ruins, and on the heights behind the Castle a mild little wood which grew away into a forest of pines through which ran a wide wild avenue that could easily have accommodated eight riders galloping abreast. On to this smooth clean beach Luc and the girls had dragged the boats up between the rocks and set them out of the reach of the tide. Already the hampers of food had been deposited at the foot of the precipice. Maman and Papa had begun the laborious journey up to the ruins and were grappling with their canes up the precipitous path. Nicolas had found himself weak in the legs after the row across and had sat down to rest.

For the first time since Bridget had set eyes upon Luc, she observed an expression of distinct displeasure settle on his face. Some of the Englishmen upon their high vantage points had begun to train binoculars upon the little party of French people who had landed upon Castle Island. Every year Luc had made excursions to the island, and it was evident that he considered it as particularly their own. He knew exactly where he wanted to eat and where to build his fire, just as he had other years.

Marthe and Julie took a hamper between them, Luc shouldered a second hamper, while Annick gathered up the two little baskets of wine. Like pirates with their loot, they started up the rocky path, followed by Charlotte and Jeannot with the remaining hamper, and Mimi and Monique with packages of *madeleines*. Bridget and Nicolas were sitting hand in hand together watching the sea rippling in and out as he rested at its edge.

It was a half hour before Nicolas had finally gained the top of the rocky cliff with Bridget, walking still with his arm across her shoulders, and they found the family settled in a little clearing in the woods. The hampers of food were open and although Luc's face was bleached with his anger everything seemed to be progressing well. The truth of the matter was that the English people had ruthlessly removed the square stones which Luc had every summer made use of to build his fireplace. In fact, some years the fireplace had remained intact, just as he had left it the summer before, but on this occasion the English visitors had under his very eyes carried the stones away while he was setting out the hampers of food.

The girls set about finding other stones for Luc's purpose, and Nicolas sat down among the family with his cane. It changed the whole look of the day with Luc's spirits thus blighted, for when a shadow fell upon his face in this way it was as depressing as if the sun had suddenly given way to dreary weather. But presently a little alert Englishman came skipping back with a couple of their stones for them.

"Oh, I say," he called out "what a delightful place to eat! We can't make our fire burn at all over there, you know. What if we set it up where it was in the first place?" he said. He looked at Luc. "Will that put you out at all?" he said. "I don't want to put you people out, you know."

Luc had no idea of his language at all and went on piecing his fireplace together. And then a happy thought struck the little Englishman.

"Why on earth should we have two fires?" he exclaimed. "I think it would be ever so much jollier if we all made use of the one, you know. You've got such a ripping fire going."

Whether it was that the Englishman read something like acquiescence into their faces, or whatever it was, he suddenly called out to the great regiment of his countrymen. "Look here," he called out. "Here's a fellow who knows exactly what he's about. He's got a perfectly splendid little fire going. What do you say?"

At this moment Bridget spoke.

"Do you really think there's enough room?" she asked the alert little Englishman who was herding his party into the moss-lined circle.

"Oh, do you speak English? Do you really?" he cried. "Well, isn't this jolly. But I do think there's room, you know," he said. "We look an awful mob, don't we? But we're only thirty-two."

Aside went the branches of the charmed circle; the deep moss groaned and perished beneath the sixty-four advancing feet, and the little Englishman threw the most indulgent smile upon the party of French people.

"I do feel as though we might be trespassing," he said in the politest way in the world.

While two members of his party occupied themselves with the preparations for lunch, the little English leader talked and talked to the others about the physiognomy of Brittany. They had come on foot from Dinan, it appeared, to see this lovely old-world spot and to witness the rising tide in the late afternoon. He had pulled aside the boughs of a thick low oak on the very edge and there, directly below them, as if he had opened a window, was the sea. Impossible to believe that they had climbed so high or that they were anywhere except upon an inland plain. It was the greatest surprise to English, French, and to the American as well to see the hard steel scales of water among the cones and needles of the pines that stood between.

"A safe enough little river from here," said he. Suddenly he leaned down and seized upon a leaf which he lifted in his narrow sharp fingers. The bough of the oak he had been holding open for them to see so far below swept back like a fan. "Oh, do see what I've found!" he cried out to his people. "Do come and see what I've found!"

"Oh, rare and beautiful," he murmured. "Not a web broken. Every thread of it perfectly reeled from the cocoon."

It was the skeleton, the magic ghost of a leaf he was holding out to show them all.

"I can't get over it being so lovely," he said. And then his sharp little fingers snapped closed in his palm and his eyes danced after the slow descent of the tufted pinch of dust that fell from his hand. Before the powder of the crushed leaf had time to reach the earth, his eyes had raced to the white silky moss and lingered upon the stalks of moss upon which it was to fall. Suddenly he smiled winsomely at the entire company.

"*De nihilo nihil fit*," he said.

The stubborn professional beetling of Luc's golden brows had succeeded in boiling the French water first, while two young English gentlemen took turns at holding the English tin saucepan over whatever bits of flame escaped Luc's vigilance. Almost at the same moment the two parties sat down in the infinitesimal space the clearing afforded them, with the woods and the beach and all the rest of the land going completely to waste. The French people sat deliberately down with their backs to the thirty-two English people and ate their hard-boiled eggs and their radishes in silence. They were not accustomed to talking much at mealtime, but had they spoken now they had no chance at all of hearing each other's voices. The other party was conversing in polite English voices and behaving in a very mannerly way, but the number of them conversing simultaneously put any other thought or speech, or any emotion, out of the question.

The meal had begun when the little fiery-eyed leader discovered that his party had not provided him with hard-boiled eggs. He was very winsome about it, and pretended that he was in the very worst kind of distress because the English women of his group had never thought of preparing hard-boiled eggs.

"Oh, I do love a hard-boiled egg," he began. Papa's back was facing him, and Maman's gloomy black parasol was opened against the entire English party, but the little leader began to throw the most charming looks into their midst. "Could I possibly wangle a hard-boiled egg from you?" he said. "I don't really need a very big one," he went on. His French was perfect when he chose to use it. "I mean to say, that one which the little girl has just broken open would be about my size."

Under the relentless eyes of her family, Mimi handed over the egg to the strange little Monsieur. In doing so she was so shy that she could have perished, but she had been taught to be polite.

The little man began to talk now. He thought it was awfully decent of them to have given him the egg, he said, and he began to tell them about the parties he took on walking trips around Brittany. He knew Brittany as well as he knew the inside of his hat.

"You speak French very well," said Nicolas, and for this Luc was ready to hate him forever. One long gleaming look of despise from Luc made Nicolas go on. "Hardly an accent," said he. Papa could hardly control himself. An Englishman speaking of Brittany as the inside of his hat! But the rebel son went on exchanging compliments with the little English guide.

"Well, I teach French to students in the University of Tibet," said he. "But this isn't a bad way of spending one's summers, you know. In fifteen minutes, by the way," said he, looking at his wrist, "I shall begin my talk on the historical legends of the Castle."

"I can give you a good one," said Nicolas. The little man leaned forward. "It was built just as you see it today," said

Nicolas confidentially to him, "about twenty years ago of machine-cut rock. Didn't you notice the brick lining under the staircase?"

The little man had gone a shade lighter. The globe of his eye was white as milk in his brown face.

"How decent of you to tell me," he said. "But, I say," he went on, "shall we keep it among ourselves and not let the members of my party in on it?"

His bright little glances darted about at them all.

"Why don't you all have a drink of cider with us?" he suggested. He held up two great bottles of the stuff and to Bridget's surprise every one of the family accepted, save Luc.

Glass by glass the family warmed up to the little man and Papa in particular was delighted with the stories he told of the castles and cloisters in the remotest corners of Brittany. It was evident that his life had been an active one and that he was accustomed to directing others. In a moment he leaped to his feet and blew on a little whistle that hung about his neck.

"Now, will the ladies be good enough to go over to that side of the wood?" he said when silence had finally fallen upon them all. "Yes, that's right. I think you'll find yourselves quite out of sight behind those trees over there, and will you be good enough *not* to return until the whistle sounds again? Thank you."

In some confusion the ladies gradually made their way off in the direction he indicated, and were presently lost to sight among the trees, while he himself led the gentlemen of his party off to another corner of the woods. The French family sat talking together, apparently oblivious to the implication of the English people's absence. Again was the sharp whistle heard on the air and immediately men and women alike began to wander back to the clearing, nonchalantly talking of the clear weather and the view, for all the world as if they had not but two minutes before been poised in the most awkward positions behind the trees.

"My fifteen minutes are exhausted," said the little Englishman, wandering back as carelessly as the others, "and I cannot abandon my legends, even for the sake of verity."

With this he led his countrymen away to the tower and there the French family could hear his voice instructing and declaiming.

XVI

BEFORE the afternoon was over it became evident that a rain storm was gathering in the air. The sea had entirely receded now, and the River Rance was a narrow little runnel flowing downward between the great wet flanks of mud. All below them now looked like a volcanic land, and far at the bend which flowed on to Saint-Malo was the storm curving up, solemn and opaque.

As it broke over Castle Island, the French family took refuge in one of the tower chambers. There sat Maman and Papa and Charlotte and the children squatting on the empty hampers in the cold stony room. Bridget and Nicolas stood together by the narrow tower window watching through the rusty bars of it the deep banks of mud such miles below them, and the thread of a river, and the swinging white curtains of rain. Luc was in fine spirits again and for the benefit of Marthe and Julie he was doing a lively Spanish dance to the piercing screams of their laughter. In and out of the doorway, and hither and yon did he go, flinging his chin in the air and knuckling his hands on his hips. Never had the old tower room echoed to such peals of pure delight.

Maman and Annick were never his enthusiastic admirers when he began to play the fool, and now they sat talking together about graver things. Annick was putting all her hopes these days upon a trip to Lourdes, the pilgrimage to Lourdes under the direction of Father Bimont which would take place in the early autumn. Their voices were almost inaudible under the bellow and rumble of the storm.

Bridget looked at Nicolas' face as he stood close to her looking away over the drenched beach, over the mud banks and the long deposits of sand. The bed of the river itself was like any earthy river bed, but with the sea washing up it twice every day for centuries much sand had been deposited and left along the surface, and the beach of Castle Island was made up entirely of what the sea had left behind.

There was no denying it, thought Bridget as she looked at him, that Nicolas had changed his mind. The romantic thing of love for themselves and for their own pride and strength had altered, and now she thought that Nicolas did not know or care whether or not she was standing beside him. He was perfectly absorbed in the spectacle of clouds and earth below him, she thought, and in some conjectures of his own mind, but without turning his head to her he suddenly began to speak.

"How do you feel about having a child?" he said.

"Let's surprise them," she said. She put her fingers tentatively through the crook of his arm. "Shall we surprise them all and have a child?"

"Are you joking?" said Nicolas. His face had never changed.

"No," she said. "I don't believe I am joking. I'm not quite sure." She stood holding his arm close to her and watching the warm white swinging curtains of rain. "We would have the money then," she said. "And we would go away."

"You're just as criminal as the rest of them," said Nicolas.

They stood watching the storm for a while, and then Nicolas said: "We have to do something," he said. "I'm not getting better here, and the family irritates me, and in Paris there are doctors who maybe could help me out. We could do translation jobs together, if we had a little money to start off."

"Well, what shall we do?" said Bridget. She was ready to do anything at all.

"I am going to ask Charlotte to lend me some money," he said. "Jean has never in his life made anyone a loan of money, but maybe he will make a difference for you and me. I want to go to Paris at once, next week, before I get worse. I'm going crazy here like this," said he.

Bridget felt her heart and her soul melting to him, her blood turning weak in her veins for him, and she flung her arm about his narrow waist.

"Yes, yes," she said, whispering in her love for him. "Yes, yes, Nicol, anything you say."

The storm had abated and the few spears of water that still fell were polished and bright with sun. Presently a rainbow sprang up from Charlotte's pond and arched over the tiny river. In a moment the family emerged from the tower room and descended the dripping steps. With the empty hampers they made their way down the path among the boulders, and now they could see the waters from Saint-Malo beginning to rise and churn far down at the bend. Miles away was the tide coming in and up the river bed to them, and Papa estimated that in not more than twenty minutes the waters would have reached Castle Island and gone past them to Dinan and then they would be able to launch the boats and set out for the homeward row.

The family made their way slowly down, for the mud was slippery as glass and the rocks as black as ink after the rain. From this distance the advancing sea seemed ineffectual enough as it came up like a widening blade between the two rolling sides of cultivated fields and winding roads and thatched towns. The sea was apparently creeping up the river bed into the very heart of the countryside, but from this distance it was such a small bit of the sea that no one feared it at all. The party of English people had miraculously reappeared, had sprung up after the rain and were crawling over the rocks of the descent to settle themselves in the best positions to view the approaching tide.

The French family settled down at the foot of the precipice they had just descended and waited for it to come. At the present moment they could almost have walked across to Charlotte's house which looked quite life-size sitting on the edge of its pond. Except for the danger of sinking in the streaming banks of mud and in the clear strips of sand, they could easily have made their way by foot to the river that ran deep in a crevice in the mud, leapt across it, and continued on foot to the other side.

Here they sat with their various thoughts and conversations when the thunder of the advancing waters began to shudder along the ground. Such a mild looking line of blue sea it was coming up the wide bed of the river with the gulls dipping and curving over it as it came. Even the gulls' cries they could hear now, and a sort of tang and whistle of the sea on the air. When it reached the wall of Charlotte's pond, they began really to see it. One straight arrow of water shot directly up the descending river's course, and behind the arrow came galloping and galloping the thundering regiment of white riders, tearing and pitching forward with the volumes and miles of blue water piled at their galloping heels. Along the edges, there was very little movement and the water seemed merely to be rising steadily but smoothly along Charlotte's wall. But in the centre was this thunderous advance of white horsemen with the gulls screaming and picking at their heads and their feet galloping steadily and relentlessly on towards Castle Island.

The island lay right in the course of the crested thundering waves which advanced abreast with the hard deep waters packed at their heels. Bridget reached for Nicolas and clung to his hand, transfixed by the glory and terror of the sea's advance. The children were close in Charlotte's skirts, and Luc, with his capable bright head lifted, was sniffing the wind. His small nostrils were spread with delight and he turned to shout something to them but no sound could be heard except the sea's wild hollow roar.

On and on came the sea, and just as it seemed that it must rear up upon the beach at Castle Island, it split thunderously apart and as if with a common will the greater number of the white riders went full speed up the river to the right side of the island with the deep blue sea behind them in full cry. Those who remained turned and snarled and splattered in confusion among the rough rocks on the beach's edge, and then in a moment turned off to the left of the island with what was left of the pack of sea behind, and thus cantered out of sight. In this way Castle Island again became an island in appearance and was again cut off from the mainland to the naked eye.

Now wherever they looked there was no spot of mud or land until the opposite shore. The closest haven was the wharf on which Bridget and Nicolas had danced one night with the country people and the fishermen, and further down stream was the top of Charlotte's wall. The waters had mounted almost to the top of it, but only twice a year did the waters really surmount the wall and flood the pond and even, at unusual times, run into Charlotte's garden. Once the sea had come into her kitchen. But the incoming tide they had seen today was the thing that had happened daily and nightly, day in and day out, for centuries. And day in and day out for centuries had the poor little river been shot through by the advancing waters and been turned completely around in its course and rushed upstream as hard as it could go.

Hardly had the first impact of the water passed them by than the family began to move down the beach. The sands had greatly diminished since high tide, but Luc had known very well how far inland he must draw the boats and they were still out of water. Into them they tossed the empty hampers, and then Luc and the girls began to drag them out towards the rocks. The sea was lapping in so gently now, sucking between the boulders with a gentle slap and throb. Julie, in her direct mannish way, was settling the oars in their sockets and swaying back and forth as she stood with her legs set far apart. Above them were the English, perched on the rocks with their binoculars, and far, far above them was the ruined tower with its windows open like eyes in exclamation, deserted and far above them in the oaks.

It was Luc who climbed upon a rock that had some footing to it and swung the family up and over, one by one, from the beach into the bobbing boats. Over went Maman and Papa in his strong young arms. He put his hands beneath their armpits and swung them lightly over. The veins bulged a bit in his temples as he lifted Papa, but the three girls were like feathers in his hands. Over went the children like puffs of wind, over went Nicolas, but not entirely, for he swung himself a bit on his cane besides. And once in it, Nicolas found his own boat was filled, with Charlotte and Bridget still waiting on the shore.

"Well, no matter, no matter," said Luc. "The others can come with me."

Charlotte protested that for nothing on earth would she let Luc lift her over into the boat.

"You could get a hernia for life," she kept protesting. But in spite of her opposition he grabbed her up and swung her great laughing figure into his boat. After this struggle he leaned back a moment against the rock to catch his breath.

"You see," cried Charlotte in remorse, "I've almost killed you!"

"But nothing of the sort," he said, laughing, and as if to prove it he leaned over and took Bridget's armpits in his hands. He swung her up against him, and as he regained his balance he held her there. Her breath had scarcely the time to come in and out, and then he set her down in the boat on the other side, but in that second of hesitation she had felt the deep bell that had been set ringing in his blood.

Nicolas and his little party in one boat had already pushed off and they could see that Julie had taken her place beside him and was pulling at one oar. And now Luc's craft began to nose quietly out through the rocks. He was using his oar as a paddle and guiding them gently out. The sea looked to them now as mild as a lake on a summer day, but they could see that Nicolas and Julie together were having some trouble ahead. And indeed once they were clear of the rocks and out in the open water, the current struck them like the palm of a hand. The senseless current struck them and swung them straight about and again the rock teeth tore sharply through the sea, covered and bare and covered again against the ribs of the boat.

But Luc was not to be caught a second time unawares. He clung to the oars as if their lives depended on it and, as he rowed, Bridget watched the sharp quiver of his strength down his body and through his braced legs to his wet bare feet. All about them the current was coiled dark and close like a great soft cobra, wrapped dark and stifling about the brittle ribs of the boat. Marthe and Annick sat behind Luc, and Annick was singing to them in her high clear voice. Before him sat Charlotte and Bridget, guiding the rudder, and Bridget looked for a moment at his fine arms tapering to the oars and then looked away. Now the water was swinging in clear ovals of milk and green about them and Luc had rowed them gallantly through the roughest piece of sea.

Suddenly they felt the boat released and they glided away over a clear bright stream. Luc leaned back on his oars a moment and then began to row with long easy pulls at the water. Presently they had outstripped Nicolas' party although Luc did not seem to be exerting himself at all. There was a burst of laughter from the children as they passed, and the family all called out to one another and waved their hands. Luc's little boat sprang lightly on towards the shaggy legs of the wharf and the others were left to follow in their quivering wake. When Bridget looked at Luc's oblivious face and listened to Annick's voice chiming out in song she had to remind herself that in that moment of hesitation upon the rock she had heard in her heart the rich ominous thunder of his blood.

". . . *t'es bien trop petit, dame oui,*" sang Annick, and her voice singing made the air innocent and pure. By the time they had drifted under the wharf with the sturdy legs of it striking the quiet water, Bridget was thinking that maybe it was a dream of some kind that she had had and that there was no truth in it at all.

XVII

ON THE following day it was that Oncle Robert drove out to them from Saint-Malo.

It was his custom to come this way upon them without a word of warning so that Maman complained to Bridget and the girls as she fled from bureau drawer to dressing-table that never by any chance did Robert find her with a clean white band around her throat or any but an old skirt on her.

"It would be such an easy matter for him," she said as she pinned fast a bit of ruching under her chin, "to send a telephone message by the doctor. It isn't as if we were cut off from all communication," said she. "The doctor is every day at Charlotte's for the baby or for Jean's injections, or for this or that, so that at times I wonder if Robert does not come with some end in mind."

"It's the only way he can see you without a collar," said Julie. She was in a soiled pink linen dress and she had no intention to change.

"It would give him the greatest satisfaction," said Maman—her moistened forefinger and thumb were rapidly pinching into place the pleats of her black cloth skirt—"to see a bit of dust that hadn't been swept up in the hall, or a dish cloth left hanging on the line."

Her mind was making a hurried and painstaking tour of the entire house, peering into odd corners, smoothing out imaginary creases here and there. She squinted grimly at herself in the small glass in her room, cawed a few words to her daughters, and hastened down the stairs. Papa and Nicolas were chatting with Oncle Robert in the salon and Maman's ardent wish was to hasten him out to have tea in the garden before his eye should fall upon the case of miniatures. She knew quite well that a coffee cup had been set down upon the glass of it and had left a ring.

"I cannot wait for any of you," she said to them. She must fly down and put herself between Oncle Robert and the case of miniatures until she could somehow manoeuvre him out-of-doors. "And Bridget," she said as she began her descent of the stairs, "your dress with the long sleeves and buttons is much prettier on you. I do not mean it as a criticism, my dear," she said, putting her hand on Bridget's arm. "But this one is perhaps a little crushed and a little bit too low in the neck for Oncle Robert."

Cawing hoarsely at her daughters, she hurried down the stairs in her high black button shoes. To get inside her head for a minute, thought Bridget as she was left in the hall, it would be a funny thing to get inside and know what was going on. Why do you put up with my low necks and my bare arms? she thought. Such loyalty to a young man who would stick you in the middle if ever he got the chance at it. The ship is sinking, old woman, the family ship is rapidly going down and you must cling to me as well as to all the other members upon board. Once you recognize in us the rats who would sell their skins to skurry from the sinking ship, all will be lost. She could hear Maman's feet striking the tiles of the front hall-way. Her words, sharpened with reproach, pierced the deep well of the stairs:

"*Mon cher Robert.*" Bridget could hear the chirping of her kisses as she pecked at Oncle Robert's face. "*Mon cher Robert*, how nice of you to have come!"

As Bridget went into her own room she slammed the door. In this house it was an offence of some kind. In this bosom so exposed to the human love of simple things, of children, of daughters-in-law, this love of the Church, she had almost carelessly, but still viciously enough, slammed the door. As she did so at least twenty doves were startled into flight from under the eaves of the mansard windows of the room, and off they went dipping and circling about the tidy garden. Bridget paused at the dressing-table and took off her dress. The grass blinds were gently blowing, and beyond them were the trees flowering darkly and richly at the windows, and presently the doves returned to the mansard eaves and were again strutting about and cooing there.

Such a cooing of ring-doves there was under the low eaves that not a tear could have been heard had it fallen. And why should I cry, said Bridget to her own face in the mirror. Why in the world should I cry? She stood watching the tears as they came up, swelling under her lids and rolling singly away down her cheeks. So much more beautiful than any smile could be, and yet they were the speech of sorrow. Nicolas, Nicolas, I could be a brave woman if I tried, she was thinking. She stuck out her tongue at her crying face in the mirror. If I were a brave woman I'd go out and make a fortune, she said. She had not noticed that someone had tapped lightly at the door and had come in. She noticed nothing but her own shameful face in the glass before her until Marthe suddenly threw her arms around her neck.

In a passion of love Marthe held Bridget close in her long naked arms, and although Bridget tried to turn soft and cling to her, she felt herself rigid and hard as bone, standing apart.

"My poor sister," cried Marthe to her in a distressed whisper. "I know why you are crying. You wish to go away. Like all of us you want to go away. Annick wants to go into a convent, and I want to go away and marry Luc."

Marthe sat down upon the bed and her hands pulled Bridget down beside her.

"I am sure, Bridget," she said, "I am sure that I am the one who should marry Luc. Annick, at heart, it is a convent she has always wanted. And perhaps you do not know, perhaps Nicolas has not told you that there are certain reasons why Julie should not marry anyone at all." Her voice whistled sharply through her teeth. "Julie is not like an ordinary girl, you know. Every month something happens to all of us, of course, but it has never happened to Julie although she is eighteen. The doctors say maybe it never will. But don't you think Luc should be told this, Bridget? Don't you think it should be Pierre's duty as our brother to tell Luc so that Luc will be able to decide? I think Pierre could talk to Luc very easily and tell him that at heart Annick would only be happy in a convent and that Julie could never be a mother, you know, and in this way it would make it easier for Luc to decide."

Marthe sat looking eagerly at Bridget through the filtered light of the room.

"Don't you think I'm right, Bridget?" she whispered. She sat fondling Bridget's hand. "Don't you think it's the thing Pierre should do?"

But now Annick's pure mild voice had floated up the stairs, reminding them that Oncle Robert and Maman were awaiting them for tea. Bridget pulled her modest dress on, combed her hair with a wet comb, and with her arm around Marthe's waist, she walked down the two flights of stairs.

"No, no," Oncle Robert's voice was politely protesting as they entered the salon, "I assure you, my dear, I am ever so much more comfortable here than I should be outside. I have not acquired that charming rustic habit of taking nourishment under the trees. The light disturbs rather than allures me and I am constantly besieged by bugs. They flit into my tea and drown there with the greatest unconcern. They relish, in particular, long venturesome excursions between my collar bone and navel——"

"Oh, Robert," protested Maman. She had been vainly attempting to whisk a lace tidy from a chair back to the case of miniatures in order to conceal the mark the coffee cup had left there two days before. And when Marthe and Bridget entered the room arm in arm, Oncle Robert turned to welcome them and behind his back Maman manipulated the rapid change.

"My dear, dear Bridget!" exclaimed Oncle Robert. He laid his frail hands upon her shoulders and with his lips pursed up he drily kissed her cheeks. After he had passed on to welcome Marthe, the clean fragrance of his soft white hair lingered, and Bridget felt a burst of sympathy and affection for the delicate old man. He turned to Maman as she sank at last with unspeakable relief into a chair.

"Now, why do you cover up that lovely miniature case?" asked Oncle Robert immediately, as if possessed. "I do declare, Auguste," he murmured to Papa with the faintest of smiles, "women would be the destruction of all aesthetics were they not the inspiration of them as well."

Across to the case of miniatures skipped Oncle Robert and with two fingers flecked the lace doily away.

"These precious things," he said, "should never have even a shadow of lace upon them. Have you examined them, Bridget dear? My beautiful Bridget," he murmured as she came and stood beside him. His fastidious hand moved absently across her buttocks. "Have you ever remarked that perfectly exquisite miniature of your dear father-in-law, a veritable masterpiece created from sixteen photographs dating from the age of six months until he was twenty-five? Hence the slight obesity about the middle which was no more than a childish characteristic that completely disappeared once he had forsaken his mother's breast, and hence also the suggestion of a moustache upon his upper lip." His hand had progressed upward and was lingering upon Bridget's shoulder. "It is safe to say that this is a speaking likeness of your father-in-law's first quarter of a century. But what a shame," said Oncle Robert in an aside to Maman, "that the servant you now have does not keep things in the immaculate order which has always been such a principle of your house!" He pointed an accusing finger through the glass cover to the miniature.

"There are several fly specks upon Auguste's brow, and

certainly someone set down a cup of something or other right here on the glass."

Fluttering his handkerchief he sank exhausted into an armchair and crossed his small neat feet before him.

"But to come to the point of my visit," said Oncle Robert as if it had occurred to him that the discoveries he had just made might be mistaken as the cause. "I want to offer a betrothal gift and a luncheon to whichever one of my dear nieces has decided to marry Luc!"

One little hand precisely rapped out the words into the palm of the other, and as he spoke Marthe turned livid, Julie made furtive grasps at the hairs that were straying as if in a high wind about her ears, and Annick looked up from her needlework and smiled.

"It is very, very good of you, Oncle Robert," said Annick.

"Not at all," said Oncle Robert mopping at the tiny beads of perspiration on his temples. "Only I have no idea how matters stand. My own humble conviction is that Annick would be the one most suited to Luc's professional ways. I am persuaded, my lovely Marthe, that you are still a bit young and extravagant, and I know that Julie's tastes run more to robust things such as *le sport*. But Annick——"

"Annick was always your favourite, Robert," said Papa savagely. His false teeth slipped up and down in his annoyance. It was evident that both Maman and Papa resented Oncle Robert's interference. Maman's silence as she plied her crochet needle indicated that she considered Oncle Robert's interest most exaggerated and most insincere.

". . . Annick, peculiarly suited by temperament and inclination," continued Oncle Robert, raising his voice as if to cry down any opposition. "But here," he said, "is tea."

"It was certainly no more than that he found he had an idle day in Saint-Malo," Maman confided to Bridget as they walked ahead of the others down Charlotte's drive, "and so came out to put his finger in other people's affairs. He is, of course, in terror of dying alone and thinks that Annick would be the most devoted and return to nurse him if he ever fell ill, but as far as any affection goes! And as for making a present!" Her voice went off in a shrill whistle of derision. "He has never made anyone a present in his life," she said. "And of course he is quite mistaken about Annick. Marthe would make the perfect wife for Luc. That is so evident that it is not worth discussing——"

Luc himself came walking up the drive as they went down. At the sight of him all Maman's worry vanished from her face, the wrinkles of concern perished from about her eyes and mouth. This handsome man, this gleaming god-like man, came striding up the drive towards them, bearing the sun in the roots of his hair even, carrying the ice of centuries of fine blood in his small shapely teeth. This man, was Maman's heart protesting, must somehow, through the flesh of one of her three daughters, be grafted to them all, be one rich fruitful bough upon the decaying family tree.

"Luc, *mon* Luc," she said.

"How solemn you are," said Luc, standing still directly before them. Over their shoulders he waved his hand to Oncle Robert and the girls beyond. But Maman could not refrain from turning back to glimpse the admiration which she felt must surely have transfigured Oncle Robert's discriminating face, turned back as well to see if the three girls were looking at their best, and there was Luc left facing Bridget on the drive. The Chinese *tilleul's* boughs dripped down into a saucer of yellow wax and Luc walked close to her and stood before her quietly with his eyes searching hers. When he opened his lips to speak she found that her hand had involuntarily risen as if to stop him from what he was about to say.

"You have been crying," he said softly. "Why have you been crying? Why have you been crying?" he said.

And then the whole family swept down upon them: Maman and Papa, Oncle Robert, Nicolas and the three girls. Down they swept, with the tittering and talking of the girls, and with Nicolas leaning on his cane.

"Ah, Luc," said Oncle Robert holding out his hand. "Not looking so well as when I last saw you," he murmured. "Have you been working too hard?"

Upon his words both Maman and Marthe burst into protest. How *could* Oncle Robert say such a thing! Why, never had Luc looked so well, *si beau*, said Maman. Marthe blushed furiously, but she dared not utter the word. Even the country doctor had been astonished this year by Luc's *bonne mine*.

"Ah?" said Oncle Robert. Now that he had succeeded in disappointing them as to his opinion of Luc's appearance, he lost interest in the subject. "I wanted to have a little talk with you, Luc," he continued. "In fact, I might say it is the object of my visit. Shall we take a little promenade along the road?"

As Luc bowed his head in assent the lovely summer afternoon expired, the shadows of the passing clouds darkened the faces of the three young girls who could do nothing now but turn and walk off with their parents down the driveway to their married sister's happy home. It was this fatal insistence of Oncle Robert's upon picking and choosing his favourites which made him in the family such an object of scorn. How they resented the right he assumed that he need only indicate who his companions should be for the others to withdraw as if in humility! A family situation in which he played his part was always dramatized by his discard and his choice, and the imposition of his preferences was the great weapon which held them at a distance and intimidated them. At this moment Oncle Robert put a detaining hand upon Nicolas' arm.

"Oh, do come too!" he whispered. "I never have a moment to talk with you and Bridget. Do come along!"

Like happy casual people on a boulevard talking and laughing and making jokes with one another, the four of them walked leisurely away. Oncle Robert had drawn Bridget's arm through his, and Nicolas walked up on the other side. Luc carried with him a blue rubber ball which the children had forgotten in the garden, and as he walked a step or two ahead, he tossed it idly from hand to hand. There were the bits of sun on them that came through the light ragged wind as they walked up the road, pruning and cooing like four clean well-fed doves. The dust of the highroad was delicately powdering the noses of their boots, and the oaks that shaded donkey carts and wagon ruts rustled and shook their heavy heads above them.

"My dear Luc," said Oncle Robert, rhythmically patting Bridget's hand as they walked. Her parasol hung over both their shoulders. "I cannot tell you what a warm place you have in my heart. You are not unlike my own boy who is now so far away." He waved his silk handkerchief at a passing dragon-fly. "*Dieu sait*, it would be charming to have you in the family."

Back and forth went Luc's blue rubber ball, idly back and forth from hand to hand.

"There are many reasons why I should like to be," he said.

Bridget felt Nicolas' hand resting on her arm, and then he lifted his cane from the ground and swung it viciously at a group of daisy heads which scattered down before their feet like white stars in the dust.

"This degenerate family needs you, Luc," he said bitterly. "We are in desperate need of quarts of new blood in every vein of us . . ."

"You'd have such pretty children," continued Oncle Robert in his vaguest and most absent-minded manner. "You yourself, Luc, were such an attractive boy. He was a great beauty, Bridget," said Oncle Robert playfully. "It may be difficult to imagine such a thing now, but he had the most beautiful hair and the biggest eyes in the world."

At this Luc threw back his radiant head and laughed. Up fled the ball from his hands into the heavy summer air, and as it dropped again his eyes turned sideways to see Bridget's eyes.

"Do you think it would be difficult to imagine such a thing?" he said. He was so like a child then, thought Bridget, looking at her with his clear untroubled gaze and playing with his ball. Suddenly it occurred to Bridget that Luc was too young, really too beautiful and young to be the proper husband of any one of the girls.

"Oh, don't get married!" she said suddenly. It seemed so important to her that he understood how aloof his radiance should remain from the good family's vigilance. "Oh, don't get married!" she said.

Luc looked at her across Oncle Robert's fresh white head, looked at her steadily through the oval shadow of her parasol.

"But *you* did," he said to her as if in accusation. "After all, you did, you know."

But whatever Oncle Robert learned from his conversation with Luc, he gave no hint of it to the family.

"Oh, my dears, what a family!" he said. He pressed Bridget's arm close to his heart as they walked. He threw his hands up in dismay. "*Quelle famille!*" he said. He hushed his voice to a whisper: "How *do* you survive," he said, "you young ones with your thirsts and appetites?" They had come down the road towards the river and rounded Charlotte's wall. Into the midst of the family they walked and Oncle Robert sank down among the cushions of the *chaise longue* in the shadow of the acacia tree.

"I have had the most delightful time," he told them all as he rearranged the disturbed line of the immaculate bang across his forehead. "The loveliest time in the world, but now I must be off. Charlotte, my dear, either the coach or the limousine will do, but *please*, I beg of you, please don't get out the sulky on *my* account."

"Oh, but of course I shall, Oncle Robert," said Charlotte. The whole family knew that Oncle Robert would never cease reviling them to other and remoter relatives if he were not driven to the station in the sulky. He admired the filly and he liked to question and gossip with the driver on his way.

But Oncle Robert had only just begun his various adieux when the little filly was led around the side of the stable, stepping lightly with her shiny black harness trailing behind her on the ground. Oncle Robert had already kissed the children, and now he pinched the lobes of their ears with more spleen than affection, embraced his four nieces, and approached Annick. He paused before her for a moment and a tender light seemed to transform his countenance.

"Annick," he murmured as he kissed her cheeks, "my dear dear little Annick . . ."

When the bright yellow sulky finally rolled out before them, Oncle Robert was at the end of the line and he drew Maman aside a moment to speak confidentially in her ear. Her head was eagerly inclined to him so as to capture every sound, but as she listened a shade of disappointment passed over her face. "*Extraordinaire*," she cawed at him. "*Extraordinaire*." But it was evident that he had not told her anything she wished to know.

He stood up in the sulky as it went slowly up the drive, waving his silk handkerchief at them, and touching his eyes with it from time to time as if tears of regret at leaving them were about to fall. As soon as the *tilleul* partially concealed him from their view, he sat abruptly down and could be seen opening a conversation with the driver and settling his straw hat precisely on his head.

XVIII

WITHIN the hour Papa and Charlotte and Nicolas knew what it was that Oncle Robert had whispered in Maman's ear. Maman had told Papa, and Papa told Charlotte in indignation, and when Nicolas had a long talk with Charlotte in her room and asked her if he could borrow some money from her and Jean, Charlotte told Nicolas what it was that Oncle Robert had said. Although no one took Oncle Robert seriously, Charlotte could not help crying when she told Nicolas. When she came down from her talk with Nicolas she kissed Bridget a hundred times.

"I'm going to talk to Jean, now," she said. "I'm going to ask him for the money for you, and I'm sure it will be all right. I'm sure, I'm sure," she whispered as if convincing herself against her own doubt.

But no one could be persuaded to tell Bridget or the girls what it was that Oncle Robert had said. That it had to do with Luc was taken for granted, and like bees about the hive did Marthe and Julie hum about Maman, trying to make her tell. Whatever it was, it had evidently given Papa food for reflection, and he had sought his little basket and cane and gone off to the hen-house to look for eggs. Annick was sitting in the garden with her group of urchins reciting their catechism before her, and around the house, through the strawberry bed, and up to the ringing torrent of the pump Marthe and Julie pursued Maman on her active way. Here she had a path to rake, here a wayward vine to train, here a rose bush to clip into obedience. Marthe was shrieking with laughter and spinning about on the balls of her feet, begging and bribing Maman with an offer to make the mayonnaise for lunch all week if only Maman would tell. Julie offered to take out the ladder and pick the cherries the first thing in the morning. It was an idle hour for them and up and down the garden they went, following in Maman's hasty steps until dusk began to fall.

Just before supper Charlotte came up the pathway to the family's house. She had a book beneath her arm and she came walking along as if it were the most natural thing in the world for her to come to them at this hour of the day. But never before had she left her own house at suppertime, had abandoned Jean and the children to come to the family's house. She sauntered up the garden with her head somewhat averted so that they should not perceive that her eyes were swollen, and with a coating of powder across her face to conceal the ravages of her weeping. They were all sitting awaiting the call to supper outside the dining-room door.

"Could I have supper with you, Maman?" she said. Had she announced that the world had come to an end the family could not have been more astonished.

"Of course you can," said Maman. Her piercing eye turned a furtive but unerring glance upon her eldest daughter. "I'll tell them to put another place," she said. She snapped her eyeglasses back on their revolving gold chain and humped away through the dining-room window which opened down to the garden like a door. And there sat the family, Papa behind his paper, Luc and Nicolas playing chess, Charlotte rippling the pages of her open novel, and Bridget and the three girls. No words were spoken, except those which touched upon the new moon and the weather, but it was understood that Jean had refused to give Nicolas and Bridget the loan.

All through supper no words concerning Jean or the children or the future were exchanged, and every mention of Oncle Robert's name brought them back to the same demand.

"Oh, Maman, Maman," wailed Marthe in vexation. "Now is the moment to tell us all what it was Oncle Robert said!"

Had not her pompadour of lightish hair risen so high and exposed such great portions of her face she might have risked more venturesome glances at Luc who sat across the table from her. But with her eyes and brow so unprotected she scarcely dared to dart a look at him from time to time. Bridget could see her, between bursts of laughter, attempting to draw down a portion of her light fluffy fringe in which to ambush her two evasive eyes.

"Nicolas won't be able to keep it from me," said Bridget. But at her words Maman's lips narrowed. Her nose hung ominously over her plate of soup and she turned a severe eye upon her son.

It was then that Papa, so far from all that had been going on, suddenly raised his head.

"Why, what are you doing at supper with us, Charlotte?" he said.

The warm soup and the few sips of cider had revived Charlotte's pride.

"I had a disagreement with my husband," she said, "and I came back to you."

She gave him a small friendly smile, and again Papa's chin sank far into the depths of his sky-blue linen stock. Slowly and reproachfully he shook his paternal head.

"What a way to speak before your sisters!" he said. His old fingers toyed absently with his glass of goat's milk before him on the table. "I think the milk's a bit sour tonight," he said with a grimace. "What's that book you have there?"

He had reached forward to draw towards him the book which Charlotte had carelessly set down beside her plate. He fumbled for his eyeglasses and with difficulty settled them upon his nose. Then he discovered that he was holding the book upside down. He cleared his throat and turned the book carefully around.

Slowly and deliberately he read the title aloud, and then as if the words as he deliberately pronounced them had struck some horror to his soul, his eyes started out of his head.

"La Révolte des Anges!" he cried again, and his voice rose high and sharp with his displeasure. *"La Révolte des Anges!"* He looked at Charlotte with his proud wounded eyes. "Charlotte, what is this?" he said.

Charlotte had no idea what it was. She had scarcely opened it, she said. She had merely glanced at the title page and was planning to read it through that night in bed. It was her custom to read for hours at night, for often she could not bring herself to fall asleep until the early hours of the morning. This was because, as she well knew, she led too trivial a life and was idle most of the day.

"If I could travel about everywhere with the children, I don't think I'd ever read another book," she said.

"But this book, but this book," said Papa.

As a matter of fact, said Charlotte, it was Oncle Robert himself who had brought her the book that day from Saint-Malo.

"My brother!" cried Papa aghast.

"Yes," said Charlotte. She made an effort to recall Oncle Robert's remarks concerning it so as to repeat them to him. At any rate, Oncle Robert had said that he had selected it for her especially, at the stationer's shop right opposite the cinema in Saint-Malo, in spite of the fact that it was obviously the cheapest edition that could be found. Oncle Robert had recommended it to her, said Charlotte, as a particularly beautiful book written by Mr. Anatole France.

"That is the man who married his cook," said Maman.

She had removed a toothpick from its little paper case and was forcing it in between her teeth.

"Anatole France!" snorted Papa. Anatole France. It hit the window-pane closed against the deep dusk in the garden and sprang back across the steaming plate of artichokes which the servant had set down upon the dining table. Anatole France, who had taken the name of his country in vain. "Anatole France," said Papa bitterly. The veins were ready to burst in his head.

Papa's intense feeling about immoral literature was no senseless thing. Even though books were placed upon the index by the Church, he saw no harm in such people as Maman and himself, who were immune to passion, in reading them if they should fall into their hands. But, as he explained to Nicolas and Bridget later, his objection in this case was rooted in the fact that Charlotte was not an ordinary woman. Charlotte was a woman of passion, Papa told them in a whisper, and he had once been dismayed to find her reading a novel which dealt with a lady's love affair with her chauffeur.

"Imagine the ideas this might put into the head of such a woman as your sister," said Papa in his proud wounded way. "I took the book out of her hands at once, but for weeks I was in terror of the harm it might even so have succeeded in doing. I even suggested to Jean, in a veiled way of course, that it might be wise to dispense with any male help about the place for a while. My one idea was more or less to isolate Charlotte until whatever effects the book might have had, had time to lose their first powerful influence."

Thus was *La Révolte des Anges* tossed contemptuously upon the serving tray and borne off to the kitchen, where Julie was despatched to see with her own eyes that it was properly burned. Charlotte had no real interest in it, and no regret, but Nicolas took the matter up as if it were his own special grievance. Whatever Luc's thoughts were he kept them to himself and devoted his attention to plucking off the leaves of his artichoke and dipping them deeply in the yellow frothy sauce.

Hate and hate and hate was in Nicolas' glance for each face at the table. Hate and hate for everyone except for Charlotte's face, but even for her he had some little irritation now because she had not protested and because she was willing to accept censure from Jean and Papa as if it were their right to dole out sense and reason to her. Hate and hate for Maman's face and her adroit toothpick spiking out great locks of shaggy artichoke at which she nibbled nervously. And hate for Luc's unfeeling cleanliness and charm. Like a man's face ill and turning on his pillow in pain, Nicolas' face turned from one to the other of them, eyeing them all. Hate for Marthe's hysteria, and hate for Annick's unselfish heart that bade her not take the veil. Hate for Julie's sullenness that was a barrier to her womanhood, and hate for his own wife who should have somehow mastered circumstances and made the family bosom but a temporary resting-place. Hate it was that made him turn upon Bridget and hold her captive in his bitter eye.

"Would you like to know what it was that Oncle Robert said to Maman?" he asked her in English. He had begun to grin. He looked at her, grinning, with bright points of antagonism shining in his eyes. "Well, this was what it was," he said. He could scarcely contain himself, so filled with hate was he for them all. "It was about you, Bridget," he said. "Did you know it was about you?"

"No," said Bridget. She watched him as she shook her head. She was perfectly sure that she didn't want to hear it now. Maman had risen from her seat, a signal to them all that she had observed from all their plates that the evening meal was done, and the entire family rose and followed her into the other room.

"Yo-ho-ho," yawned Maman as she smartly whipped the shutters closed across the open windows. Charlotte had caught up with Bridget in the salon doorway and pressed her hand.

"I'm going to bed, I think," said Charlotte smiling brightly at her people.

"He said he was very much surprised," said Nicolas lazily as he lingered in the door, "that a person who seemed so very much a lady should wear the kind of earrings that you wore."

XIX

CHARLOTTE'S limousine quivered under the portico, the nickel buttock of the spot-light elongating the chauffeur's mirrored nose until it hung reflected like a fresh sausage between his moustaches. Once Nicolas and Bridget had settled back in it, it leapt away up the drive. Up it nosed between the rose trees and the beds of grass, slowing down and crying out sharply at the open grill. The children scampered after, waving and screaming after it.

"Good-by-ee!" they screamed after their aunt and uncle. They were learning English with Bridget. "Good-by-ee!" they screamed, proud of the English Bridget taught them every afternoon. "Good-by-ee!" before they were finally lost behind the umbrella trees as the road whipped away.

"Aren't you a little ashamed to be a governess?" said Nicolas, lighting a cigarette. "Doesn't it debase you a little, grain of sand?"

But Bridget was feeling far from that, going off as she was in elation with Nicolas, escaping from the family with Nicolas to buy some stuff to make herself a dress. Every Monday in Dinan there was a market in the streets and here they were going off with the money Charlotte had paid her for lessons to have a day together and to buy herself some kind of a dress.

"But after all you are an American," said Nicolas with his most pointed smile. "Every situation you find yourself in must be turned to account."

"How malicious!" said Bridget. She took her hand away from his. The world flowed past them in the windows, broken apart at cross-roads or sharply scarred by a wall.

"I'm not interested in little pieces of money," said Nicolas.

Without turning her head to him she could feel the intense gloom of his profile riding beside her. His mouth went down at the corners as if he were tasting something sour she knew. In her gums and her jaws she could almost taste the queer acrid sourness of his despair. And what days there had been together, she thought! What days when the horses' feet had sped over the firm red California clay and the carpet of portulaca flowers! What mornings when Nicolas had stood half-naked at the pump on the ranch drenching himself with the coldest water the earth possessed! Some stream they now fled past made her remember the wooden trough of dark quivering water which had always stood brimming in the yard before the timber house with the

California clouds reflected in it crimped tight as a judge's wig.

"Nicol," she said. She took his hand back again between her own. "Let's go away and be ourselves again," she said. "It would really be wonderful, you know, to have a baby, and then we could go away. We are really going to have a wonderful life, you know."

"I get no satisfaction out of words," said Nicolas. He managed to stifle a yawn. "As long as you want a baby so badly, Bridget," he said, "why don't you have it with somebody else?"

After he had said this in his black weary voice of gloom, his spirits seemed to revive.

"Well, why don't you, Bridget?" he said. His speech had turned as airy as thistledown and was blowing lightly back and forth between them. "If you have a child, Papa would pay us the money. That doesn't mean I have to have a child. There are lots of people," he said, "who have no disease in their bones. What a solution!" he said. He had begun to laugh aloud. "Such a simple way out of it all," he said. "Why didn't we ever think of it before?"

He sat beside her with his lip drawn back from his teeth, smiling, his bright eyes pursuing the telegraph poles and tree trunks that raced steadily past. Here he was peeled and fresh again in the lovely summer morning, with a veil lifted from his features and his eyes washed clear and young. At exactly the same moment they perceived the immense nest of mistletoe that was hanging in the oak.

"Oh, look!" cried Bridget.

"Oh, look!" said Nicolas.

"What a huge one!" said Bridget.

"What do you think of that as an idea?" said Nicolas. The sight of the great bunch of mistletoe hanging up there so isolated and so far from any holiday or any feeling of Noel, had made him put his arm around her and draw her close. "I couldn't bear having an ill child, you know," he said.

He wanted the money very badly indeed, thought Bridget; he hated his people and he wanted to go away, but still she knew this idea of his was just a pretence of his own bitter wit. It was never possible that the devotion of the good family had brought him to this.

"You're not a bit funny," she said.

"I'm not trying to be funny," said Nicolas. He drew himself away and sat hunched and wounded in his corner of the car. He felt he had been rebuked. He sat all hunched in the corner against the window, staring away. And suddenly Dinan was flung out of the curve of the valley, more beautiful than any living town could be. The houses of it were clinging to the deep hillside, with a few venturesome ones advancing to the River Rance, edging down in the heat to the cool trough of water. Nicolas looked at it all as if he had seen it too many times before.

"You don't seem to realize the position we are in," he said angrily to her. "You take things so much for granted. You'd sit on here all the rest of your life living off my family, taking a few sous from Charlotte who gives them out of charity. I think I'll kill myself," he said, "and leave you here where you're so happy with them all."

Bridget thought that if she did not speak that perhaps his anger would spend itself. But she felt that she would hit his sour face if he said those words again. The family, she thought, who had been motivated by the one thought of bringing them closer to each other as husband and wife had only succeeded in setting them apart.

"You wouldn't so much as lift your finger to help us get away," he said. "And it's mostly your fault too that we're here. It was your idea that we come to France. I know I couldn't have gone on with my work where I was, but we didn't have to come here, did we? We didn't have to come back and get caught with the family, did we? That was your idea. Well, now it's up to you to get us away."

He sat tossing his shoulders, hunched up as he was in the corner of the car. They were passing by the clear canal and along it the creamiest of silken oxen were dragging the loaded barges. Charlotte's car soared up the hill into the market place and deposited them among the great stacks of square white wheat.

"Well, here we are," said Nicolas.

Down they went into the crowded place with the high hoarse voices of the merchants calling out all around them across the stalls of food and cloth. At one place they ate some scorched country sausage and fresh bread, and finished up further on with hot *galettes* dripping with new sweet butter. All through the meal Nicolas stood in silence beside her, leaning on his cane. When Bridget wiped the running butter from his chin, he looked immovably off into the impersonal distance of the market place. He had no use for her. She had involved him in a nasty mess, and now she must get him out. And not one smile to be cracked in the doing of it.

How awful not to feel this, thought Bridget. How terrible not to feel the desperation and gloom of their situation in life. At the sight of the bolts and bolts of materials to be bought, her heart was ready to wing from her bosom. She flung her arms around Nicolas' neck.

"Darling, darling, I love you," she said. "I am so happy to be alive with you that I could die with joy! I am so happy we are together in spite of, in spite of everything, that I could die with joy!"

"God knows what kind of feelings you have," said Nicolas. He had turned away from her, but something like a smile had come into his eyes.

They walked together down through the cattle square, avoiding the fresh warm islands of dung. One young calf had broken loose and went frisking down before them, waving the remnant of his tether rope as he gambolled down to the portico of the church and went frisking back again to the corral. They stopped to watch him for a moment, the palpitating pink heart of his nose and the crisp hair which freedom had startled down his spine. The clear thick eye which seemed pierced with light turned upon them as he rocked like a wooden rocking horse down to the church piazza, waving his ragged end of rope, and, eyeing them wildly, frisked back to the edge of the corral. And then they fairly ran into the Englishman who was teaching French to students in the University of Tibet.

"Fancy," said he. "I must have left my penknife on Castle Island!"

"Well, that will give you an excuse then," said Nicolas, "for coming back to see us."

The little man threw up his hands in despair.

"Oh, it's miles too far!" he said. "Of course it's quite too far for me to go with all the other trips I have to do. I'm taking a party to Mont-Saint-Michel tomorrow. Fancy!" he said. "You people are practically *there*, if you know what I mean, but for me it's quite a journey, you know."

He nodded brightly at them as he spoke, turning his head this way and that to look at all that was going on round about him. For the first time Bridget perceived something rugged and windbeaten in him, something of the weather in the burned flesh beneath his ears.

"I might row over one day and have a look around," said Nicolas. Bridget wondered why Nicolas was so polite to this little man.

"How nice that would be of you!" exclaimed the Englishman. "It wouldn't be a bit of trouble to you, would it?"

When he had given them his address and gone on, they proceeded to the church. Nicolas' legs were beginning to get weary under him and he sat down on one of the yellow wood prayer chairs which were crowded in the small damp nave. In the baptismal vat Bridget found a school of fish in bronze clinging to the depths of slime which had collected on the sides. With Charlotte's sous she bought three long candles which she pierced upon the iron pins in the Virgin's chapel: one lighted for Nicolas' health, one for a good job for him, and one that he might love her all his life.

"If I don't find the penknife," said Nicolas, "I'm going to buy him one and write him a letter asking if he can do something about getting me a job sitting down in the University of Tibet."

He had crossed the church to her and was watching her settling the candles in place.

"It's too bad you weren't born a Catholic," he said. And then some feeling of the devil rose in him and he said: "I think the

Englishman rather liked you. What would you think of him as a *pater familias*?" he said. He stood grinning at her below the Virgin's sweet mild face.

A new thing flashed through Bridget; an instant of anger, of rancour and despise. She snatched the third candle out of the high burning bouquet and spat upon its flame. With hard quivering hands she broke it into two pieces and flung it down at Nicolas' feet.

"There you are," she said. "There you are."

She bit her lip with her teeth. She would not cry, she thought fiercely, she would not cry. She looked up at the mild wooden statue of the Virgin, wishing that this woman of wide repute would come to life and damn Nicolas adequately for his venomous ways.

"Don't ever tell me you love me again," she said. She looked into his black motionless eyes. "I hate you," she said. "I am going away."

She turned from him quickly and fled out the door. Up the market place she went and through the strange bright world. And where could she ever flee to, she thought, except into the very bosom of the family? Up to the booths of dress materials she made her way, and picked out yards and yards of bitter black. Black would her dress be, she thought; black for her broken heart and for her love that had perished. Black, and black. All her life would be a mourning for her love for Nicolas which had died. Long tight sleeves to her wrists and buttons up to the chin.

"You'll be a gay figger," she thought. "You'll be a joy to the young."

XX

At three o'clock that afternoon Luc was going away. His vacation had finally drawn to a close; he had not spoken; the end had come. At three o'clock that afternoon the year would breathe its last full breath of wonder and of wealth, and then interminable days of misery faced Annick and Julie and Marthe. Already the sorrow of it had bleached Marthe's face and it was evident that she had cried all night. She had written to Pierre urging that he speak of Julie's shortcomings, and on the previous day his response had come. She brought it to Bridget's bedroom and read her every word that Pierre had penned in answer.

"I in no way consider it my duty to inform Luc of such matters as you suggest. Even though I am a doctor and Luc's associate, I consider that it would be entirely outside my province. . . . On the contrary, it seems to me the height of wisdom on Luc's part to wait until he has fully made up his mind which of you girls means more than a sister to him. . . ."

She looked with queer old faded eyes into Bridget's face.

"There is still one thing that can be done," she whispered across the bed to Bridget. Her under lip hung almost lifelessly down. How beautiful is love, thought Bridget cruelly. She imagined an entire regiment of naked Cupids piercing Marthe's heart with love. The divine passion had penetrated her soul and turned her eyes into dripping wells of rank despair. "There is one thing remaining to be done before he leaves, Bridget."

Ah, Marthe would surely have him, she would get him finally, thought Bridget. The sight of him escaping her now was almost more than Marthe could bear. She must have him somehow, in some way promised and betrothed to her before he went away. How else could she bear the months ahead if there were no hope in sight at the end of them? These years of terror must ultimately end, with Annick retired to her convent, Julie immersed in her sturdier occupations, and she herself to the altar on Luc's arm.

All the smug arrogance of Madame Roland, all the high poetic reasoning of that other French lady of letters who brooded full length in Marthe's bedroom, all swelled and persisted in the eyes washed pale by tears. "I know I am the only one who could make you happy," Madame Roland had written. The record of that arduous engagement she had submitted to with Roland had stirred hopes in Marthe and lent nobility to her lot.

"She lost Roland ten times before she finally married him," said Marthe. "Ten times. Bridget, there is still one little thing that you and Nicolas can do."

She pressed her shoulder against her quivering chin.

"You know we each of us have the same dowry," she said. *Dot* was the word she used. "*Dot,*" she said. "For Annick and Julie and me it is exactly the same. Now, you yourself can see how difficult this makes it for Luc to decide. It is very unfair to put Luc in this position, after all. How can anyone expect him to make up his mind?"

Outside the world was a hot aggression, an insult to their flesh, but in this room they lay at peace in a charmed shadow of tranquillity. Marthe had drawn herself up against the footboard of the bed and from there she surveyed Bridget, so like the great lady of a house, holding her head high with ceremonious but nervous smile playing about her mouth. Surely she was visualizing herself now as the married lady in her *salon*, as Mrs. Luc speaking intelligently with strange callers and wittily referring to this or that.

"Ever since I was a mere child," Marthe was saying, "I have lived in a world of my own in the books I read. In that realm there are greater loves and more beautiful relationships, you know. Never in real life have I found a single person who would do a really great and magnificent thing for anybody else."

In the shaded room the evidences of her grief were less visible and her eyes less piercing under her full lids.

"This is what I wanted to ask you, Bridget dear," she said. "Of course I know that you and Nicolas intend to have a little baby. You would not wish to wound Papa, and it would be so nice for you to be able to go away. Of course we all know that you intend to have a little baby. Maman was talking about it last night and she said: 'It is such a joy to me that Bridget is so anxious to please us all.' "

Her voice had begun to shake a little in her throat.

"Now this is what I wanted to ask you, Bridget," she said.

She had abandoned the rôle of proud mistress of the house. She had slipped off the bed and down upon her knees by Bridget's side. With her bare arms she clasped Bridget's waist. "I want to ask you to lend me a little money," she said. So tightly she held her that Bridget could scarcely draw a breath. "Not very much," she said. "You could easily lend me ten thousand francs out of the money Papa has promised you for your baby. Ten thousand francs would be nothing at all. And then it would no longer be a problem for Luc to make up his mind. Ten thousand francs added to my *dot*, Bridget, would make it so much more than Annick's and Julie's that it would be an easy matter for Luc to make up his mind. You see that, don't you, Bridget?" she said. She held Bridget tighter and tighter in her arms. "You see that, don't you?" she said.

"Nicolas doesn't want to have a baby," said Bridget. She tried to get up but Marthe drew her firmly down upon the bed again.

"Don't talk like that," she whispered. "No, don't talk like that. You know that Nicolas will do whatever you say."

"But he doesn't want that," said Bridget. "There's no use in talking about it at all."

"Yes, yes," said Marthe. "Yes, there's use. Nicolas can't refuse his own sister. He can't refuse me that little thing, Bridget. It means my whole life, Bridget, you understand. You can't just throw a person's life away without a thought like that. You've got to think of other people in your life, Bridget. That's what the Catholic religion teaches us. That's why people who aren't Catholics haven't the same feeling about things. It's part of the religion to think of other people," she said.

"Nicolas doesn't want to have a baby," said Bridget. She could think of nothing else to say. She put her hands upon Marthe's naked arms and tried to wrest them away.

"Oh, it's so hot," she said. "Shall we get out in the air?"

But Marthe pursued Bridget across the room.

"Listen, Bridget, you've got to do something," she said. "Just because you're married you can't forget about everybody else. Before you came I thought you were going to be closer to me than all my sisters. I wrote letters to you such as I have never written to anybody else. You can't just put me aside this way, simply because you have a husband."

Suddenly she collapsed against Bridget's unyielding side.

"You've got to do something, Bridget," she whispered. "You must talk to Luc," she said. "You are a married woman and maybe he will tell you what his feelings are. You must promise me that you won't let him go away like this."

After Bridget had promised they got dressed together and went down into the garden where Maman and Papa and Nicolas and Jean were playing bridge. All about them were seated the other members of the family, the girls and Charlotte with their needlework, and Luc idly smoking a cigarette. When Bridget saw him there with his head back blowing soft rings of smoke into the air, the speech of all she had to say to him sprang to her lips. But there it faltered, while her disturbed heart spoke clearly out: "Oh, fly, escape!" her heart cried out to him. "Oh, save yourself from all they would condemn you to! If you alone amongst us all would remain faithful to your years and not to sentiment, some glory might survive!"

Beside her walked Marthe, clutching her indignant hand that had essayed escape into the folds of her dress.

"Remember you have promised," whispered Marthe in her ear. But how, but where, thought Bridget, and what am I to say?

Nicolas was smartly snapping his tricks into line.

"Do you remember the only *bonne* we ever loved, Charlotte?" he was saying. "We used to roll our hoops out to Chateaubriand's tomb with her at Saint-Malo. Jean, your spade."

Jean had revoked again and they must stop and sort over the tricks that had been played. Maman's sharp fingers pounced mercilessly upon the cards.

"She died in childbirth," said Papa, stifling a yawn behind his hand.

Maman's shoulders disposed of Papa's words. She cried out sharply: "Auguste! *Fais attention à ton jeu!*"

Her eyes paused upon Bridget to ascertain if she had understood, and passed on to Charlotte's soft contented face.

"Your father," she said, "is a little beast."

Nicolas played his card.

"They tell me she protested too loudly against the course of nature and her husband rushed in and split her skull with an axe," said Nicolas quietly.

"Faugh!" exclaimed Papa, flinging down his cards. He looked in fury into Nicolas' face. With dignity he forsook his chair, and with his hands twitching under the tail of his coat, he turned and went down the drive. Maman laid a restraining hand upon Nicolas' arm.

"The husband was mad," she reproved him. "Why do you say such things? Everyone knows that the husband was quite mad."

She looked mildly at Bridget as though her own refusal to be disturbed should somehow diminish the importance of Nicolas' words.

"Nicolas does not think," she said.

"Or thinks so much," said Nicolas blindly over his cards, "that his mind is twisted and fixed in agony in his head. . . ."

Charlotte, glad to abandon her needlework, rose to follow after and console Papa for this outrage to his feelings. It was a great grief to Maman as well as to Charlotte and Annick that neither of Papa's sons could get on with him at all. Julie took the place her father had left vacant at the card table and picked up his hand. Nicolas turned to look over his lean shoulder and smile grimly at his wife.

"I've been looking at Luc," he said in English. "What do you think of Luc as a father of the race?"

"I'm sure you're talking about me," said Luc lifting his gleaming head. "What were you saying, Nicolas?"

"I was saying that you and Bridget never got well enough acquainted," said Nicolas. "And here you are going away this afternoon."

But Luc was not deceived and he closed his eyes half-way, as if against the sun, and set his stubborn jaw.

"Next time I come she'll know more French," he said, "and we'll be able to understand each other better."

"It might be faster if she gave you a few lessons in English," said Nicolas. He was being very funny and everybody laughed.

Bridget herself laughed. She knew that she was very slow and stupid about learning French. Only Luc sat stiffly and stubbornly in their midst without a glimmer of humour in his eye. But in Marthe's laughter was a quivering note that was more a sharp whimper of despair. Not once did her desperate eyes abandon Bridget's face. It was almost the hour for Luc to be driving off to his train.

"Well, let us begin now," said Bridget shyly. She stood up and stretched out her hand to Luc. "Come with me around the pond as I do with the children," she said. "You must begin by learning to say 'good-bye.' "

"Good-bye," said Luc in English. He waved his hand gaily to the family as he walked away. "Good-bye," he called out again to them as he and Bridget went out the little gate on to the river road and disappeared behind the wall of Charlotte's house.

It was low tide and the pond was quite shallow as they made their way around the wall. Out beyond the great wide reaches of mud ran the thread of the river. At the door of the pond the shrimps were leaping like crystal grasshoppers out of the water and back into it again, and Luc squatted down on his handsome legs and attempted to scoop some odd ones up in his hand. Never had the air been so soft, never the hills so mural-like beyond, never the sky so clear. Presently the sea would be returning with the gulls screaming in after it and the sharp prow of the tide driving a furrow through the River Rance, but for the moment they were moving through a wide landscape of peace.

"I think we should begin the lesson," said Luc as he walked a step or two ahead of her. "There are a great many words in English that I want to learn to say."

But this kind of talk was leading them to nothing at all and in her heart Bridget was thinking: "Now I must speak of Marthe to him. Now, now at this moment I must speak." But the only words that would come to her mind were: "Luc, Luc, you must save yourself, you must run away."

She wanted to be just to him, and above all just to Marthe who had put her confidence in her, and she knew she must speak out and tell him that Marthe loved him with all her soul. She must advise him to take Marthe to his bosom and make her his wife. But when she tried to find words for these thoughts she found herself thinking:

"Luc, Luc, do not relinquish the miracles of your self to these women. Do not give them one moment of your life, one drop of your rich blood."

But Luc was carrying the conversation on, turning to look at her and talking to her in his youngest and most innocent way.

"It would be the greatest help to me in my work, if I could speak your language," he said. "And there are other things, besides, there are other things I would like to say—I mean, to you."

It was this remark which shaped the resolution of Bridget's intent, for ever since Luc had intimated to her by glance and speech that there might be something more between them than there was, she had determined that there should be nothing at all. If it were chaff, or if there were some kind of gravity to it, she did not know. Because she was Nicolas' wife she knew she had no right to know. And now there were so few minutes left to them before they would have to turn and make their way back again around the wall.

"Luc," she said, "I have come out with you to talk about Marthe."

"And I came out to talk to you about English," he said. Even through his banter she could see his stubborn jaw grow firm. "I have talked about Marthe all my life," he said. "And I've never been able to talk for a minute to anybody about you."

He stooped down and then in a moment he came back to where she was making her way along. He was carrying a frenzied little black lizard to show her in the palm of his hand. Beneath the frantic lizard were all the bold lines of his hand marked out: the heart line strong and unbroken, the head line a little short and thick, and the long unwavering life line curving deeply down to his wrist.

"Put him on your dress," he said, "and watch him change colour. Isn't he funny?" he said. "*Amusant.*" He looked with such eager interest at the little black animal, now with a shade of blue on his belly, scrambling across her skirt.

"Luc," said Bridget suddenly out of her dry throat. His head was so close that she could have touched his brilliant hair with her fingers. "Luc, I'm sure that Marthe would make you very happy."

She spoke with great intensity but in shyness she turned her eyes away to the curve from which the sea would presently emerge. Her blood was kindling with the shame of thus interfering in other people's lives.

"I am sure you would be very happy with Marthe," she said.

But even as she spoke she knew that she had destroyed any beauty which remained in the day, and she was angry that she had lacked the courage to say out what was in her mind to say. Now she saw clearly how dull and filthy was the water of the pond beside them, how thick and odorous the long slippery banks of mud. Even the castle on the island seemed more artificial than it had at any other time.

"Oh, Luc," were the words she could not utter, "what are you doing in this barren country with people who would wrench children from you? Oh, flee from them while you are still able to combat them! Oh, Luc, do not submit through reason or despair!"

"Is it really true that you want me to marry Marthe?" Luc was saying. He was standing looking at her under the big hat which fell around her eyes. Every separate piece of her face he looked at very carefully, at the eyebrows, at the cheeks, and at the freckles across her nose. He was very close to her and his underlip was trembling like a child's. "Is this the lesson you came out to teach me?" he said. "Is it really so that you want me to marry somebody else?"

"I think if you want to marry now, I think you should marry Marthe," said Bridget deliberately. She kept her eyes turned far away on the safe distance of the sea. "I think she loves you the best," she said. "I think she loves you more terribly than the others do." *Terriblement. Terriblement.* Yes, *terriblement* was the word.

"But do you want me to marry anybody?" persisted Luc. "Do you really want me to marry anybody else at all?"

"I can't see what difference that would make," said Bridget.

"It makes all the difference," said Luc. Because she had turned as if to walk back towards Charlotte's house he had to pursue her for a few steps along the rugged wall. "Listen to me, Bridget," he said. "It makes all the difference, because you can do whatever you want with me. You know you can do whatever you want with me, Bridget," he said.

He had caught up with her and the sight of his clean tan feet suddenly keeping pace with hers was almost more than she could bear. To escape with him into a new life, she thought, with his capable, stubborn jaw and his bright beauty holding the world at bay, would be a thorough way of abandoning Nicolas to his disease and his despair. At the thought of this she turned upon Luc.

"You've had enough years in which to make up your mind," she said to him, "and now you can't make it up this way by putting it on to somebody else."

"If it hadn't been for you," said Luc gravely, "I think I would have proposed to one of the girls this year."

They walked along for a little while side by side and then Luc said with a certain delight as if he had finally caught her in a trap: "You see, you have a certain responsibility. You must tell me what it is you want me to do."

She had opened her mouth to speak again, but Luc interrupted her.

"No, no, not now," he said. "Because I want you to think about it. I want you to think about the thing that is really true, I mean, that you can do whatever it is you want with me, and I'll come back again and then maybe you'll be able to tell me what it is you want me to do."

A regiment of crabs was hastening along ahead of them, rattling over the stones of the wall with their queer shifty gait. Into the water of the pond they sidled, one by one, and at the sight of them Luc threw back his head and laughed.

"Ha, ha, ha!" echoed Luc's laughter over the stretch of water. It struck the wall of Charlotte's house and rippled back to them. "Ha, ha, ha!"

XXI

AFTER the evening had finally closed down, there was no doubt in anybody's mind that Luc had gone. All the afternoon it had seemed that he must surely reappear around the the drive, or come suddenly through the doorway, in spite of the fact that they had all seen him step into the train.

That Luc was gone there now could be no doubt. All the afternoon the filly had waited and stamped her small impatient feet in vain. And when darkness began to fall and it became evident that Luc would not appear, she set up the wildest neighing in her dreary stall. Peal after peal of bell-like neighs invoked the unresponding air, and suddenly she began kicking with mad intent, as if the whole stable must collapse if Luc did not sing out "Who-oo yep!" and fling the easy saddle over her.

Surely the minds of the three girls were filled, as Bridget's was, with thoughts of Luc alighting from the train at Rennes, crossing important busy streets, and taking up the threads of his arrested life again. The barren house was hollow for the sound of him, the garden in the evening was in harmonious complaint. For all they knew they would not set eye on him again till Christmas, and perhaps not then, for usually they had to bide their time until summer came around.

Nor could they expect letters from him for three days at least, for being dutiful young women they had been brought up to know that a man's work in life comes before all else and that he would have a great deal to do. Hence the girls wandered as far afield as possible, avoided the postman, made calls upon the poor. And Nicolas, as if infected by some of the contagion of the uneasy atmosphere, announced that he was going to try to find the penknife which the little Englishman had left behind.

Against the advice of Maman and Annick and Jean, and in spite of Papa's predictions of disaster, Nicolas and Bridget packed up their lunch one morning, climbed into the *doris* and set out for Castle Island.

They had their fishing-rods and a net for shrimps, and the sea that was there between the mainland and the island was really a very harmless-looking sea. Nicolas had no trouble at all in rowing the boat across and beaching it. What a relief, thought Bridget, to be doing these active things with Nicolas instead of being at home with him and his contempt! No gentle words had passed between them since the day they had ridden off to Dinan in Charlotte's car, but here with the sea and the strong bright air between them there was no need for speech.

They laid their fishing tackle and their lunch away in the rocks near the foot of the great rocky cliff, and they started up the climb. Nicolas used his cane and progressed slowly, saying nothing, but in his whole demeanour scorning any aid. Bridget climbed ahead of him, but slowly too, turning back to look at the world below them at every step of the climb. All along the edge of the beach were little ruffles of sand packed hard in the coast as if a broom had briskly swept them into place. The few rocks that still had water about them were black with seaweed, and mussels hung like bunches of dark rich grapes upon the rocky boughs.

The path they walked was oozing with fresh damp things, steaming under the mild sun with the pungent odours of earth and mosses. Every rare blade of grass along the side was coloured a strong bright green and pointed sharply like a turtle's tongue. As they climbed higher and higher out of the salty air some small unknown flowers began to blossom. Among these strangers were the little orange star-like ones which everyone knew meant death to rabbits; and blue ones quite faded out before they had fully opened, bleached there for lack of sun or too much of it on the moist side of the hill.

Whatever this higher earth-life had as complement, it had no link with the rough, ragged shoreline and the sea below. The wan blue flowers here were strangers to the ebony *moules*. It had no part in all the marine life that flourished in brine below it in the water that lingered out in coils about the rocks. In the bushes of this underbrush were leaves as tender and sticky as any springtime foliage, for into the depths of it there came hardly any sun at all. In the branches were birds and their nests, and hence the mainland sounds of unadventurous forest birds, and even the usual sulphur caterpillars humping their silky green hides along the edge of the wood. How far from the sea-gulls and their appetites! but not so far, for on certain ledges of the cliff was the spotless snow of the sea-birds' droppings piled up in shallow drifts and hanging here and there in icicles of lime. Here and there was this record of the sea-birds' contempt for the immovable land.

All the light airy green contained in ferns and in the grasses led on to darker richer shades. First were the oaks, rooted as only oak roots could be, reaching out to grapple with the air and drawing sustenance as strong from it as they could from any other soil. And beyond them stood the forest of pines, glittering in their black spangled armour, moaning and shaking their lean heads in dignity and reproof at the spirited wind. Far, far below them all was the same wind on the water patiently braiding and unbraiding the tangled skeins of the shore.

Not a word did Nicolas and Bridget speak as they climbed up the precipitous side of the land. Once at the top they set about looking for the penknife that the Englishman from the University of Tibet had left behind. They walked through the deep pine needles with their eyes searching the ground, walking in circles under the tall bony trees. From time to time Nicolas stopped to rake the needles this way or that with his cane.

It was Nicolas who found the penknife.

"Here's the penknife," he said with a certain satisfaction in his voice. "Here it is."

He slipped it into his pocket and then he lit a cigarette. They went down the side of the cliff again in silence. In complete silence they ate their sandwiches upon the rocks, and after Nicolas had wiped the last crumbs from his fingertips, he removed his socks, rolled up the cuffs of his flannel trousers and set off with his cane and his fishing-rod for the edge of the sea. Bridget threaded her own fishing-rod and started off farther down the beach. From then on she saw him only at moments when she returned to where he was perched on his rock to select fresh bait from his tin can. He sat there fishing in silence, with his profile set against the water, and not an eyelash flickering in his set dark face. Finally on one occasion he spoke to her.

"I've caught three big ones," he said.

"I haven't caught a single one yet," said Bridget. She sat off by herself, fishing alone.

After an hour or so she saw Nicolas sliding down from his rock and with his cane he came across the packed damp sand to her.

"If we're going to do any fishing after *moules*," he said, "we'd better do it now. It won't be long before the tide will be turning."

He put his fishing tackle away and the little bucket in which swam his three handsome fish. He set them all back safely against the cliff out of reach of the tide, and armed with a shrimp net and a basket for mussels he set off into the sea. Deeper and deeper he waded into the bright shallow sea, striking out for the rocks that horned out of it with their polished growth of *moules*. Bridget rolled up her skirt about her hips and started wading after him. He had come to the first rocks and was beginning to twist the sharp mussels from their sides.

When Bridget had caught up with him she began to pull at the mussels too. They grew in such strong bold vines, mingled with seaweed, up and down the rocks; and save their lives they would so that picking them off was no easy thing. They clung like demons to the rocks and to each other. They snapped closed their brittle jaws. They knew they did not want to go; and before long their resistance had split the ends of Bridget's fingers and set them to bleeding, while Nicolas picked silently and competently on around the laden vines. His basket was filling rapidly up with the juicy black fruit of them and he was growing bolder and bolder and making wider and wider detours through the sea and over the little stranded beaches of sand.

The whole receding tide, as far as the opening far down at the curve, was striped and broken with long slim beaches of sand that only served to encourage one to go farther and farther away from shore. Like a deadly wasp was Nicolas voyaging from rock to rock storing the honey away, the sweet warm honey of the yellow-fleshed *moules*.

"Nicolas," called Bridget after him. Her fingers were so torn that she had lost interest in plucking off the mussels. "Maybe the tide will be coming up soon," she said in warning to him.

But he paid no attention to her, although he must have heard her voice across the little expanse of sand and sea. He would not even turn his head, as though no word or thought of hers could ever touch him again. The thing is, thought Bridget as she sat upon the rock holding her knees and watching him plod here and there with his cane, that I have brought him back to France and the heart of his family and now it is up to me to get him out. Everything that had happened to him had been a wound and an insult to him, she thought. Everything had made him despair. She saw so clearly the wounds in his spirit from which he would never recover, the terrible death wounds of his father's offer to him and of Jean's refusal of a loan. The unforgivable insult that they had let him be born at all.

Down at the mouth was the sea beginning to run like a white thread towards them, and Nicolas in his white clothes was standing shading his eyes and regarding it in the sun. He stood out clear and bright-looking against the qualities of sea and sky and sand. And as she watched him he turned towards Castle Island and began to make his way back to her over the sand. Down from her rock slid Bridget and fled through the water to meet him, splashing the sea all about her as she leapt and cavorted down.

"Hurry back, hurry back, Nicol!" she cried out to him. "Hurry back before the tide!"

But Nicolas had almost imperceptibly changed his course, and although he was still coming inland his steps were taking him more and more to the cliff side of the island. He seemed to be going directly and wilfully into the shallow water at the sheer side of the cliff, and from that side there could not be any escape at all.

"But there's no need for this," said Bridget under her breath. "There's no need for this, Nicol," she said.

She saw so clearly what it was he wanted: to evade them all completely, to get away from them all into death. When she saw that this was the truth she stood perfectly still in the water, watching his progress through the sea and the thin islands of sand. To the left of them was the tide approaching and at the sight of it so near she began to be afraid for Nicolas and the weakness of his legs.

"Come back, come back!" she shouted, but he pretended that he had not heard her at all.

Down through the sea she splashed to him. If she held his hand, she thought, surely he could run faster with her than quite alone. Surely no tide could have them if they clasped hands and fled from it side by side.

"Nicolas, Nicolas, Nicolas," she cried to him.

"Eh?" he said, lifting his head to her as if in irritation. "What is it you want?"'

"Come back, come back," she shouted, "the tide is coming in!"

"Well, what about it?" said Nicolas. She was coming close to him now.

"Give me your hand, Nicol," she said. "You must come back."

"Why should I come back?" said Nicolas. He stood looking at her in his dark gloomy way. "What reason is there for me to go back?"

She had grabbed his hand and his cane firmly in her hands and was trying to pull him back through the water.

"You don't want to be killed, Nicol!" she cried.

"Why not?" said Nicolas drearily. "Why shouldn't I want to be killed?"

"Because I can't live without you," said Bridget. At this he relented a little and took a step or two forward.

"It isn't true," he said.

Bridget was tearing wildly at his hands.

"Yes, it is true, it is true!" she cried. "Nicol, Nicol, you make it so hard!"

Whether for fear at the actual sight of the water coming along, or whether because of her words to him, Bridget felt him suddenly yield to her and her direction. In a moment they were running at top speed together across the beach. Through the coast of rocks they splashed and stumbled, and on to the final beach of Castle Island, with the waves of the sea blowing and gallivanting a pace behind.

Only when Bridget had hauled him partly up the path of the ascent did she turn and look at him. With her two hands she pushed him down upon a rock. She stood before him looking at his exhausted panting face and at the faint smile which was lingering about his eyes.

"Why didn't you let me be killed, Bridget?" he said. But the usual despair had left his voice. "You would have been much better off."

XXII

FORWARD moved Charlotte's sweet round nose and chin. On and on she sailed against the hedge and the wheat-fields which flowed by the limousine window. Beside her sat Nicolas, talking about America. Beside her and beyond her he sat with his long nervous hand hanging from the armrest's grey brocade.

"Yes, yes," agreed Charlotte with her pale grave mouth. "Yes, tell me, Nicol. The colours in the rocks there! The red earth! Tell me, Nicol!"

Ahead was the wall and the great gate and the worn stones of the houses gathering there in the windshield. Bridget watched the roofs of Saint-Malo clustering about the chauffeur's white linen cap.

"Oh, it sounds beautiful, really it sounds beautiful!" said Charlotte. She lifted her hand and made the sign of the Cross upon her brow and bosom as they passed the graveyard of St. Servan. She listened to him but it was evident that her thoughts were upon other things. Her hands jerked over the little girl's smooth hair. She straightened the white square of the little boy's collar.

Only when they had all descended from the car and settled upon the sand in the shadow of the town wall, did she give her real attention to Bridget and Nicolas. Her shy furtive smiles took courage. She leaned forward and covered Monique's thin bare knees with neat little patches of sand.

"Nicolas, my darling," she said. Her face was low and shy and quivering over the trembling fingerfalls of sand. Nicolas was always more at rest with Charlotte, always easier in his heart when his older sister was there. And today he had a certain sense of achievement as if it had not slipped idly past like every other day. For the chauffeur had been sent off to despatch the penknife and the letter Nicolas had written to the professor at the University of Tibet. With it had gone Nicolas' college certificate and an outline of all the work he had ever done.

"Nicolas, my darling," said Charlotte, so occupied with her little puddles of sand. "I have been going over Jean's business affairs and I find there is a place open to you in North Africa if you will have it. I want to know how you would feel about taking it," she said, speaking with great haste to him. "It is not true, it is not true that you will not get well," she said. Her voice quivered over her deep handfuls of sand. "I know so well that you are going to be strong again soon," she said. "But in the meantime I can't bear the strain to be so terrific for you. In this place on the *estancia* it doesn't matter if you can walk a great deal or not. Whether you could get out a lot or not, it wouldn't matter. It is work you could supervise," she said.

Nicolas sat quite still looking at the water.

"You mean on one of Jean's *estancias*?" he said.

Charlotte's fingers released the burning threads of sand.

"Yes, yes, but it is no form of charity, Nicol," said Charlotte. "I thought of you because it is your sort of work. It would be a future for you, Nicol," she said. "I know, I am sure."

Slowly Nicolas turned his face away from them, but there was nothing to do to prevent them from seeing what had become of all his vanity and all his pride.

"Oh—oo!" exclaimed Monique. "Tonton Nicolas is crying!"

Charlotte bit her lip and the tears fled from her eyes.

"Ah, don't, don't, Nicol," she said. She sat speaking softly to him over her trembling hands. "It is the natural thing, my Nicol. It is so natural that we should offer it to you and that you should go." Her voice was lost in the soft storm of her tears. She reached out to clasp Nicolas' and Bridget's hand in her agitated fingers.

"I am so glad," she said smiling at them through her clear unhidden tears. "I am so glad." Her small teeth shone in her pale quivering mouth. "I am so glad it is so," she said.

"Charlotte," Nicolas was trying to say to her. "Charlotte . . . Charlotte . . ."

The bleat of the children's voices as they played was following up the wind, and the big brilliant sea gathered softly under Charlotte's chin.

"I shall speak of it soon to Jean," she said firmly, blowing her small nose. "I may have a little trouble making him understand," she said. "But it's going to be all right. Everything that I suggest to him at first, it takes him a day or two to understand."

Monique crouched back on her heels, watching them all. And suddenly Charlotte began to speak again to them.

"There is something else too I want to tell you," she said, watching Bridget shyly. "There is something else . . ." she said.

She sat looking shyly at Bridget.

"Did you know . . ." she said to her. "Did Maman tell you yet?"

Bridget looked into Charlotte's eyes and shook her head. Charlotte's lids lifted for a moment and then drooped again. The white flesh of her bosom approached the sun-stained crescent which lay about her throat. Bridget suddenly and distinctly knew.

"I'm going to give you another little nephew or—niece," she said. She had turned a rosy red and she was laughing.

"Oh, what a wretched business!" said Nicolas in real distress. "Lolette, you're only thirty-two, and five of them already! Isn't it time you decided whether your responsibility is to the living or to the unconceived?"

It was all a sort of joke to Charlotte. She sat in the sand shaking her head and laughing.

"One more won't matter," she said. "It's my life, isn't it?"

Upon the homeward ride Nicolas shyly took Bridget's hand and drew it through his arm.

"How will you like it? How will you like being in North Africa?" he said. His voice was soft and whispering close in her ear and neck, hidden from Charlotte and the children in English words. He spoke as if in great humility to her, shy and apologetic, scarcely daring to look into her face.

"It will be too wonderful," she said. He held her fingers tightly in his palm. He sat close to her, holding her hand as though there was so much he wished to say to her, but not a word of it could he force from his lips.

"I have been terribly worried, Bridget," he said. Suddenly he lifted her hand against his cheek. "I have been crazy with worry about what we should ever do," he said into her palm.

"Oh, sweet children!" said Charlotte to them, teasing them and laughing as they sat holding hands in the deep cushions of the car. "Now I see you happy!" she said. "But now that things are arranged, I can't ever let you go. I shall die without my Bridget and my Nicol," she said.

Bridget had not yet really thought what it would mean to go, but with Nicolas' words and Charlotte's talking of this to her, it became an actual thing. To go. To go away. To go away to another country. To go so far away.

"To go so far away from what?" she asked herself. All the way home in the car, up the white road and down the valleys, soaring, screaming out at turns, all the way home she sorted the litter, the bits of ribbon, the remnants of disorder in her mind. This feeling of relinquishment in her was foul as a rat-trap and stiff and relentless there like a dried bouquet. This is what becomes of idleness, she thought in anger. She wanted the whole summer back again to make it all anew. Why am I having these bunches of old lavender, these dried knots of garlic infecting the thoughts that I have? Why this chop suey mess of uncertainty in me?

Down the drive they swept with a splatter of gravel upon the bridge table and the family as they went past. To go so far away from what, thought Bridget as she looked through the window at the faces of Maman and Papa and Jean and the three girls. To go so far away from what, she thought, as she stepped out of the car. But before she had time to take a step towards them, the girls had rushed up to her waving their elation in their exultant hands.

"Luc, Luc, Luc!" they cried as they surrounded her. Each one of them had a letter from Luc and before Bridget could have her tea even she must sit down with them and listen to every word that Luc had to say. "Luc," they said to her, as if it were a caress; Luc, as if the mere dwelling upon it could prolong it into syllables of sound.

Luc, thought Bridget as she sat listening to them reading out his polite small words. Luc, Luc, Luc.

To Marthe his letter was a sign to walk slowly out into the dusk that followed upon it, to walk along the road that had been built by peasants to go from field to market, and from farm to farm, and which did not linger by the side of the Rance. Castle Island was a melting vision between the tree stems, for Charlotte had been allowed to plant them this way to conceal the dock's stone walls. Luc in Rennes now strong and bitter as stone, to be washed against by little ripples of love, to be caressed by cloud kisses. Marthe's face flushed with shame at the thought of this, but now it was begun and ringing in her. She would be soft as the flowering crest of the river's salted wave, soft as the evening and the dry floury sand for all that was doctor, shell, competence in him must be breaking in him like a heart for gentleness.

To Marthe it was a sign to come to Bridget's room and look in the glass for a long time at her face, at the front and the side of it and to put the combs back and forth through her hair until she grew angry wanting to escape from the face before her. Then she would almost see it herself, the witless way her lower lip hung down when she was absorbed in anything, and between her eyes that would not stay back in her head the look of a calf with his brow swollen from blows, the glazed dull look as if he were slowly understanding slowly why he was there. This way she stood looking into the glass and drawing her lips into place when she saw them and saying without compromise: "Luc."

To Julie it was a warning to her own hidden soul to crouch deeper and deeper into the flesh, to hide more perfectly than ever from any prodding eye. Her shaggy top-knot slipped lower in her neck, her ears were covered, she kept her lids down so as neither to see nor to be seen. Her hands, thrust away into great masks of gauntlets, gripped a cane which she followed out around the high-water mark along the banks of sour aging foam. Her shoulders were stooped as if her back were hollow; like the curved side of a 'cello her ruddy chest contained the deep loud chuckles of her laughter. She slapped the leather of the wind with the side of her walking-stick; she could be seen from the windows of Charlotte's house walking with her head lowered and her face turned to the cold company of the pond. What of it? A letter from Luc, *qu'importe*? In front of them all she had turned the colour of a ruby and torn it up into little pieces. Before them all, "*chère*" and "*mer*" and "*amitiés*" had fluttered away across the lawn.

Annick alone had retired to her room, with Luc's letter among a little sheaf of correspondence, folded away between pink blotters in a tooled leather case. She had selected a book marker to send him to mark his pages, always of such use to a student and to a doctor with reference books open at his elbow. She undid its folds of tissue paper to show it to Bridget, hand-painted on thinnest ivory the figure of Saint-Roch showing his plague spot to a bevy of cherubim who had never seen anything like it before. "The thought of embracing a calling wholly devoted to others, such as yours," was but a part of all she wrote to him before she retired, "draws me more every day. Men can be doctors, but for women there is but one way to serve and that is in the convent." This so gently, so admirably written to him, and in such innocence that entertained no thought of threatening Luc with what his indecision might lead her to do.

XXIII

In Charlotte's salon the card table thrust its green baize corners at the four players: at Papa, at the silver head of Jean's cane, at the embroidered buttons of Maman's front, and at Nicolas' white sweater. Charlotte herself was squatting on the floor cutting out Bridget's perfectly black dress. Annick was seated on the sofa, quietly stitching at some strong serviceable garment, with her grieved gaze lifting from time to time to dwell upon her family. The bridge games were scarred deeply in Annick's heart, and although Maman's hands continued to work unfalteringly at her knitting, the waste of time as well as the sullying of it by a few gamblers' tricks, grieved Annick sorely and wounded her.

In the creases of Papa's mouth a little of his breakfast chocolate still lingered. His watch-chain strung across his vest caught and held captive five fine links of light. His hands moved ponderously over his cards.

"Is black quite suitable for such a young woman as Bridget?" said Papa as he played his card.

"And why not?" asked Nicolas sharply.

"I love it," said Charlotte touching the cloth. She was leaning forward upon her two round elbows. The scattered pages of *Femina* were all about. "I'm going to make every stitch of it myself," said Charlotte firmly.

"Ah, well, times have changed!" said Papa. "I should never have wanted to see my young wife in a gloomy dress. And of course little babies can't bear to see black. Every young mother is told that she should never dress in black on account of her baby's dislike of it. It isn't appropriate at all."

"And neither is chocolate a proper beverage for an old warrior," said Nicolas with a gleam of contempt. "Imagine a wrathful old colonel sipping hot chocolate!"

"Nicolas!" said Maman in reproof.

"The thing is," said Charlotte with a deep sweet smile at

Bridget, "that maybe you won't have much occasion to wear it where you are going. But it will be nice to travel in."

Jean's face looked up in mock distress.

"But, Bridget," he said, "you're not going away?"

He sat at the card table imitating the small passing sorrow of one of his own children, with his blue eyes filled with mourning and his mouth beginning to turn down.

"Ah, that's a secret!" said Charlotte. "It's something we have to talk about, Jean."

"I don't want to talk about Bridget and Nicolas going away," said Jean. Maman was listening as she settled back to knit while Nicolas dealt out the cards. Miraculously all the needlework in the two houses had blossomed into baby things over night.

"What's this, what's this?" she said with her old sharp nose. "What's this, Bridget? Shall I have to be making bootees for another little grandson too?"

Riquet was watching his grandmother and bumping his round felt toes against her chair.

"Bootees for Riquet," he said in such a grown-up way that they all burst into laughter.

"No, no, not for Riquet," said Maman as she curved fatuously over him. "For a little, little brother or sister who will come to play with Riquet. Maman is going to buy him this winter at the Galeries Lafayette," she said.

In his small strong fist Riquet grabbed and held firmly the pleat of flesh that sagged in his grandmother's throat. The blood rushed to her face and her words were strangled in her mouth. She sat in her chair with her face swollen, gurgling as her grandson strangled her. Charlotte leapt to her feet and slapped his rosy hands.

"*Vilain!*" she cried. "*Vilain!*"

Once she had freed Maman and the *bonne* had borne Riquet away, Charlotte put her handkerchief to her mouth.

"Oh, I am feeling so ill!" she said. She turned away from them and hastened out of the room.

"You see, it's beginning," said Papa darkly. "Poor girl! She won't be able to eat another mouthful now for six months.

How she is ever strong enough at the end of these confinements to bear such beautiful children," he said, "I do not know."

Nobody, indeed, knew. They all agreed it was an affliction peculiar to Charlotte. Six months ahead of her stretched out on a *chaise longue*, murmured Maman.

"Sometimes I think that Charlotte's nerves make her exaggerate just a little about how badly she feels," murmured Maman so softly that one could scarcely hear her. "After all, all women suffer, all women bear suffering for months and months," said Maman. She turned the heel of the bootee and started courageously across the sole of the foot.

"But anyway, Pierre might examine her and give his opinion," said Nicolas.

"Tut, tut," said Jean. "Let's not have any doctors here messing about. My case ought to prove to you, Nicolas, how little they know about anything. You modern people have such a belief in scientific things."

"Charlotte has five healthy children," stated Maman.

"Jeannot and Mimi are weak as water in the legs," said Nicolas.

"Weak as water or not," said Papa with decision, "they are the joy of existence, Nicolas."

"I don't see what joy any one of your offspring has ever brought to you," said Nicolas sourly.

"Enough, enough!" cried Maman. But two weeks later she wrote to Pierre and asked him to come and see his ailing sister.

Pierre replied, in no great haste, that he would run out within a day or two one afternoon. He was really too busy to take a vacation that year, and it was even difficult for him to get away for the day, but he would do his best, and although no mention was made of Luc, the hope began to grow that Luc would come as well. In this expectancy the days took on a gayer tone, and the little group around Charlotte's *chaise longue* wore fresher dresses and kept their hair in curl. Hour after hour Charlotte lay patiently wrapped in a blanket, retching into her little basin of bile.

They were all settled beneath the acacia tree in front of

Charlotte's house. Papa was reading the *Ouest-Éclair* with his ears pricked up for any sound of steps coming down the drive. Every drop of his blood was restless and impatient and he stirred and shifted with his paper in his hand darting fierce furtive glances over the edge of it at his daughter who was feeling so badly in her *chaise longue*. With all his aged contempt he was ready to fling to scorn the medical knowledge that Pierre would bring. He had known him, a mere scrap of flesh wetting his diapers, and now he was coming to antagonize and patronize him.

And then the sharp crackle of steps rounded the shrubbery and came down the gravel drive. Papa bridled to the hammer of Nicolas' words. His eyes sulked below his lids, avoiding the sight of his two sons coming arm in arm around the acacia tree. Pierre was carrying his gun with him, evidently hoping to enjoy a bit of hunting upon this unavoidable visit to his people. When he had come in among them, he set his gun against the tree and embraced his parents. Then he kissed Charlotte's pale brow. He sat talking a minute with them, the small bones of his shapely hand pressed down on the fresh dark knee of his fine hunting breeches. He had come alone.

The family sat in silence about him. Suddenly Maman removed her nose-glasses with her sharp impatient fingers. The sun which danced upon them flashed across Pierre's intelligent sharp face. He looked up uneasily as if it were almost painful for him to bring himself to look upon the alien countenances of his family. His head was lifted and his nostrils withdrawn as if to escape a bad odour that assailed them.

"Pierre, I wrote you about Charlotte," said Maman. "What can you prescribe for your sister, my Pierrot?"

Her voice was brisk and casual as though she could by this feint of natural spirits and affection between them create a sympathy which did not exist. Pierre turned his head to regard his sister pleasantly, and she smiled wanly up at him from her chair.

"I hoped for better luck this time," said Charlotte as if in apology for putting him out. Jean smiled under his great moustaches and tapped the yellow leg of the reclining chair with the side of his cane.

"Eh, Pierre, *mon vieux*," said Jean with a gulp of laughter. "This is the godfather of all my children, this varnished animal!"

"Of course you won't eat eggs?" said Pierre pleasantly.

Charlotte's face contorted and Papa tossed back and forth in indignation in his chair.

"Eggs!" cried Papa contemptuously.

Pierre shrugged his shoulders and gave his attention to a minute examination of his small, clean nails.

"It is like this, Pierre," said Maman. "She eats toast and a little pink jam."

Charlotte groped below her for the porcelain basin and retched over the low arm of the chair.

"I think I had better be left alone for a minute," she gasped. Pierre turned pleasantly away. "Nor milk?" he said, when she was done. "All I can say is what I have said to you before, Charlotte," he said patiently. "You should eat eggs, drink a great deal of milk, and you should stop vomiting."

Maman threw up her hands.

"*Mon petit* Pierrot," she said. "Doesn't she suffer enough, doesn't the poor child suffer enough? Let her have her toasted bread and *confiture* if it gives her any joy!"

"Let me have peace, let me have peace!" cried Charlotte wanly.

"You have wounded Papa with your impatience, Charlotte," said Maman. Over the rims of her glasses she watched Papa's retreating and agitated back. Annick put down her work and slipped quietly away after him. Charlotte lay moaning in her chair.

"After five confinements, Pierre," said Charlotte. As though suddenly reminded of the others, Pierre looked up and brightly about.

"Ah, where are the children?" he asked.

Bridget and Nicolas went off with him to the pond where the children were skimming small bits of blue slate over the surface of the water. Beside them sat the *bonne*, crocheting with a great amber needle that gathered up the thick lilac wool in its beak. Pierre smiled absently over their heads, running his white palm up and down the gleaming muzzle of his gun, his eyes prodding sharply at the remote closed crescent of the sea.

In answer to his questions Nicolas told him that the tide would be starting up soon. Between the pond and the basin emptied for the sea were meadows of sour sea-grasses and long wet naked banks of mud. It was very like the afternoon that Luc had walked around the wall with her, thought Bridget. But at the far edge of the pond in the sea-reeds there was a movement like the passing of the wind, a sedate and austere rift furrowing the briny blades apart.

When Pierre lifted his gun to fire the children scurried with joy to Bridget's skirts. Beyond the clear water of the pond and the dam wall was the high grass sagging slowly away. They all stood silent as if a spell had been cast upon them by Pierre's short amiable command. Across the pond the reeds were pressed apart and a mammoth marsh crow walked shortly and busily forward, swinging his head through the blades and picking here and there at the roots of the reeds in search for stranded fish to sweeten in his dark belly.

Pierre fired twice.

"Delicious meat," he said as he led them delicately around the wall of the pond. "Best when served not overdone so that the tang of the flesh is preserved."

He picked up the bird whose breast he had shattered open, holding the dark scaled feet of it securely in his palm. In silence they all followed him back around the water. He walked lightly on the balls of his feet over the great sea-scarred stones, swinging the plumed bleeding body far from the fine cloth of his breeches. From time to time he turned his head to talk with Nicolas who walked beside him, and his keen eyes would go beyond to examine the distance and the thin edge of sea uncurling like an opening finger.

"Gulls," he murmured.

Jeannot stroked the blood-torn breast of the dangling crow.

"Can you eat gulls?" he asked respectfully.

Pierre smiled. "Eat gulls? Eh? Oh, no. But what of feathers for your bonnets? What of wings for the little girls here?"

He indulgently pinched a cheek below him, and Mimi and Monique swung on Bridget's hands and averted their shy faces in laughter. The gulls were coming steadily on with the sea, scattering and dipping before the advancing wave. Nicolas and Bridget and the children followed Pierre on back around the pond.

XXIV

"WHY," SAID Charlotte suddenly, "why do you suppose the nightingale never came back this year?"

She lay on the great bed with the richly embroidered sheets turned down below her chin and her dark eyes suffused with injury.

"I want the nightingale!" she said in a high childish voice. She beat her feet with irritation in the bedclothes. "I'm sure that Pierre shot it down last autumn after we had gone back to Saint-Malo! Bridget, I want the nightingale now," she said. "I want him right away. Last year I didn't have you and Nicolas, but I had the nightingale." Her eyes were filling with tears. "Last year I didn't have you, but why should I have to choose between you. He was so lovely, Bridget," she said. "You have no idea. He was as soft as a feather himself, and you could see his little throat rippling when he sang."

Bridget and Nicolas and Jean were having their coffee and cigarettes in Charlotte's room.

"I want to get the sea-gulls in," said Nicolas. "Their wings must be broken. They're floundering around out there in the pond."

"*Ben*, Nicol," said Jean. "Let them be. Pierre's a good shot."

Through the window of Charlotte's bedroom could be seen the three fallen gulls that Pierre had shot the afternoon before. They were floating clearly and quietly on the water. One was drifting with his wings spread widely apart and his small smooth head moving slowly with the slow lapping rhythm of the water.

One was washed steadily up and then down upon the sea wall, first up on the wall and then sucked down again into the vacuous edge of water. And the third one was managing to arch his slim neck and peck from time to time at passing objects as he drifted.

Bridget stood beside Nicolas at the window watching the filling pond and the poplar row shuddering along the beach. The sky was grey with foreboding and there was a fresh wind combing the waters.

"Jean, I want the nightingale!" said Charlotte's querulous voice behind them.

"What a spoiled child you are!" said Jean with a convulsion of laughter.

"What shall I ever do for my tongue?" said Charlotte. She called Bridget back to look at it, thrusting it out at her white as wool and slightly speckled with toast. "I can't bear being ugly!" cried Charlotte suddenly. She pressed the palms of her long white hands into her eyes. "I can't bear being horrible and smelling bad!" she said. "I don't want to be left alone!"

"Oh, Charlotte," cried Jean. "No one is going to leave you!"

The soft expanse of his forehead was abruptly furrowed with distress. The great wide hairless hands stroked at the sheets of the bed.

"Don't be sad, Charlotte," he said. "No one is going to go away. We are all here and so happy together," he said. His vast face had slowly begun to collapse. "Nothing is ever going to change, Charlotte," he said. "Look up at Nicol and Bridget. Don't be sad."

"But Nicol and Bridget must go away," said Charlotte. She took one of Jean's hands in hers. "Of course, Jean, you know that Nicol and Bridget have to go away and make their living somewhere."

"I don't see why they have to go away," said Jean. His great chin had begun to tremble.

"I want to talk to you about it," said Charlotte. "I want to talk to you about it now."

"But you're too ill now," said Bridget. "No, wait, Charlotte, until you are better soon."

"No, I want to talk about it now," said Charlotte petulantly. "I want Jean to bring me the papers about the *estancias* so that he will understand and we shall talk about it now."

Jean looked at her in bewilderment and she patted his hands.

"There, there, Jean," she said, "you must understand how things are, you know. We must all try to lead better lives the way people of the world all do. And, Jean, you must promise to take me away after this. We'll go to Paris and we'll go to the theatre, and it will take the bad taste from my mouth. We'll see *Mon Curé Chez Les Riches* and *Mon Curé Chez Les Pauvres* and, whatever Annick says, I want to hear Chevalier sing. We could go out when he began singing his bad songs, Jean, and just once we'd go for the *apéritif* to the Café de la Paix."

"Charlotte, Charlotte," Jean began to whimper. He had taken out his handkerchief and was beginning to wipe his beautiful mild eyes. But the arrival of Maman in a state of extreme agitation gave another turn to his attention.

Down sat Maman by the side of her daughter's bed. Her old fingers fumbled in her skirt and drew out her crocheting. Her hands were always a happy independent couple in themselves; in themselves a complete *ménage* continuously occupied in some rapid work they shared between them and in which the old lady herself had no part. Now did these two elderly members toss the wool back and forth, weaving and working in and out in perfect accord and as if with minds of their own, while Maman's detached face looked gravely on and finally addressed Charlotte and Bridget and Nicolas and Jean.

"The most extraordinary thing has happened," she said in a rapid undertone. "Really *extraordinaire, extraordinaire.*" No one else could give it such a flavour. "Oncle Robert has written a letter to your father making an absolute offer to add fifteen thousand francs to Annick's *dot* if she gets married within the next six months."

Every pigment of colour sapped from her face as she spoke these words to them. Her voice had turned hoarse in her throat. It was easily the most astonishing thing that had happened in the family since the day that Nicolas had married a foreigner.

This news could mean nothing else, surely, but that Annick was as good as betrothed. There could be no question now, as far as the family was concerned, as to what Luc would do. The girls' dowries were handsome enough as it was, but with fifteen thousand thrown in to boot, there could surely be no more doubt as to how Luc would make up his mind.

"Ah, poor Marthe!" said Charlotte softly.

"Yes," said Maman, as if it had echoed the fear in her own soul. "What can we do for poor Marthe?"

"If only someone could give her that much too," said Charlotte, "to give her an even chance!"

She turned her head upon her pillow but she did not look at Jean. With delicacy and tact she looked away across the running sea. But her words, although not addressed to him, had caused a distinct change to alter his countenance. His eye diminished and his chin grew firm. He set his face as if against some sinister force which, the more because he could not comprehend it, he knew he must stubbornly resist in silence to the end. If his mind's eye did not perceive legions of unmarried sisters, aging relatives, sick brothers-in-law trespassing upon lands that were his, at least some sense in him made him suspect the intention of their presence near his home. Here was his defeat for them all, then, in his whole shrinking face which was presently reduced to a small relentless fist before them. His triumph lay in flapping his loose knees together, clinging to his cane and looking as if he had not understood. His softening brain could, in the miracle of silence, finally outwit them all.

"How does Annick take the news?" asked Charlotte.

"She wished to write to Oncle Robert at once and suggest that he transfer his offer to Marthe," said Maman. Completely unobserved in her lap, her hands were turning the sleeve of a baby jacket. "But your father and I persuaded her that it would not do to appear to be critical of Oncle Robert's choice. She has always been his favourite and I must confess that now I consider he has done enough to merit her tending him in his last illness when the time comes. I only hope for all our sakes that it won't be a lingering one so that Annick will not be long away from home. Your father is writing to inform Pierre," finished Maman, "so that Luc may know at the earliest possible moment how things stand."

The excitement of all this was too much for Charlotte and by the time Papa had joined them in her room she was gagging over the porcelain basin beside her bed. Papa watched her darkly as she sank back upon the deep pillows in their embroidered jackets. The pages of *Vogue* and *La Femme Élégante* had glided down over the quilt and collapsed on the floor. Charlotte smiled gently up at him and held out her hand.

"Will you open the shutters a little, just a little, Papa," she said, "on that side so I can see the acacia tree?"

XXV

NICOLAS leaped out of bed into the middle of the bright morning, wiped his feet on the square of sunshine and began to shave.

Never had such a beautiful room been theirs. The bed was shining like a golden throne, and over the long golden mirrors the cupids floated endlessly away with their cheeks swelling to the trumpet-tubes and their toes curled close on the architraves of the fluted pilasters. Nicolas flung wide the shutters and the warm thick air of the September harbour fell in upon the floor.

Beside the bed squatted the valises, their sleek leather jowls rubbing against the petticoats of lace. Nicolas' fingertip drawn down the surface of the mirror as he shaved before it, left a gleaming pathway through the infinitudes of dust. The night before they had pulled the shrouded covers from the gilded armchairs, and now the brocaded satin of them, stuffed fat as pigeons, swelled smooth and glossy in the morning light.

"This is our honeymoon," said Nicolas.

He was transformed with peace and gaiety in Charlotte's and Jean's bedroom in their house in Saint-Malo. Beneath them was the nursery, empty except for a headless doll and a scattered string of beds. "This is our honeymoon," said Nicolas, and Bridget thought of Charlotte stirring upon her pillows and discussing whether this year they would return to the house in October or if they would linger on in the country until she was up and about again, perhaps even until the *Toussaint*. . . . But in the meantime, Bridget and Nicolas must have a week of it, for the harbour and the sea there were like none other in the world. "Before you go to Africa . . ." said Charlotte. "But will Jean ever be persuaded?" said Nicolas, in doubt. "Oh, but that goes without saying," Charlotte had answered. "By the time you come back from Saint-Malo that will have been decided. . . ."

"This is our honeymoon," said Nicolas. He took her hand as they walked down the stairs of the empty house, each hollow step of it reproaching them for their intrusion. Six months it had been since the house had been closed away, and in all the rooms there was the faint humid scent of early spring. The salon was shrouded like a tomb, and the family portraits veiled that hung upon the walls of it.

In spite of all the words there were to say, even at coffee that first morning on the strong sea wall the conversation turned again to Luc, and every time a passing sail or thought disturbed the trend of it, back it came to "Luc lived here, and in this corner house Luc was born, and in this villa which was a hospital in time of war Luc had lain side by side with Nicolas for two months and Annick was the head *infirmière*." Bridget felt a certain resentment in the thought that Annick had been there to nurse them both when she was far away.

Nicolas was so contented, drinking his coffee in the shadow of the café awning and talking there. He told her about Chateaubriand and pointed out the island, the closest one, where they had buried him. And beyond was where Conrad had lived the first year of his marriage, but they would need a boat to get to it. There, on that hard packed beach, Nicolas and Charlotte had rolled their hoops together.

"Do you think Luc will marry Annick?" Bridget suddenly said.

Nicolas sat puffing at his cigarette.

"Maybe he will," he said. "Fifteen thousand more means a lot, you know. Pierre has been talking about a new wing on the clinic for some time and he and Luc could use that money very well."

"Do you know what I want to do, Nicol?" said Bridget in a moment. "I want to go to a bird shop and try to find a nightingale."

All morning they spent in climbing over the dark strong rocks, exploring the two beaches and discovering clearer and clearer pools of sea hidden on the outskirts of them. It was unbelievable that salt water could be so thin and clear, so fresh that it was difficult not to lie down beside it and drink great draughts of it. Here and there were fish poised static a moment in the little basins of sea and then darting off under the roots and caverns of the rock. In the running waters were occasional minnows woven into the movement of the flowing weeds, transparent fish opening and closing their crisp short fins.

This was the most wonderful morning of all. Although it was late in the season they went in to swim. Under the water there were stalks of white coral like polished skeletons, and branched fangs of rosy coral hung with glassy ornaments of the sea. When they grew hungry before lunch they pried open quantities of yellow clams and ate them off the tip of Nicolas' knife. In the afternoon they went to call on Oncle Robert.

Oncle Robert was in a state of exhaustion incident to the endowment he had made upon his favourite niece. Scarcely a whisper of his voice could be heard from the depths of his velvet chair and the folds of his satin gown.

"Dear, dear children," he murmured. He laid an expiring hand in each of theirs and then he closed his eyes as if he were about to swoon away. "Tell me how each member of our dear family has taken the news," he said when he had again recovered sufficient strength to speak. "I wonder if it was wise of me," he continued, "to have put my finger in the matrimonial pie." There was almost a shade of regret in his voice. "Oh, dear," he murmured. "At times I fear my spontaneity makes me actually imprudent!"

"Annick has decided not to take the veil for a while at least," said Nicolas, "and spent the entire day upon her knees thanking the Father, the Son, and the Holy Ghost."

"The dear girl wrote me a few sweet expressions of her gratitude as well," said Oncle Robert with a deprecatory smile, making a gallant gesture with his hand as though the real honour belonged to the Holy Three. "I love Luc as I do my own dear boy, and rather than see him united with that absolute serpent of a Marthe who would consume him so completely that there would be no virility left to pursue his high career—or with that guffawing graceless creature who is half-man and the remainder quite indescribable, I refer to Julie, of course—rather than see him united to either of those two monsters of womanhood who shy like skiddy horses at the sight of a man, I prefer to sacrifice my entire fortune, small though it may be, and enable him to marry a good and lovely woman who has washed enough behinds in hospitals to take a husband as a matter of course."

Oncle Robert was seized with a fit of ague, and interrupted himself to ring for tea.

"But we enlightened ones," he continued with his tedious cough, "must use our wits to guide the lives of others who are less gifted. Thus I have, like Fate, indicated as best I could the way that it would be best for events to dispose themselves. My dear brother Auguste has just telephoned me that Luc is expected for the week end. I fully expect this will mean an engagement formally announced within the week."

The words dropped like bitter pills from off his dry sharp tongue, and Bridget put down her tea cup with a clatter. Luc in the country, and they were here in Saint-Malo! Luc in the country, riding the filly bareback, bringing in hedgehogs rolled tight as chestnut burrs. A whole week end of Luc in the bosom of the family. Forty-eight hours of gold squandered in handfuls, and she not there for a single moment of it.

"And Charlotte is feeling better," continued Oncle Robert, "and sat up the entire afternoon. The horror of that affair!" said Oncle Robert as he sipped his tea. "That's one thing I can never forgive your mother, Nicolas," he said. "Your mother is a woman who considers she knows best about every matter that comes under her nose. She never could see any harm in Charlotte marrying Jean. Of course the whole explanation of Charlotte's sieges is Jean's disease. Everyone knows that there should be no children from such a union at all. They are all doomed to it, and it poisons Charlotte like the plague. How wise you two children are!" he murmured. "How wise of you, in spite of my brother's tempting but most indelicate offer, to have no children at all."

In spite of his spoken approbation of them Bridget felt there was a gleam of censure in his eye.

"Now Luc is another matter," said Oncle Robert. "What a husband for any woman!" he exclaimed. "Too bad you can't marry him, Bridget," said Oncle Robert playfully, "for you would really be a charming pair." He laughed lightly and with the greatest agility turned the conversation back to Jean. "But as for Jean," he said, "of course he should be burned alive for being a dullard, and Charlotte should be put on the rack, if she isn't there already, poor thing, for having married a nit-wit." He wiped his fingertips in his silk handkerchief. "Oh, dear," he said, "how people do abuse their lovely, lovely lives! Now you two handsome ones are going to do something perfectly gorgeous, I'm quite sure. I can see in your eye, Nicolas, that you're just on the verge of doing the most amusing thing in the world!"

Oncle Robert shook his finger playfully at his nephew whose eye, in truth, was particularly grim.

"You see, I'd never dream of offering you two anything because it's so evident that you just couldn't get into straits of any kind. Such a relief to have competence, *and* charm, in the family for once in a way!"

And thus Oncle Robert disposed of any necessity of doing anything for them. He looked at them sharply over the porcelain edge of his cup, just on the point of speaking of other things, for it was perfectly clear that he did not want the conversation to go on in the way it was going. It had clearly occurred to him that they might just say that they had nothing in the world to do and that they thought he might let them have a little money. But this he solved for the moment at least by passing his fragile hand across his forehead.

"I'm really feeling much more fatigued than I should," he said. "I can't imagine what it is except that I must be getting old."

After this there was nothing to do but go. They went out of his house on to the wall, and there was the afternoon already moving down the beach to sunset, slipping away from them in cool clear tides of light. They walked into the precipitous streets of the town and sought out a bird shop, for Bridget was determined to buy a nightingale.

By the greatest stroke of good luck, they found a solitary nightingale in the first pet shop they entered. He was put into a little unpainted wooden cage and they carried him out with them into the open square. Behind them was the sea wall, matured and bosomed with dusk, and before them in the street a military band was passing by. The little pieces of bottle glass on the court wall of the mediaeval prison yard were bladed with the last rays of sinking light. They sat down with their bird at a little tin table on the terrace of a café.

Never before, thought Bridget, had she felt such desolation in her heart. Never before had faces looked so grim and decorous, never had complexions seemed so sallow and worn. Nicolas was wearied and gloomy after his conversation with Oncle Robert and he sat sipping glumly at his ruby drink. Bridget thought of Luc's short bright moustaches, of his thick square lashes, and of his scalp scrubbed clean as a timber floor. Great expanses of gold had been splashed on him as if from a brush dripping with fresh paint. Splash had gone the brush on the crown of his stubborn head. Splash, splash went the brush and gave him his yellow brows. " 'The twilight attempered Hyperborean Apollo,' " she thought sadly, " 'gleaming at times with a supernatural brightness, and exposing to those who love him a golden thigh.' "

Not even the sight of the nightingale perched in his small wooden cage could revive her fainting heart. There sat the little bird with his merciless eye upon her, clutching the perch in his dark naked feet. He had turned a sharp censorious eye upon them from the outset, and not a leaf of lettuce would he consider, judging moreover the tiny grains that they had scattered for him as fit only to bear his droppings. A critical small bunch of feathers turning this way and that upon his perch and uttering no sound.

XXVI

THE SHARP September darkness was awaiting them as they stepped down from the train. Autumn was coming in like a wet leaf blown across their faces, a sign for the blood to turn to wine in their veins, a promise of new countries, and winds, and faces. There was always this jubilation in the changing of the seasons, and now the thought of winter on the *estancia* where they were to begin all over again made shivers of delight pierce Bridget's heart.

Outside the station there were stars. Far above them the stars were hanging in the darkness, and near by the night was puckered like golden silk about the bright lamps of the sulky. Charlotte's coachman leaned in after they were seated and adjusted the rug snugly about their legs. Then he too climbed up and took the reins. With a chirp of his tongue he flecked the whip across the filly and her hoofs started out in a tentative rhythm on the road, her uncertain ears quivering forward and back in the cones of light. Forward they would go, pointing with distrust into the perilous night through which she must advance, and then back they would flash revealing their soft lining to the gentle cluck of the coachman's tongue.

"The night throws her out," the man said to Nicolas.

Nicolas stirred beneath the carriage robe to find Bridget's hand. Before them they could see the pure bright ripple of the filly's buttocks and the nervous flash of her cropped tail across her rump. The dainty dance of her hoofs was rapidly diminishing the distance that lay between them and the good family.

"Are you glad to be coming back?" asked Nicolas.

"Yes," said Bridget. Everything would be settled now, she was thinking. Now Charlotte would tell them that Jean had agreed; Annick would tell them that she was engaged to Luc; everything would be determined in its own unalterable fashion. She thought of two pictures she would like to paint before she went away. In her mind everything was settled and arranged: the mornings that were left to them would be spent in oil painting and the afternoons in walking over the cliffs and woods that now would be so altered by the severe September nights. In this determination her mind was like a stranger to her, a freshly starched object, agreeable to the eye. How long before you wilt, she asked herself. There'll be no wilting, she said sharply. Smartly the coachman's whip splintered the air.

Down the road chattered the bells of the filly's harness, and her sharp, nervous hoofs danced in the gate. Maman came quickly down the steps to them, came hastening around the syringa bush with the three girls following behind. A week they had been gone, and how the weather had changed! The hall stove was so choked with last year's soot that they couldn't get a stick of wood to burn in it! In the salon chimney only were there a few tongues of flame licking inadequately at the cold.

As she removed her hat amongst them all Bridget could hear the filly snorting away through Charlotte's grill and down the drive. Out in the night she could hear the soft puddle and snort of the filly's muzzle and the chirp of her bells.

"How's Charlotte?" asked Bridget. "I have brought her a nightingale."

There were glassy cracked moons upon each one of Papa's knuckles as he spread his old hands at the fire.

"No wonder you two never have any money!" he said grimly. "Buying nightingales!" His old shoulders were withdrawn from the chilly room. "Charlotte is naturally much better," he continued in a moment. "In spite of Pierre's efforts to inveigle her into his clinic in Rennes, we, in our poor humble way, have managed to make her practically well. She was up most of the day today."

There was no word, no hesitation, no silence hallowed there

for Luc. No one so much as spoke his name. Bridget looked at the faces of the three girls hoping to find some record of his visit there. But their eyes bespoke no elation and no despair.

"September shutting its jaws on us," said Papa. "We'll see its teeth before morning."

Nicolas walked back and forth in the firelight, rubbing his hands and nosing the sharp eager cold.

"It'll go off in the equinox rains," said Nicolas. Papa wondered about that.

In the morning only Monique could remember how many sour-balls Charlotte had eaten the night before. Charlotte herself lay perfectly hidden beneath her lids.

"After such improvement!" said Maman. The happy *ménage* of Maman's hands continued their uninterrupted life below her, occupied in making a bonnet for the head of Charlotte's unborn child.

Papa's voice was ominously narrowed at the door, hushed to the importance of telling them that he had been to the village to telephone Pierre, and that Pierre had refused, refused point blank, to come. Jean was relieved. He settled back in satisfaction under his moustaches and then suddenly he leaned forward and cried out to them:

"Family! Leave her alone! You and your Pierre! Do you think I want my wife carried off to a clinic? Do you think I want my child to point out a clinic as the place where he was born?"

Maman's false but ringing laughter attempted to restore the normal tone. Only her eyes, swelling like amber beads against her nose, betrayed her indignation.

"By way of precaution, Jean," said Maman judiciously. "We are merely discussing, you understand, discussing the wisdom of . . ."

Bridget remembered that Charlotte had once shown her over the entire house, explaining every stick of furniture and its history to her, pausing at the prayer-chair in her bedroom to point out the hollows cupped in the plush of it by the devotion of the ancestors' knees. And every day Jean prayed there, she had said, entreating God to render him more patient and more tolerant of others. Jean's eyes were gentle as larkspurs, but Charlotte had smoothed out the bruised plush of the chair and remarked that Jean was not a patient man. "He prays for it," she had said. "For patience, patience . . ." patience to extend like a gentle and forbearing hand upon his brow.

Papa sat in his shabby old lavender coat, his breath sweet with port and his chin relaxed upon the shredded velvet of his coat lapels. Behind his head was a small oblong of landscape which one of the ancestors had hung in place. "Corot, before he discovered picnics," Charlotte had said of it with her small brilliant smile.

"My children!" cried Maman. "You all forget this is no new thing. Why all this to-do about it? Why are you grave, my Auguste? Why is my Marthe weeping . . . ."

But in spite of all that Maman could say, Charlotte had become a stranger to them in her own house. Behind that closed door she had become a presence which they spoke of in whispers. Bridget felt that if she went in to her that she would find an alien creature, for even Maman's laughter could not soothe them. But Maman insisted that they go in, that they sit upon the bed and talk with her, that they speak of ordinary things and show her their needlework. Bridget went in first to her and kissed her warm bewildered brow.

"Darling," said Bridget as she kneeled beside her. "Here is the nightingale. Look how lovely and soft he is."

Charlotte stretched out her hand towards him but she was frightened when he flew startled against the bars of his cage. Her lids had grown so heavy that she could scarcely lift them from her eyes.

"Isn't it funny, Bridget," she said. The quality of her voice had changed and her words came slowly as if drawn singly from a mire of weariness. The putrid odour of her breath transformed her tender mouth. "I can't possibly lift my eyelids, Bridget," she said.

After this she was too tired to say any more. But she had such a lovely long sleep all that day that no one disturbed her again and everybody was reassured. At supper Papa suggested that as long as Pierre was so busy, that perhaps Luc might come out and give his advice, and it was decided that if Charlotte were not completely herself by morning that Luc should come.

"But wasn't Luc here over the week end?" said Nicolas, as if suddenly reminded. "Oncle Robert told us that Luc was going to come."

Maman's fingers set the silver straight under the shadow of her soup plate, the blade of the knife approached the last fine tooth of the fork and the spoons were crossed precisely below the fluted glass of cider.

"Luc was expected," said Maman, "but Luc was detained. He had to wait for an estimate on a new wing they are considering adding to the clinic. He was very anxious to come, but he was delayed by this estimate which required his presence there."

Across Maman's nose was a flushed saddle of colour which she stroked with her fingertips, telling Bridget that this mark had afflicted her at the time of her second pregnancy and that it returned to her now at moments where she was overwrought.

"I am very nervous now," she said. "For some reason, I am very tired."

She recounted to them that she had laced her corset so tightly at that time, in order that none of Papa's associates should suspect, that she had fainted quite away. It had been at a dinner party, and everybody had been so delighted and so amazed to learn that the young Colonel's wife . . . and only seven months after the birth of baby Pierre! Papa laughed out loud at the remembrance of the water they had dashed on her and the bodice slit open by the blade of Capitaine le Beaufils' sword. Little unborn Charlotte, always too nervous, Papa said. Taut as a fiddle-string.

"Nerves, nerves, nerves," murmured Papa. "Always nerves. . . ."

Charlotte had even broken down in the convent play, with the *Noëlists* so sure of applause, and little Charlotte at twelve collapsing in "Poet and Peasant," a piece she knew backwards and forwards. . . .

"Ah God, ah God, ah God," Maman cried out and covered her eyes with her hand as though she suddenly knew.

"No, no, I am all right," she said to them. "We shall all say our prayers very well tonight and go to bed. I am worn out. I am tired."

For once her hands had collapsed and lay idle in her lap. She did not move again until she led the family from the table to the salon where the candles blazed and re-blazed in the mirrors. And there, as if life had revived in her, she sat abruptly down at the piano.

"Par-umph!" she banged out on the keys. The candles twinkled about the weary lines of her old faded hair. Slyly she watched them all over the fatigued slope of her shoulder while her fingers searched sharply on the keys. "The talented young musician who married your father . . ." she said. "How ravishingly she played for him on their first meeting. . . ." Her fingers selected the notes as they would, tinkling along in smooth flight of sound. "Oh, we had such a bridal suite with a real gold piano! And Monsieur and Madame dined together on their first evening. . . ." Tinkle, tinkle, tinkle went the old piano. "And now would Madame have the goodness to play a selection on the pianoforte for Monsieur *son mari* before retiring? My poor Auguste . . ." She crashed the notes with her laughter. "The talented musician he had married had no notes with her and could play nothing, but nothing, from memory!" The tuneless old piano could scarcely express her mirth. "Out he went into the street, your father, and to make my tears stop flowing he bought me a little red and yellow cap, children . . ." Her hands abandoned the keys for a moment and she swung about on the stool to face them. "Do you remember the little red and yellow cap, Auguste *cheri*?" she said. She cocked her little old head on one side.

Papa tossed his elbows on the arms of his chair.

"I don't remember," he growled at her. For nothing on earth would he show her that he was amused.

"Oh, Auguste," cried Maman. "The little red and yellow cap, *voyons*!"

Maman crashed the notes one final time, closed the piano, blew out the candles which burned upon it, and stood up and looked at them all. She looked at the girls who were tired, and at Bridget, at Nicolas, and at Papa. She looked at them all. And then like an old general she gave them their orders, her wise protective orders, as though she were saving and intrenching them for the coming battle.

"Take your candles and go to bed," she said. "Get some sleep now."

Presently Papa and Nicolas and Bridget were left alone by the fire.

"What of Pierre?" said Nicolas.

Papa's eyes started up from the fire.

"Eh? Oh . . . Pierre . . ." he said. His hands fell down on the arms of his chair. "He wanted Charlotte to come to Rennes," he said. "He spoke of operating. That won't do."

Nicolas leaned forward, striking his palms softly together.

"But shouldn't Pierre be the one to know?" he asked.

Papa stirred in his chair.

"But she'll eat, she'll eat," he said impatiently. "She's been this way before. You don't know. You've been away the other times, Nicolas. You'll see, she'll eat tomorrow . . . or the day after . . ."

"Has she been as bad as this before?" asked Nicolas.

"Eh?" said Papa vaguely. He was looking at the fire again. "Eh? Oh . . . yes. She's been as bad as this before."

They sat like three survivors of some storm, huddled close to the fire with the rosy curtains of the salon drawn against the night.

"But I think you should have Luc or some other doctor come," persisted Nicolas. "Will you let me go to the town and telephone for somebody else in the morning?" he said.

Papa started a little at the sound of Nicolas' voice.

"Oh . . . Luc . . . yes," he said. His head had sunk lower on his bosom and he was smiling softly, inexplicably. Suddenly a snore escaped him. "I think I'll go to bed," he said as he started up.

XXVII

THE RAIN, which had been imminent all week, suddenly smote the ground. A high wind accompanied it and swung the giant trees like mad Ophelia's over Charlotte's lawn. Over went the garden benches and the bright clay pots which covered the bleaching heads of chicory. The wind could be clearly seen streaming up the river and flinging the crests of it sky-high. From the windows of the billiard room the great livid banks of mud were speared with rain.

" 'The four and twenty sailors,' " read Jeannot's precise tried voice across the page, " ' that stood upon the decks, were four and twenty white mice' "—his impatient eyes darted over the edge of the book which Bridget held, to the click of Jean's and Nicolas' billiard balls—" ' with chains around their necks.' "

Jeannot's blue eyes wandered all over the green baize table, examined Nicolas' hand squared below the polished cue, drifted off to the small white umbrella that was progressing over the head of a little girl who was carefully making her way in the rain over the mill-wall. Deliberately and slowly Bridget shaped the words for Jeannot: " 'Robin and Richard were two pretty men. . . .' " His sweet patient sigh fluttered across the pages as he turned to her, and then he said suddenly:

"I hate English."

"I hate English," said Riquet like a parrot. In his red felt slippers he strutted about the room. "I hate English," he screamed. Nothing could silence him. The nursemaid slapped at his bulging thighs and his father pounced on him with a gulp of laughter. "I hate English," he shouted. It was all of no use.

The skin of Charlotte's children was fair and beautiful and their hair was as soft as flax. When they opened their mouths to wail or shout they revealed red velvet caverns studded with priceless pearls. Their ears were neatly buttoned to the sides of their heads, and their eyes were stainless like the clearest marble. They were as clean and warm as spotless young rabbits in their nest of hay. A round green ball of candied sugar popped into the jaws of their yawning jewel boxes would cause them to snap into silence in the twinkling of an eye.

"Pierre is not a father himself," said Jean when his younger son had quieted down about a sour-ball, "or else he never could have suggested to Charlotte that she go away. It's terrible," he said, "to have to leave your children."

Pierre's pleasant medical manner suddenly took shape in Bridget's mind. She saw him quite distinctly balancing before them on his heels, holding in one hand an immaculate pair of black kid gloves which he slapped repeatedly against his thigh. He had just concluded a successful operation in Rennes, seconded by Luc. "The twins on the operating table labouring in the womb of the unconscious woman," he had said. "Magnificent as Wagner torn with his Tristam and Ysolde. We removed the cist, replaced the womb in the woman's body, and three hours later the normal birth took place. . . ."

"Listen, Jean," said Nicolas leaning on his billiard cue, "maybe it would save Charlotte's health forever if Pierre operated now?"

Jean looked at him in bewilderment as if the injury of this was more than he could bear. His mild, gentle eyes were brimming now with tears.

"Do you know what they did to me last night?" he said. "They told me I couldn't sleep in the same bed with her until she gets better. Everyone is turning against me," he said, "and turning against poor Charlotte now that she's so ill."

The imaginary figure of Pierre exposed his small bright teeth to Bridget. "My hands," he said prettily, "are tied. . . ."

"It's against my wishes that the family has telephoned for Luc," said Jean looking at Nicolas with his mild injured eyes. "And when he comes I don't want to see him at all," he said. "I don't want Luc and a strange doctor in my house doing things that will only be harmful to Charlotte. At first Papa was on my side," he said, "and now he's turned against me too. I know he's the one who told you to telephone for Luc. Now that Charlotte's ill," he said, "there isn't anybody to take my side."

So Jean sat quietly up in the billiard room with Annick and the children when Luc and the little white-bearded doctor came. Into Charlotte's room went the two medical men while the family waited and did their needlework in the adjoining room. There was a sense of peace and assurance now that the medical men were here. Nothing could happen now. The lines were smoothed out of Maman's face, her hands had resumed their active life again.

And then, delicate as a flute, Charlotte's voice sounded through the door to them: "*Il n'etait qu'un petit navire, pet-it na-vi-re-e . . .*" And Papa burst into shouts of laughter. He looked from one to the other of them in bright vindication.

"Lullabies!" he exclaimed in triumph. It was quite evident that Charlotte was singing lullabies.

Slightly muted with laughter, Charlotte's voice sang on behind the closed door. "*Qui n'avait ja-ja-jamais naviagé . . .*" she sang, and the whole family burst into laughter. Even while she laughed the tears streamed down Marthe's cheeks, and Julie shouted with deep guffaws. Papa shook in his garnet vest and the links of his watch-chain slid up and down upon his belly. Maman's teeth gripped fiercely over her lip with laughter.

"Charlotte," said Luc coming out the door and closing it behind him, "is much stronger than when Pierre saw her last."

Maman's fingers abandoned their work and clasped one another tightly across her bosom.

"Oh, children, children, the champagne we'll drink when Charlotte is up again!" she said. "The gay dinner we'll have for her, children!"

"It is her head that is a little bit light," said Luc, "from not having eaten enough all this time."

Luc was wearing a dark blue suit and a stiff white collar and he was looking more severe than they had ever seen him look. When he walked across the room he took great strides and rubbed his hands together in the most professional way. But whatever he did, the attention of everybody was turned upon him, and the girls sat looking and Bridget sat watching him as if they could never see enough of his fine ways. When he reached the window some kind of a change came over his face, and he stooped down by the table and looked into the nightingale's cage.

"Oh, here is the nightingale!" he said.

He squatted there, balancing on his heels and looking through the brass bars of the family's cage at the little bird which he had terrified and which was making short hurried flights here and there. He whistled softly through his teeth to it, and the little bird cocked his head and eyed Luc with a shrewd eye. Presently the feathers about his neck began to rise and ruffle in delight as if Luc's serenade had spurred his flagging pride. He sat quite still and turned the small black crescent of his ear to Luc's ceremonious tongue that chirped and chuckled words of highest praise.

But if the nightingale had succumbed to Luc's sweet wooing, Maman and the girls were outraged that he should be spending his brief time with them in squatting whistling before a wild bird's cage.

"Come now, Luc," said Maman. "Tell us what we are to do for Charlotte and when she will be able to get up."

"We are all of the opinion that she should go to Rennes," said Luc. He stood up and pulled down his cuffs in his sleeves. "I think you ought to make up your minds to that."

"Jean won't hear of it," said Papa. "There's no use talking about it at all."

"There's no use talking about it at all," whistled Luc through his teeth. "Bridget, I think the nightingale is lonely," Luc said.

In the midst of the family he turned to face Bridget and he stood before her lighting a cigarette and looking into her eyes. She was trying to knit a necktie for Nicolas and now the stitches of it went running like drops of water off the needle.

"I think the nightingale's heart is probably breaking," he said. "What are you going to do about it?" he said. "What do you think you will do?"

"I think I will have to let him go," said Bridget.

When she looked up into his face she saw a tremor of pain cross his eyes.

"Oh, but you can't do that!" he said. "You're responsible for him, you know. You can't just turn him off that way. But I think you ought to see that he's not alone," said Luc. "Something very silly might happen to him, you know. He might grieve away for love, or for the lack of it," said Luc.

Such health, such fortitude faced Bridget, such well-shaped hardy bones, such distribution of solid flesh that she mistrusted any matter could fall into decay, could pine and perish for love or lack of it. Even the nightingale, for all his fragility, had a certain wise pre-eminence which could survive an accumulation of restraint. But for the moment Luc had lost the courtly ways which had always been his obeisance to each member of the family.

"Ah, well," he said to Bridget. "You can't just *give* freedom. It's a much more complicated thing than taking it away."

And now, if ever, thought Bridget, must they come to understand each other. She thought of the money Oncle Robert had promised Annick and of the wing that the doctors wanted to build in Rennes. She thought of Marthe's fast avaricious love. Whatever respect she had, thought Bridget, it was for Julie's proud indifference and what it served to conceal. In all of this was Luc, who could have been, who might have been the rainbow, the horned stag with honey in his hoofs fleeing obscurity and its demands upon him and turning all he touched to gold.

"Well, it is just *that* that I should like to give him," said Bridget. She looked at the little nightingale. "Instead of bits of groundsel and grains of corn," she said, "I should like to give him that."

XXVIII

If there were books written, things said, women to talk wisely of other people in the preparation of an atmosphere which would give a grace of mind and action to those who are too young to be prepared; if there were a tradition of gentility that could stand without the prejudice of inexperience in each person who upheld it, it would be a good thing. A tradition is an explanation, is in itself an education which people should be proud to carry on but should not sit down within and make no effort to assert. I cannot, thought Bridget, support the tradition of the family, for it has no pride to it, and it has not made them lift their chins a hair's breadth higher. I should have liked, she thought, to have had heroes behind me with which to have shamed them. Men who gave up family, fortune and whatever the world could then offer them to discover a new planet, a radium, or to fly alone across the Atlantic at a time when no one had flown across it. With these men behind me I should have carried on in smaller ways their grace. I should like to have had successful ancestors, by which I mean that they could have died sick, ill, or despairing but whether they knew it or not they had still got the best of the details which take you by the flesh and wear you to the bone. Had they succeeded in writing two lines that declared them, or lived in any shiftless way, I should now have some indignation inherited with which to confront Nicolas' people.

This, she thought, is the crafty way of the young in putting the blame upon the old. This is the way, she thought, that Nicolas himself is blaming his family but what I blame them for is something else again. There was my grandfather, she thought, and whether I could live with him or not he was a fine arrogant man, and perhaps with a legion like him behind me I could now lift my head among these people. But through lack of education and that tradition of old warriors I should have relished, I resent the purpose of the good family, for I myself have no purpose at all.

She was sitting in the billiard room of Charlotte's house making a very pretty darn in the heel of a sock, while Nicolas was idly knocking the spotless balls about the table.

"Do you know what I've been thinking, Bridget?" he said. He was in a sour temper and he drew his cue rapidly back and forth before he gave it a vicious shot at the ball.

"I've been thinking that if anything happened to Charlotte that our chances of going to the *estancia* would be in a bad way," he said.

The brightest crackle of balls followed this remark. He was smiling rather bitterly as he stood examining the balls for his next play.

"Everything we touch vanishes into thin air," he said. "I suppose you've noticed that?"

It was in such moments that Bridget thought that, had she refused and challenged and antagonized the family from the outset, things might have taken a better turn. All by himself in his resentment Nicolas was getting nowhere at all. Nicolas' own particular gloom had once seemed a thing of distinction to her, but the bitterness of it had increased to no purpose, and when things were holding out no promise to them it possessed and poisoned every moment they shared.

"What do you want me to do?" she said. Riquet was gravely watching his Tante Bridget finishing off her darn.

"Perhaps you could have a little talk with Charlotte," said Nicolas with his sour shameful smile. "I mean now," he said, "before she gets any worse."

It was then the nursemaid came into the room and said that Charlotte was asking for Riquet.

"Do you think I could take him?" said Bridget. She had picked up the little boy in her arms. "I haven't seen her for two days Do you think it would be all right if I should go?"

Jean was off playing bridge at the family's house and Bridget went down into the dark stench and terror of Charlotte's room, carrying Riquet high like a torch in her arms.

The blinds were drawn and in the first moment the one visible thing was the porcelain basin waning like a dim moon in the interminable gloom. Gradually the bed took shape below them, luminous and unstirring and heaped with confusion, with one thick braid of ebony hair lying across the pillows. Bridget stood with her arm under Riquet's small close thighs, watching that motionless braid curved across the linen. And suddenly Charlotte loomed slowly up out of the darkness, loomed up upon them with the loose flesh of her face sagging down on her jaws as she rose.

"Charlotte . . ." said Bridget. "Charlotte, Charlotte, my love . . ." she said. The tears rained down her face.

But Charlotte squatted below them with her face peering up from under her dark puzzled brows, her dark offensive face attempting to fix Bridget in all the chaos of her sight. Slowly she lifted one hand to shade her eyes, and from under it she peered suspiciously up at Bridget. There she sat crouching in her bed, peering cautiously up through the obscurity, crouching there silent and dark and offensive with odour.

"*Embrasse,*" said Riquet, leaning softly down with his hands outstretched. "*Embrasse,* Maman."

Suddenly Charlotte's mouth was blurred and swollen with sound, with apology and explanation, with no words that could be distinguished, but with a blind fumbling flow of sound which sought coherence in the small gestures of her hand. She was apologizing, Bridget could make out, for her condition. She was apologizing to them because she could not form language any more. She showed them her tongue, and then she deflated upon her pillows and the inarticulate voice tapered out in her small weary smile. In the darkness she lay smoothing the polished brow of Riquet's hair and he patted her cheeks with his open palms and listened incuriously to the black torrents of her mouth.

For a moment Charlotte lay watching Bridget, and then she thrust her head up on her neck and held it there in poised offensive strength. Her tongue was swinging thickly in her mouth, and the acacia was moaning at the window in the wind. Through the ribs of the closed shutters Bridget could see the dripping white globes of rain which clung there, slid, and dropped away. Charlotte's loose mouth had fallen open and sagged upon the back of her hand.

"The acacia," she said. She spoke it in a deep stricken voice, and the sound of her own words so startled her that she gave a cry of fright. Holding her loose jaw in place with her hand, she sank back and turned heavily to the pillow, averting her face and the violence of her weeping from them both. Her lips hung wide and loose about the deep snores of her sobbing, and Riquet burst suddenly into tears. He pulled fiercely at the lace of Charlotte's gown, crying aloud, and drawing her nightgown down from her full shaken shoulder. The terrible snores of Charlotte's grief resounded in the room, and now the nursemaid tiptoed lightly in.

"Oh, dear, oh, dear, how naughty, naughty!" she whispered. She picked Riquet up and bore him rapidly away.

All night long the wind shook at the house and smote the walls of it with great blasts of rain. In the morning when the family hastened down for news of how Charlotte had passed the night, they were halted by the sight of the great acacia fallen and lying enormously across Charlotte's drive. The whole family stood aghast before the awful sight of it snapped off like a reed to the very stump, the great acacia that had stood for centuries of bad weather before Charlotte's house. The world itself might have splintered about them and they would have been no more surprised. There lay the mammoth beast, with its thick dark trunk gaping and ripped wide with fresh wood, and the sap running out like syrup all over the ground.

After the first moment of horror the family picked their way around it under the rain, stepping gingerly over the stout branches that only yesterday had swung like demons high above their heads. Jean was having his hot chocolate in the dining-room. He had passed, he told them, a terrible night.

"*Ben*, the tree crashing down and Charlotte screaming like a maniac," he said. Papa said he had always expected it to happen sooner or later. He wiped his shoes carefully at the salon door. Jean sopped a long crust in his chocolate and bore it dripping to his mouth. Maman was humping slowly away upstairs to see her daughter.

"She's quieted down now," said Jean as he ate. He hadn't closed his eyes all night.

Bridget and Nicolas stood at the window together watching the sea-foam which had gathered at the water's edge below the esplanade. The wind would sweep suddenly down upon it and lift up mouthfuls of the foam in great quivering gulps, shattering it against the bars of the grill and the window pane. Splatter, splatter went the foam in a million rainbow bubbles before their very noses. And the sea itself looked as though it had no humility left in it, and that its clear intention was to rise upon them and possess them all.

"Anyway, it'll give us enough fire wood for the winter," said Jean of the acacia. "We'll have a young tree planted in February and, you'll see, in two hundred years it will amount to the same thing."

He spoke of those two centuries as if they were years in which the children would be growing up, and Charlotte's hair turning grey, and even Nicolas and Bridget still there to pull off the acacia blossoms and the leaves of it for the *Fête Dieu* every summer just as they had this year. Every year was fixed there in his mind, mild and unalterable, with Bridget and Nicolas eternally visiting, Luc returning for his *vacances* every summer, and Charlotte giving birth again and again unceasingly just as she had always done. His greatest sorrow was that the hard red wine of the country had a restrictive action upon his intestines and therefore he could not drink as much of it as he would have liked. North Africa and the *estancias* had certainly never for the last ten years entered his calculations as an actual place.

But here, without turning away from the sight of the rearing ocean, Nicolas took up his words.

"But doubtless we won't see, as long as we're going to North Africa, Jean," he said.

"Going to North Africa?" said Jean. "*Ben*, that's a funny idea of yours, Nicol." But something canny and suspicious had crept into his eyes, and when Bridget smiled at him he said: "*You* don't want to go to North Africa, do you, Bridget?"

"If we could make a living there," she said.

"Oh, it's horrid!" said Jean. He shook himself in his skin like an animal unpleasantly wet. "Ugh! No water closets!" he said. "And bugs! Such horrid things!"

"But Charlotte spoke to me——" began Nicolas. His face had turned as white as chalk.

The sight of Maman walking in on them stopped him short. She seemed to have grown smaller. She had shrunken in her clothes, a small withered old woman whose fingers could manipulate no coherent work but which buttoned and unbuttoned endlessly the opening of her corsage, whose hands must fold and crease and tremble over whatever chanced to fall beneath them. She removed the tortoise-shell pins from her old hair and as promptly restored them to their place among her locks.

"My daughter," she said hoarsely, "my daughter is very ill. We must send for Pierre at once, Jean," she said. "We must send for Pierre. Pierre will come with his ambulance and I will go at once with her to Rennes. We must resign ourselves to the operation, Jean, I see that now. We have not made any mistake at all, Jean, we have been wise to wait and see if the operation was really a necessity. And now I am convinced, and I am quite ready to accompany Charlotte to Rennes."

Nicolas was dispatched in the limousine to telephone Pierre. He was to tell his brother that the family would now consent to anything, only Pierre must come.

"And now Charlotte must be dressed," said Maman. Her hands were shaking in the ribbon of her pince-nez, her fingers pecking furtively at nostrils, scalp, at the corners of her eyes. "Charlotte must be decently attired," she said. As she went here and there picking at this and that about the room, Jean sat huddled in his chair, shuddering and watching her with apprehension from his easy chair. His larkspur eyes never forsook her for a moment as she moved about the room, turning in blind faith to the aged general who had always mustered them before. Now that a sinister attack was being made at their very gates, he turned to her for counteraction and for a successful peace.

Up the broad stairs went Bridget and Annick and Julie and Marthe to dress Charlotte for her ride to Rennes. Here were the stockings to put on her, and here the embroidered shirt. Here was the blue sweater that Maman had made her under the summer sky and by the warm sea in the mildest of garden winds. Charlotte lay quietly in the elaborate sheets which she herself had embroidered so long ago with a C and a J and the most innocent of cupids piercing their two hearts. Bridget lifted one sweet leg, and Annick the other, and on they pulled the warm cotton hose. Like the limbs of a doll they were, carved motionless, as stiff and artificial as the impersonal limbs of a wooden doll. Into the sweater went her doll-like arms, and over her head went the magnificent shirt. Stiff as a doll she lay between her sheets with her eyes half-closed, waiting quietly and unprotestingly for her ride through the lovely Breton countryside to Rennes.

XXIX

SOON AFTER lunch the ambulance snorted at the grill and glided down the drive as far as it could before the fallen acacia tree barred its way. The agile young internes leaped out and walked in their leather coats down through the rain, bearing the encased stretcher between them. Gravely, and gleaming in his rubber cape, Luc came behind.

Down the drive he came and into the house with a dignity and a presence that set their hearts at rest. Whatever it was worth, thought Bridget, this sweet gravity alone deserved a homage, this stern grace in one so limited and young was rare enough to merit loyalty. To him and his activity could be given a devotion which more sensitive men did not require. Of what use am I to Nicolas, she thought as Luc came across the room, of what use?

Papa sat sunken in his chair with his chin dropped upon his stained cravat.

"Ah, but what sense is there," he said, "in taking her off to Rennes this way? Why take her away from all of us who love her?"

Luc spoke to them all, and then made his way up to Charlotte's room. When he came down to them again he spoke rapidly but without alarm.

"I want to talk to Pierre on the telephone before I undertake the trip with her," he said.

Papa rose stiffly up, bracing himself upon the arms of his chair.

"What do you mean, sir?" he said. He was quivering with authority, arrogant with all the tattered remnants of his military manner. "You have your orders, have you not?" he said. He stood trembling, erect with authority, facing the young man.

"I am ordered," said Luc pleasantly, "to use my own judgment."

Papa nodded.

"Yes, yes, very well," he said. Slowly he sank down into his chair. "Yes, yes," he said. He watched Luc bow slightly as he left the doorway. "Very well," he said. He sat down small and impotent in his chair, vanquished and deflated. And slowly the ambulance backed up the drive and snorted away to the village telephone.

All the afternoon the two houses waited in silence. The ambulance had rolled quietly back down the drive where it too waited in the rain. The two internes sat upstairs in the billiard room, smoking and watching casually from the window. Pierre, Luc said, and the other surgeon were on their way.

There was no weeping, no display of grief. Maman packed her bag and made her preparations to go. With great precision she ironed out her grey silk frock and sponged and pressed her travelling suit.

"Does an illness in the family make any difference about *fêtes*, about weddings or anything like that?" asked Marthe. She was curling her hair up on the irons which she heated on the coals.

"How could illness make any difference?" asked Maman wearily as she spat upon the sizzling flat-iron. She passed it briskly over the steaming cloth.

"Of course I know a death makes a difference," said Marthe. "But I was just wondering if the illness of a close relative makes it necessary to postpone things."

She was talking in the most casual way in the world and curling up her bang before the kitchen mirror.

"Of course I know that in the case of a death," said Marthe, as if she were speaking of things in general, "everything is put off for years, isn't it?"

It was almost dusk when Pierre's black car nosed swiftly down the drive. His face could be distinguished smiling and undisturbed above the wheel. The small white-bearded man who rode beside him was the same surgeon who had come before. He bowed ceremoniously to the entire family who had gathered in Charlotte's dining-room, and then the three doctors passed up the stairs.

The sight of them all and what they portended had sent Marthe off into a paroxysm of grief. She clung to Bridget in the hallway of her sister's house, sobbing, while the terrible moments ticked away. Beside them in the corner stood the great clock with its setting sun and its rising moon and its hemisphere of stars. Across its disc limped the jerky little tin clouds which obliterated minute by minute the time as it crept past.

Suddenly Maman came down the hall with fresh starched blouses hung across her arm. Her face was grey but marked with no emotion.

"Here . . ." she whispered to them as she passed. "They have decided to do it here . . ."

Next it was the turn of the doctors to go by. First the experienced old gentleman with his precise goatee; then Pierre, almost smiling; and then Luc. They carried their black cases of instruments, and left behind them an odour of anaesthetic and polished steel.

Bridget put Marthe's mackintosh about her shoulders, and with their arms linked they walked up Charlotte's drive. The children and their nurses had been banished to the family's house and there Marthe and Bridget joined them in their games. The maids were sitting with their wool and needles by the fire and the four children were playing cards. Riquet was a trial to all of them, for his part of the game was to grab the cards and fling them upon the burning logs. Nurses and sisters, and now aunts scrambled after him. To scream and shout, to fall, to slap, to reprimand, to soothe, was easier by far than any thought or conversation could be. And sing they must, Marthe had decided. She sat at the table singing out the words of some French childish song.

"*Frère Jacques, frère Jacques,*" shouted Marthe, and Monique came to lean against her knees and sing the words with her.

"*Frère Jacques, frère Jacques,*" sang Jeannot with them too.

Darkness was beginning to creep in upon them and now the candles were lighted and set like yellow tulips blooming across the mantelpiece. The *bonne* moved carefully in with a tray of hot milk for the children and a heaping platter of meringues.

"*Frère Jacques, frère Jacques,*" went Marthe's piercing voice in keys that none of them had ever heard before. In a moment they all joined in.

"*Sonnez les matines, sonnez les matines,*" with voices ranging upon every note and never coming near enough to chime. "*Frère Jacques,*" insisted one small high voice while the others had moved on to other verses. "Ding, dang, dong," sang Marthe with hollow foreboding. "Ding, dang, dong."

Julie's deep clanging voice sounded suddenly up the garden.

They sat suspended, struck silent by the sound of Julie's boy-voice praying aloud as she ran up the garden to the house. They all sat in absolute silence while she ran through the kitchen and down the hall. In burst Julie upon them with her hands lifted in the air, praying as she came, and Marthe's head fell down upon her knees where she sat, her fingers thrust into her ears as if to keep the terrible news from penetrating there. She clutched her head tightly between her knees, shuddering in agony, and closing them all out so that she need never hear or know.

"Down on your knees!" cried Julie as she made the sign of the cross. "Down on your knees for your mother!"

Down she fell praying against the table, and the children who had burst into tears, fell down upon their knees in fright. Bridget held Monique pressed close against her as they kneeled, and softly did the children and the nursemaids wail under the deep shaken voice of Julie praying deeply in the room. Out clanged the words from her brazen throat, challenging God, beseeching and imploring him.

When she had done they all went slowly and quiveringly out into the early darkness of the garden. Across the streaming road and down through Charlotte's drive they went, walking two by two. Shining over the river and Castle Island was a great luminous light which threw an astonishing clarity upon everything they passed. Every drop of rain that clung to leaf and bush was gleaming with it, and every blade of grass was like a needle of ice. This was no soft forgiving dusk, but the bitterest revenge of daylight refusing to succumb. Even the Chinese *tilleul* had become a menacing figure to the little group which filed so grimly by.

Down they came to the giant tree laid low by the storm and lying there across the driveway. All about them was murder and devastation, drenched but not revived by the interminable grieving of the rain. Over the proudest crests of the acacia tree they trampled with their ruthless boots, and across the threshold of Charlotte's house.

Annick led them up the stairs and while they waited before Charlotte's door, she wiped the children's noses and dried their eyes. Silently they waited there, Bridget, and the sisters, and Charlotte's children waiting in the shadow of the door. Presently Maman opened it to them. She stood fumbling her rosary, her fingers shaking incoherently over the great carved russet beads.

"There is still hope . . ." she murmured blindly to them. "There is still hope . . ."

She widened the door to them and the children walked calmly into the roar of Charlotte's death.

XXX

THE GIRLS were working about the boiling cauldron in the wash-house, dipping and turning their garments in the bubbling black water. Everything they possessed had gone into it without a murmur: white stockings, blouses, skirts, coats, sweaters. Only when it came the turn of the red fox did Marthe make any protest.

"Do you think furs have to be dyed black too?" she said. The lovely orange beast with his yellow belly was rippling like silk in her hands.

"Of course," said Julie. It was a bitter day and Julie's nose was running. Around her mouth her skin was slightly chapped from the cold.

" 'Of course!' " mocked Marthe. "You don't know anything about it! I'm sure you can wear whatever colour fur you want when you're in mourning, as long as the rest of your clothes are black."

She was kissing passionately the wrinkled leathery nose of her beautiful fox.

"I should think he would be better black," murmured Annick as she stirred the great boiling mass of clothes. Ever since Charlotte's death a terrible mask of sorrow had fallen upon her face.

But the matter had to be taken to Maman for decision, for Marthe remained unconvinced. Letter after letter was Maman penning at her desk, and down upon them all Marthe opened *Vogue* and *Femina* in an attempt to persuade her that coloured furs were really quite appropriate worn with mourning.

"It will make his hair so stiff and horrible afterwards," said Marthe. She had wound the fox close around her neck as if she would never let him go into that boiling mass of gloomy clothes. "I think it's awful for a young girl to be completely in black," she said.

The cold autumn garden beyond the windows of the little room where Maman sat held no rebuke for her defiant daughter. Even the sky had capitulated and was hung with deepest mourning, while not a leaf had turned red. The little tin table in the garden bore the meagre feast of Annick's new blue purse varnished black for the funeral, and the tan pumps which Julie had bought just last week and never worn, and the chauffeur's leather *casquette*, all varnished black.

But the same devil which possessed Nicolas at times, was heaping fuel upon his sister's recalcitrant heart.

"It's hard enough on us all anyhow, Maman," she said. "Especially for us young ones to be in black for one whole year.

You've worn black for years now so it isn't such a sacrifice for you. Even if we wanted to, we couldn't get engaged or anything for a year now, could we?"

"I'm sure you wouldn't want to," said Maman quietly. But Julie had come into the room and was wiping off her nose on the back of her hand.

"Of course she would," said Julie harshly.

"My girls, my girls," said Maman looking up from her deep-bordered letter paper. "Is this the time to go into such discussions?"

In two strides Julie had crossed the room and snatched the fox from off her sister's neck. Down the hall she flew and out through the garden with the fox's fat yellow tail blowing hither and yon on the wind. Marthe sprang after her in pursuit, but Julie had gained the wash-house before Marthe had rounded the syringa bush, and into the boiling cauldron went the gleaming fur. Down went the fur among the jackets and scarves, swirling and bubbling and sucking down with all the rest. By the time Marthe had rushed sobbing in upon them there was not a yellow hair left in his beautiful hide.

Monique was delighted when Tante Marthe slapped Tante Julie smartly in the face. In the past two days, life had become a much more amusing thing. She loved to press close against grandma's knee and watch the elegant incline of the letters as she penned them between the black rims of the paper. When grandma told her solemnly that Maman was going to be taken away and put in a hole in the ground, she jumped up and down and clapped her hands. She had always wanted to see the big black wagon back up at the door. Besides she was charmed with the crêpe hat they had bought her in Saint-Malo and she stood still playing with grandma's string of dull jet beads while the old lady for the twenty-eighth time wrote "consoled by the faith that we shall meet our dear one . . ."

Papa came down to join them now, and Nicolas came in and stood looking away out of the window. He was holding a letter in his hand.

"I have just had an answer from the Englishman who teaches

in the University of Tibet," he said. "He says he can't do anything for me at all."

There were all his diplomas and his documents returned. One by one were the doors of escape closing, one by one. No future on the *estancia,* and no hope from the Englishman they had met by chance on Castle Island. One by one were the issues from the family narrowing down.

"There is still Oncle Robert," said Nicolas as he stood looking out of the window. And with that forlorn hope of borrowing money he turned away from Annick's flushed countenance as she passed by the windowpane. She was proceeding up the garden with her armful of dyed dripping clothes. Her hands holding the bundles of limp black forms were raw from the rinses of cold water at the pump. One elongated sleeve of a dyed sweater trailed behind her on the gravel as she walked.

Papa suddenly wiped his eyes and loudly blew his nose. His grief lay in threads of water caught in the grooves and wrinkles of his sorrowing face.

"To think, to think," said Maman suddenly in anguish, "that I shall never again see Charlotte coming up the garden in her blue dress!"

She sat dry-eyed at her desk with one capable hand shading her face. The two old people sat talking together about Charlotte's death, talking, but somehow unconvinced that this had happened to them. Papa spoke of the broad-cloth riding habit that he had brought Charlotte from London when she was twelve years old. He had never been able to fathom her fear of the Mogul horse, he said, for animals were not to be feared but to be corrected. He talked of the hair ribbons of moire-antique that he had bought her in Strasbourg. When he recounted little anecdotes of her early days, he cried and laughed aloud at the same time.

His heart was broken; whatever would happen now, his heart was broken. He could talk of nothing for ever more but the ways and the words of his second born. Step by step he went over every hour of her illness. He blamed every member of the family, he blamed the government for encouraging people to have children, he blamed the Catholic religion, he blamed the whole unfeeling countryside which continued about its ordinary duties, for Charlotte's death.

Out on the line in the garden hung the ghastly row of mourners: skirts that had been green, dresses, sweaters, scarves, tam o' shanters that had been blue, red, yellow, hung like drenched crows upon the blowing line. And here amongst them all was the little hide of Marthe's fox reduced to a stringy ribbon of black dripping upon the sharp October air. Bridget walked out into the garden thinking of Charlotte who was dead now, and wearing the dress of gloom which Charlotte herself had made for her. There seemed no promise of good weather anywhere, none in the closed sky and none in the direction of the wind. Tomorrow five motor buses of mourners would be driven out from Saint-Malo and from Dinard and Saint-Servan and Paramé to walk behind the bleak wagon of death.

In the afternoon the grave-digger came to the family to tell them that he had opened the vault and found that it was flooded. Jean's mother and father, it appeared, were quietly barging about underground. To drain it would mean a certain sum of money and two or three weeks of work, while in the natural order of things the water would drain off by itself the following summer.

Jean discussed the matter with Maman and Papa and they ended by deciding to pray for good weather and put their faith in God. Had God seen fit to flood the vault, it was perhaps outside the sphere of a husband to take any contrary action about it. Nicolas could not refrain from mentioning the famous trip by river from Saint-Malo when Jean's father had distinguished himself by his gallant manipulation of the sails. Nicolas had then been only eight, but he remembered because it had been repeated to him so many times, that his uncle's presence of mind had saved them all. How wildly had the boat rocked on that perilous voyage when the sea and an electric storm had overtaken them simultaneously, and the ladies, with hands clapped to bustle and bosom, had retched in unison over the heaving side. Papa had managed to open bottles of salts and tend to the children, but Nicolas' uncle, with his sideburns bristling, had brought them all into the home harbour safe and sound. When they were finally all upon land once more it proved that there was no more serious damage done than Maman's bonnet blown to ribbons and a pair of suspenders snapped off between Jean's father's shoulder blades.

"He's probably much better off cruising about that way," said Nicolas.

Papa was too done, his heart too broken to reply. But as the acacia tree had been dragged away by four stout horses and a magnificent black and silver canopy hung upon Charlotte's door, Maman told the grave-digger that they would go on with their plans.

"*Quand même,*" she said as she stitched fiercely at her yards of mourning. It was impossible to think of keeping Charlotte above ground for a fortnight. "*Quand même,*" she said. "*Quand même.*"

XXXI

THE ENTRANCE hall was in itself as cold as the tomb and smelled of the sweet strong calla lilies which bloomed austerely now in every corner of the house. The salon had been rendered as black as night by the sable cloths the undertakers had hung to banish every remnant of day. In the centre of this obscurity was set the dazzling altar on which the coffin lay. To walk into the aura of this light was as if to walk into the burning centre of the sun. The brilliance shed by its five hundred candles could have illuminated an eternity of winters, and within it, like white butterflies, were a group of nuns in woven dresses with their hands fluttering over their great ivory beads.

"*Je vous salue, Marie pleine de grâce,*" chanted the nuns with one voice, and the haloes of the candles trembled perilously before their gentle breaths. "*Vous êtes benie entre toutes les femmes,*" they said. Four of them were kneeling at Charlotte's head and four kneeling at her feet.

Behind in the darkness were stationed Maman and the girls and Bridget, and standing beside them the four oldest children gaping at the magic light. On the other side of the undertaker's curtains, in equal darkness, waited Papa and Jean and Nicolas and Pierre and Luc. They, with the exception of Luc, were the immediate members of the family awaiting the arrival of the motor buses with the relatives and friends. Into the male section would the men mourners go, and into the place behind the coffin where the women-folk waited would file the weeping women.

"*Je vous salue, Marie pleine de grâce,*" cried the little nuns. Tante Dominique, who had arrived the night before, came in and kneeled down amongst the others in her black frock. As she fumbled in her skirts for her rosary she nodded cordially to all the little white-clad nuns about her. She smiled, she nodded brightly, she blew her nose. Death was no grave or bitter thing to her. This was the ceremony prescribed by the Church, but had God Himself been there she would have wrung His hand. They were all good, simple, gentle-hearted people, God and Tante Dominique and the Holy Ghost. There was nothing in death to chill one's heart, nothing to appal one, nothing to fear. She even rapped the fine oak of the coffin with her twisted old hand and nodded with satisfaction. Good solid oak it was, and nicely turned.

"*Vous êtes benie entre toutes les femmes,*" she began chanting with the others, "*et Jesus le fruit de vos entrailles est beni.*"

But as time passed it became evident to everyone that something had happened to detain the motor buses. Not a mourner had as yet appeared and their arrival had been scheduled for a full half hour before. On and on chanted the kneeling nuns, shifting their weight from one knee to another, swaying and singing, and telling their beads again and again.

"*Je vous salue, Marie pleine de grâce,*" they say. "*Le Seigneur est avec vous.*"

It was almost an hour later that Oncle Robert, having skipped down ahead of the others from the first bus, rushed into the house of mourning with a yellow leaf blown flat against the side of his derby hat. In his eagerness he hurried into the women's section and began to pour out the whole story to Maman. The buses had taken a wrong turning and gone fifteen kilometres off the route! Naturally it had been over the roughest road in the country, and only the day before he had been almost too ill to lift his head!

"How I survived, I do not know," he managed to confide in a penetrating whisper before Annick took him off to the gentlemen's division.

And now they could hear all the relatives and guests entering the corridor, wiping their feet, as Charlotte had done so many times, upon the iron mat at the door. Presently they all came in, filing one by one past the glittering coffin.

"Je vous salue, Marie pleine de grâce," the little nuns cried out, encouraged by the new arrivals. *"Le Seigneur est avec vous."*

In came the women, one by one, shaking out their short crêpe veils. They came sobbing across the room to Maman and her daughters, kissing their wet faces and clasping the bewildered children in their arms. The awful moan and choking of the women's suppressed weeping filled the darkness of the room. Annick was standing close to Bridget, crying aloud in the darkness like a little child.

Across the room came the fumbling unknown forms of the women, and Bridget embraced a hundred unseen faces. Sobbing these strange women took her into their arms and pressed their streaming faces against her cheeks. She wanted to wail aloud and beat her breast with them, but she could only stand shaking as if in the teeth of the cold, and there was no relief.

And then down the garden rang out the clear thin voices of the choir boys as they walked down the drive with their hymns soaring high above them into the trees. Out thundered the priests' response to them, and as if in terror the little nuns cried softly:

"Le Seigneur est avec vous!"

The gravel drive unrolled, swept clean as a palm before them, and the family and the relatives and the mourning friends went out into the cold October air. The little choir boys swung furiously their pendulums of incense, sang out in high unnatural voices, turned red as winter cabbages in their thin armozeen gowns and their coarse white lace. The limousine with its steel lamps masked in crêpe bore Maman and Papa and Nicolas and Jean and Bridget to the church. Behind them the double row of mourners, the women preceded by the men, picked their way carefully through the mud and the flurries of wet leaves which the wind was startling up in the road.

Once in the church Oncle Robert rose in his pew and fluttered his hand wanly to Bridget and Nicolas. Never, he murmured to them as they took their seats beside him, had he seen such ropes of chrysanthemums or seen such dahlia *gerbes*. At this season of the year the colours in the latter were more than he could understand.

"But in such poor taste," he added, "that your respected mother included *'fleurs naturelles'* in her announcement. Who, indeed, would have dreamed of sending artificial ones?"

The mass for Charlotte's soul was being sung when he leaned close to ask them if Maman were serving chicken or duck for the lunch.

"Chicken," thought Nicolas, and Oncle Robert gave them an approving smile.

They could hear the rain driving steadily now against the coloured glass. They could hear the wind wailing in the high rafters of the church. From where Bridget knelt she could see the clear line of Luc's bright head bowed proudly upon his hands. She saw the arch of his neck and relentless purpose of his jaw. But his wrists were delicate enough to be snapped in two and his hair itself was no stronger than the finest silk. Behind his rosy ears were the most vulnerable spots that had ever been left to flesh and bone. And how can anybody save you, thought Bridget, what can anybody do? It was Charlotte who had escaped and maybe she was smiling now, thought Bridget, the canny part of Charlotte smiling because she had evaded them all so well. She thought of the corners of Charlotte's mouth drawn up in her polished cheeks.

"I would have made a better corpse by far," said Nicolas as he kneeled beside Bridget. He grinned sidewise at his own peculiar wit. Even when he took his turn at shaking the little sceptre of incense and holy water over Charlotte's box, he smiled. He stood leaning on his cane, shaking out the little staff of drops upon her with his queer sardonic grin set beneath his nose. And then down rattled the great wet clumps of clay upon the handsome timber; little by little the enormous earth closed Charlotte away.

Oncle Robert was seated between them at lunch. Sixty-five other mourners were seated the length of the dining-room, and a hundred and fifty more were being fed in Jean's enormous dining-hall. Better fed, had been the general feeling, and there had been some little display of disappointment when so many had been ushered into Maman's humbler home.

"Death," said Oncle Robert as he divided his smile between Bridget and Nicolas, "is after all like philosophy, an axe which cuts two ways."

While Nicolas pondered this, Oncle Robert turned brightly to other subjects. It was evident that Charlotte's death had, in one sense, lifted a great weight from his mind. He looked at Annick with as kindly an eye, but now he was under no obligation to her, for naturally there could be no marriage in the family for at least another year. There was no denying that Oncle Robert walked with a firmer step and was disposed to take a lighter view of things than he had for some time past.

"And where will you two be off to before long?" he said.

"But we remain," said Nicolas bleakly, "as far as I can see. What, my dear Oncle Robert, would you suggest?"

"Curious," said Oncle Robert. "I had thought of you, Nicolas, and then doubted your interest. A delightful way one acquires at my age of creating another's attitude. And one which led me to refrain from speaking to you of a rather amusing offer. I had concluded, somehow, from something you had said, that your future was quite a settled thing."

The blade of Oncle Robert's knife bisected the thick morsel of fowl.

"But if such is *not* the case," he said, "I assure you I shall keep every sense alert. One does sense these things, you know. The one I speak of was odorous of parchment. One case I saw packed with prunes of 3000 B.C. The seals were done in wax from the ancient amethyst bees and the bee wings themselves were crystallized like flakes of ice. The work consisted of listing these curiosities for an extravagant persuasion."

Nicolas laughed a rather unsteady burst of laughter.

"Any offer, my dear Oncle Robert," he said, "would become glamorous in your description of it!"

"When," said Oncle Robert with sudden decision, "will you come and lunch with me?"

His fingertips, dry as powder, caressed his nostrils. He looked up and down the row of guests.

"I shall lavish you with my singular affection," he said absently. "Lavish . . ." he said. The word in his mouth was dwarfed and dry with precision. "Do tell me when you will come and lunch . . ."

Maman rose with the suggestion in her brows that the ladies proceed with her into the salon. Her back was bowed and weary under her burden of grief.

"Ah, poor, poor Charlotte!" murmured Oncle Robert as though he alone had remembered. "Poor, poor, Charlotte, poor martyred child!"

XXXII

THE SUN shone down the narrow path between the two even rows of round blue beaver hats. The orphans of Saint-Malo were proceeding along the sea wall and obliterating the horizon and Conrad's white island. Oncle Robert's elbows, slightly lifted, were withdrawn from contact with these strangers as he and Bridget and Nicolas edged through their midst. He was discussing across the orphans' hats the hour when the orchestra would begin to play at Dinard and the cherries in the cocktails after tea.

As he talked, his frail hands moved over the bay, the Casino, over Saint-Malo and the fortified island. In unison the box pleats of the orphans' skirts opened and re-opened. Oncle Robert breathed deeply and patiently at the interruption, and then lapsed into a genteel silence until the procession had outstripped them and passed on towards Paramé.

"I do prefer you two, your type of youth, to the whole display of *jeunesse*," he said when they could again breathe freely. "Your distinction . . ."

Oncle Robert and Nicolas walked arm in arm. All afternoon Nicolas had been leading up to the consummation of Oncle Robert's love for them.

"You can, then," Nicolas now said, "understand our unfortunate bondage . . ."

"Oh, how completely, how perfectly!" exclaimed Oncle Robert. He faced Bridget suddenly and looked emotionally into her eyes. "My dear child, how happy you two in your union! I'm sure, I'm *so* sure that nothing could ever take you two apart! International alliances," he began as he took up his stride again, "—but you mustn't miss those garnet sails passing, my dears. . . . I shudder at the breath of a generality, but I must confess to it that rarely have I seen international matches retain their bloom." He lifted his hand as if to forestall any protestation. "But I do not believe, I do not believe that one can be expected to focus perfectly in more than one personal *milieu*. Your personal *milieu*, for instance, Bridget dear, in which your God is concealed in some intangible section of your person, or Nicolas' *milieu* in which God offers the flesh and the blood of His Son for digestion. International alliances," he repeated as he cleared his throat, "are most gracefully handled by good breeding, not intentions . . . details for which you, my dear apostates (and fortunately), have no possible use. I am touched, so touched," he pursued, "that you who have forsaken so much have not forsaken one who is no longer young in body. . . ."

Nicolas looked away over the water, seeking some means to bring back the unaltered fact of their bondage with his people.

"You understand," he said presently, "how much we want to

go away and make our living. Which can only be made possible by some outer aid. . . ."

"And which," said Oncle Robert promptly, "I am convinced will come to you."

Bridget felt Nicolas' fingers quiver on her arm. Oncle Robert suddenly clasped his little hands.

"Oh, the Newfoundland boats, my dears!" he cried. "Oh, aren't they lovely, the Newfoundland boats! And how romantic going out for their six months of battle with the elements!"

They stopped on the wall and watched the dark deep bellies of the fishing boats swelling out over the water. The long strong masts of them were green with lichen and the red sails were patched with yellow and blue.

"Oh, lovely!" sniffed Oncle Robert holding his fine little head and his lean chin high. "Oh, lovely, the odour of it!"

Presently Nicolas spoke again to him, but now without ease, with his fingernails pressing into Bridget's wrist.

"My plan has been," he said, "to get away to Paris. The centre of things. I feel sure I could make a start there. But to get there and have enough to look around for a bit, that's all I need. For the rest, I'm sure. I'm sure I could find something and make a start. I don't need very much," he said, with his nails biting into Bridget's wrist, "and I'm sure I could pay it back."

"Dear children!" said Oncle Robert softly, "dear children!"

He went on beside them with averted head, as if to conceal his emotion from them. In a moment he tossed up his little head in the wind.

"How you have touched me," he said. He stopped to blow his nose discreetly into his handkerchief. "You have touched me deeply by caring to confide in me. It is all so beautiful and tender to me," he said. He looked fully and deeply at Nicolas. "You are so young and so right in your wish to gather and hold your little family close to you, Nicolas. But I do feel this. I do feel that in isolation you are excluding some very profound and precious things. Your father has expressed his wish to you that you should have a child and he has offered furthermore to make it possible for you to do so. By not complying with his wish you are excluding the devotion of your family, a devotion which cannot easily be replaced; no, I do not go too far in saying that it is a devotion which can never be replaced. You are deeply wounding your mother, and you may wound her beyond all healing. You are in rebellion against the hand of God, a hand which, in my humble opinion, is not a negligible one."

Nicolas walked coldly and quietly between them.

"My advice," said Oncle Robert in a lighter tone, "is to permit things to flow naturally and logically on. . . ." He smiled winsomely at them. "Do not dislike me for these words of counsel, plucked carefully from the soil of a more mature if less colourful wisdom. The advice," he added gently, "of an old man."

"And the advice," said Nicolas with his grin, "of a canny lawyer as well, my dear uncle?"

Oncle Robert laughed delightedly and shook his finger at his nephew.

"Ah, that!" he cried. "Ah, that is another matter! For that one pays, my dear Nicolas! For that one pays a fee!"

"Let me escape, let me escape," murmured Nicolas. He turned suddenly upon the old man. "You're a small mean little fellow," he said. He had turned as white as chalk. "I'd like to break my cane across your head," he said. He looked with his dark terrible eyes at his uncle. "I don't feel it, I don't feel there's any of the same blood in the two of us," he said. "Ah, what a small awful mean little man you are!"

His rage had turned him thin and sharp and stiff as a whip. Never had Bridget seen him so bewitched and blackened with it.

"I'd like to spit in your mean little face," he said. Oncle Robert was standing up like a fierce small bantam.

"Nicolas," said Bridget, holding his arm and his hand with the cane trembling in it. "Shall we go home now, Nicolas?"

Oncle Robert began to smile. He settled his coat upon his shoulders. Then he burst into laughter.

"Dear, dear," he said. " 'April showers bring May flowers.' " He was proud of his little flight into English. " 'April showers,' " he repeated vivaciously. He bowed to the two gentlemen who were passing, lifting his hat slightly from the damp fringe cut neatly on his brow. "Age," he remarked to Bridget, ignoring Nicolas who had turned away without an adieu, "has laid a withered hand upon the hearts of my contemporaries. They have forgotten how to laugh.

"They have forgotten how to laugh, and I must teach them," he said. "They have forgotten how to crack their cheeks and split their sides," he said.

And so it was the sounds of his sweet echoing delight which pursued them down the steps into the marketplace of the town; the clear bright ageless notes from his old throat rivalling the sun, the sea and all their complements, and making the tram they mounted a dull refuge from his sparkling attack.

Nicolas sat in the rocking car savagely chewing at the end of his cane.

" 'I ask a wreath which will not crush my head,' " he said as he looked blindly through the car window. " 'I shall have, doubtless, a boom after my funeral, seeing that long standing increases all things, regardless of quality. . . .' "

They swung precariously around the corner to the station.

"Help me," said Nicolas suddenly turning to Bridget. "Help me, mountain. I don't know what to do, I don't know what to do at all."

In the sunny afternoon he looked to her as bleak and out of place as an hour of dawn set down in the middle and warmth of day. There were lines of grieving and despair about his mouth; his face was sallow and lighted with no design of hope; his eyes were extinguished. He had given up. He looked at her and she thought that tears were gathering beneath his lids.

"I hate them all, I hate everybody," he said. "There's not a person alive that matters. I hate everybody, everybody in the world," he said.

They had come to a stop before the station and Bridget helped him down from the car. He put one hand on her shoulder and put his weight upon his cane. Then he put his arm through hers and they made their way across the dust of the open square to the station door.

"My God, what beasts, what swine, what cattle!" he said. He elbowed his way through the crowd of his countrymen who were waiting to buy their tickets. He looked from right to left into their antagonistic faces. Once at the window he bought two places for them, third class, back to his family in the country. At this moment Bridget decided what it was that she would do.

XXXIII

IT WAS Luc who was awaiting them, mounted on Charlotte's filly who was dancing daintily on her hoofs and cocking her wild head at the engine and the string of cars.

He had come up from Rennes all unexpectedly to spend the last week-end with them, he said. He slid off the little horse's back and put her reins through his arm while he shook their hands. The chauffeur had opened the door of Charlotte's limousine and after they had entered Luc put his foot in his stirrup and prepared to mount. But the filly flung her head high and leaped back on her heels. With a lovely tremor she shook Luc off as though he were a blue-bottle fly, but his hand on her mane had never wavered and her reins were securely threaded through his fingers. She leapt backwards with the most agile grace, in great long springs, with her hind legs lowered and her haunches quivering with delight. This was all a part of the game she played with him, so obviously playing at being stricken with terror and in such apprehension as to what he might do.

Not a nerve of Luc's was shaken by her display; he stroked her neck and when she had backed herself into the bushes, he gave her a smart slap with his open hand on her gleaming haunch and swung lightly up upon her back as she jumped sideways with a snort of fear. Down the road she fled with Luc setting his feet into her stirrups, and then as they watched she arched her neck and sprang into the air. She reared so prettily, carrying her whole weight so perfectly upon her two delicate ankles, and tossing her head so gaily from side to side, that there could have been no maliciousness in her, and surely no wish to do him any harm. Luc turned her head and brought her down again facing them. He was smiling at them through the window of the limousine which was waiting until he had quieted her before starting off.

Just as she passed them she shot her heels up in the air, snorted as if a field of whitened dandelions had blown into her nostrils, and raced down the road. The flick of her tail and her ears cocking warned them that the sight of a humming-bird even would be sufficient to make her shy across the road.

October deep and blue was burning from both ends of its cool stalk to the cold core of winter. It would be the last weekend in the country with the family, the last short windy days. They found the family seated in Charlotte's fading grasses, their woollens buttoned to their chins, and the thin scoop of the lawn descending from beneath their feet. Beyond them the sea was pieced solid between the elm boughs. The last days—and next week the sea wall of Saint-Malo would be across their windows, all winter the sea wall dappled with foam against their eyes.

"I shall sit all day in the sun," said Nicolas in despair as the limousine bore them down to the family, "all day all winter in the sun with the *Ouest-Éclair* and the stereoscopic views of Lourdes."

To Bridget it seemed that there were added signs of mourning upon the faces of Maman and the three girls. When Marthe rose at the sight of them and came across the grass in her black clothes, she looked the bearer of terrible tidings. Bridget looked into Marthe's face and as she did so she felt her hand fly up upon her bosom as though to protect her heart from some unexpected blow.

"Has Luc told you?" said Marthe in anguish to her.

But Luc had told them nothing, and now, still mounted on the prancing filly, he was doing a courtsey and ballet across the esplanade.

"Luc is going to Indo-China," said Marthe. She held Bridget's hand in a terrible grip. "He has been offered a post in Indo-

China," she said, "and unless something can be done he is going away."

In every face it was stamped with certainty that nothing could be done. Papa shook his head in disapproval and prophesied in vain. In vain, in vain did Maman detail the evils of malaria and the desolation in being so far from culture and society. But Luc was skipping away into the stable and putting the horse into her dark cool stall. He had been offered an unheard-of salary and he was right, said Annick mildly as she manipulated her crochet hook in and out, to follow his calling. There was a pure mild light of understanding shining in her eyes.

That Annick was about to enter a convent was the news which Maman reserved for the last breath of day. Papa was not to be told for it would be too great a cause of suffering to him. Annick would begin by paying a little visit to Tante Dominique. Gradually, gradually, thought Bridget, were they all making their escape. She saw Julie taking her place in Jean's house, giving her ungracious orders to the servants and her hard devotion to the children. Step by step were they all getting away.

The morning which followed their long sleep was the clearest and most beautiful of all. They came out of their rooms with an energy and beauty they could not explain. How out of place were their black garments in this spiced glittering day; how incongruous their grieving faces and their eyes which turned to heaven and yet denied its power to eventually restore to them their dead. All week long Castle Island had been lying across the water like a promised land to them, and now they decided that before returning for the winter to Saint-Malo they would have one last day upon the cliffs of it. Maman alone remained home with Jean to supervise the packing of the final things, and Nicolas and Papa and Luc escorted the three girls and Bridget and the children.

It was a terrible moment for them all when Papa threw himself flat upon his stomach and insisted upon reaching far, far out and down to capture for them the little star-faced flowers that were blooming down the side of the cliff as straight as icicles in the wind. So like edelweiss they were, but in spite of Marthe's insistence, Luc said they could not possibly be edelweiss in this part of the land.

Never had Castle Island been so rich and beautiful, so laden with wonders and so buffeted by a carousing wind. What a relief, thought Bridget, to come out this way into the broad autumn sunlight and escape the look of each other! Here on Castle Island they could see for miles around over the expanses of beach, and far, far away into the distant sea. On this day the highest tide of the year would be coming in, and this added to the wonder of leaving the mainland behind. Even at this early hour of the day there were no boats to be seen, and the whole river bed seemed to be draining itself dry in anticipation of the great advance that was to come. The sky was deep with colour and clear and cloudless as a bell.

In spite of the wisdom of all this, there was the necessity of building a fire and hanging the little aluminium saucepan over the flames of it. The children gathered up the twigs and sticks and helped Luc put the stones in place. To add adventure to the preparations, he borrowed a mirror from Bridget's bag and ignited the paper from the rays of the reflected sun. The children cavorted about him. When he squatted down, they came close to him and with their open hands they stroked his cheeks and his shiny hair.

Everything was proceeding in the most natural way in the world. Annick had wandered off to commune in silence with the giant trees, and Papa was expressing to Nicolas his conviction that she was presently to be killed by a falling bough. Marthe and Julie were playing nearby with the children, and Bridget was attempting to crochet a long black silk tie.

"It would simplify life for you, Papa," Nicolas was saying sourly, "if Annick perished beneath her halo. . . ."

Papa tossed his shoulders. He removed his great watch from his vest pocket, stared at its face for a moment, and then cleared his throat.

"The tide will be coming up in half an hour," he said. And then Luc spoke his final and terrible words.

"*Mon Dieu,* it would be nice to have some clams to start off with!" said Luc. He looked directly at Bridget who was biting her lips in her efforts to put the needle hook through the splitting silk.

"Come down with me, Bridget," he said, "and dig for clams with me before the water starts coming in."

His eyes had suddenly pierced the day like stars. He had picked up a bucket to carry down and he was looking with all his luminous bright charm straight into Bridget's eyes. Everything he looked upon seemed to Bridget to burst into flame and now she felt that she too had been ignited by his gleaming radiance. She felt that sitting there she must have been transfigured by the brilliance his eyes cast upon her, and that surely every eye had seen the avowal in her face.

All, all of them had seen it, thought Bridget. It must have been a glaring evidence to every eye, that piercing radiant beacon of her heart. But the grim relentless smile she felt hovering on Nicolas' lips was the severest judgment of them all. And have they succeeded in putting in me too the fear of judgments? she thought in anger. If any dignity can survive them, then let me possess it now to turn my imperious profile upon them, flog them with my despise, let loose the torrents of my impotence. Let me go down the cliffs and cross the beach with him. By all means, Luc, let us go after clams.

By all means, Luc, let us escape them, she was thinking. Let us go at once while we are consumed with it. Suddenly she jumped up and took Luc's hand, and down through the pine woods they ran together, fleeing over the mossy stretches, their hands clasped, down the precipitous path to the sea, away, away. Skipping like mountain goats they slid down the treacherous path of slate and pebbles, clutching at the frosted oak leaves that had turned red on the low branches. Down, down, down they fled with their blood racing through them, and then they saw that the wild sea was galloping up the river bed.

Never had sea been so magnificent, so rich in foam and thunder, never had an entire universe of sand and fields and trees succumbed to such an advance. Even the gulls that usually screamed and dipped below the towers of it were flying high and far ahead as if they had changed their minds at the sight of it and were making for the land. Its own wind whistled with it, singing in their ears as if they themselves were winging through the air. And the great cannon of the current bucked its thunder at them out of the river's narrow flute.

Bridget and Luc stood transfixed on the path above the beach watching the black twisting storm of the approaching sea.

"Listen to it, Luc," said Bridget, shouting above the thunder of its approach. "Listen to the sound of it!"

The first waves of it were as if striking a thousand harps along the side of the shore. And while they stood listening and holding each other's hands as if they could never relinquish each other, a perfect music-box tune of water quivered across the edge of the tide and with a long whistle the sea went screaming over the wall into Charlotte's pond. The black booming of the water knocked miles away at Charlotte's gate and then turned back upon itself as if in its final throes and came tearing up the river bed. When it struck the river, the little stream of fresh water shot straight up like a geyser into the air. Then down went the sea waters over it with an explosion that would have roused the dead, curled up like foaming necks of steeds, and galloped on again. Out of sight went the white breakers, around the edge of Castle Island, galloping and whistling into the very heart of France.

Luc was quivering beside her as if every drop of brine and lash of wind had stung his flesh. And now a sudden peace was blooming upon the surface of the swelling tide as it stretched out for miles and miles below them, gentle, obliterating, but filled with depths of black deception, lapping gently in all about Castle Island and lifting their anchored row boat higher and higher.

"Bridget," said Luc. He was holding her hands in his quivering fingers. "Bridget, you know you are coming away with me," he said.

The tenderness that shook him, the sweet bright soft rebellion in his eyes were gifts to him, thought Bridget, gifts she could spare to him who had been a poor man with no intention but to marry in a small ungracious way. Even the words in his mouth were gifts to him which would be his forever. She had given them and surely it would only be his passion and his love for another woman that would ever take them away. What was the nightingale's small liberty to the deep wide exemption she had given Luc, she thought. His mouth had been marble and his perfect limbs as unaware of conquest as a Greek man's alive in an alien time. Let Rennes, let Marthe, let Annick, and let Julie lie like cast-off skins for which he has no further use, she thought. She had breathed into his nostrils and he had revived.

"No," she said. "I cannot do that. There's no way of doing that now," she said. He was so close and living that in another moment she would be submerged. "Listen to me," she said. Her own decision was fixed there in her mind. "It's too late for that. Do you know what I am going to do?" she said. "Nicolas and I are going to have a child."